*A September Day and Shadow Thriller*

# SHOW AND TELL

## *Book Three*

# AMY SHOJAI

# Copyright

Second Print Edition, February 2017
Furry Muse Publishing
Print ISBN 978-1-944423-21-6
eBook ISBN 978-1-944423-22-3
Hardcover ISBN 978-1-948366-37-3

First Published by Cool Gus Publishing
First Printing, December 2015
COPYRIGHT © Amy Shojai, 2015

FURRY MUSE
PUBLISHING
P.O. Box 1904
Sherman TX 75091
(903)814-4319
amy@shojai.com

**September & Shadow Pet-centric Thrillers**
**By Amy Shojai**

LOST AND FOUND

HIDE AND SEEK

SHOW AND TELL

FIGHT OR FLIGHT
Introducing Lia, Tee, and Karma

HIT AND RUN

WIN OR LOSE

# Chapter 1

Eighty pounds of German Shepherd vaulted onto her bed and startled September from a sound sleep. She froze, mouse-quiet in the dark. Her heart trip-hammered in concert with the dog's low, bubbled growl that shook the bed, the vibration more felt than heard.

The downstairs clock struck five times. Clouds moved aside for moonlight to spill through the wooden blinds, painting the room silver with black shadows. The dog leaned closer. White-bright fangs glistened from his sooty muzzle, and September didn't need to see Shadow's expression to understand the dog's warning.

Shadow had good reasons for everything he did. He'd saved her life more than once.

The big black dog licked her face, and she pushed against his muscled chest, urging him off the bed so she could rise. His hackles continued to bristle despite her soothing touch, a warning she couldn't ignore. He was concerned, but not in full protection mode. Probably a furry trespasser. Better to see what had him on alert. She hadn't said a word, and didn't need to. The two partners were so in sync with each other, they might as well have read each other's mind. Shadow's tail flagged with excitement, anticipating her command to *check-it-out,* his signal to investigate and ensure no danger loomed.

Before she could move, a coffee-dark streak of fur leaped into her arms. The cat's bottlebrush tail echoed Shadow's concern, and September's mouth turned dry with fear. She briefly hugged Macy and brushed aside her long disheveled locks that matched the Maine Coon's fur. Even the stark lock of white hair at September's temple matched Macy's snowy bib. The cat's tilted green eyes, twin to September's, glowed a stoplight warning. Macy shivered. Even the cat reacted to Shadow's concern.

The dog's concern heightened the foreboding that had lived inside September as long as she could remember, despite knowing the ghosts from the past couldn't hurt her. It had taken a year since moving home to Texas for her to begin to heal. Shadow's solid presence and the purring warmth of Macy anchored September in the here-and-now. *They* were real. *They* were chosen family. The crawly sensation on the back of her neck mocked her newfound confidence.

September jumped out of bed, berating herself and silencing the what-ifs. Shadow's alert had been silent, not the full-on bark-warning given for a household intruder. Besides, the house alarms hadn't triggered. She took a calming breath with that realization. Clear the house, and then check the grounds outside.

With a plan in place, September hugged Macy again, and plopped the cat back onto the bed. Best to lock the cat in her bedroom and keep him out of harm's way. Macy didn't need more stress on his heart.

She showed the cat her closed fist. He obediently sat and began self-grooming, a way to calm himself down. September wished she had the ability to self-medicate with purrs.

September cautiously opened the bedroom door, stepped outside with the dog, then closed and latched the door. Shadow pressed against her, and she knelt and gave him a quick hug before signaling with the silent hand-wave command to *check-it-out.*

He bounded ahead, a silent black wraith invisible in the dark. She could track his progress from his thumping paw-jumps down the stairs, claw scrabbling on the wooden entry, and huffing breath as he tasted the air from room to room.

Finally, after clearing the house, Shadow raced back up the stairs, sat before her, and barked once. Her shoulders relaxed, and her grin nearly split her face.

"Baby-dog, what a good dog!" Not such a baby-dog anymore, with his first birthday nearly here, just a week after Valentine's Day. Her first shepherd Dakota taught her to love again, but Shadow became her heart.

She followed him down the stairs, encouraged when her knee gave barely a twinge. After surgery repaired the injury, physical therapy—what she called specialized torture—had her nearly back to normal even though she hated water therapy. After weeks of therapy, she could tread water for twenty minutes without breaking a sweat.

September paused in the office/music room. Playing her cello honored the memory of her old instrument. The gift from Combs and her new circle of friends meant perhaps a new life was possible, too.

September debated calling Combs to come check out the house. But no, she had to take charge of her life. Calling for help meant her stalker still controlled her from his jail cell. Courage meant moving forward despite the fear, and she wanted to be independent.

She still couldn't believe someone like Detective Jeff Combs—handsome, smart, accomplished—wanted to be with her. He'd promised no pressure, yet he wouldn't take no for an answer. So after several "not-a-date" casual lunches or dinners with friends, a couple of coffee meetings, and countless phone calls and texts, September surprised herself by saying yes to a for-real formal date.

Butterflies threw a party in her midsection. It felt good.

The kitchen's stained glass windows usually splashed the slate floor with peacock colors but sunrise wouldn't arrive for another two hours. Several phone messages beckoned on the landline reserved for her pet tracking and behavior consulting business, and September resisted the urge to review them. They could wait.

Shadow insisted something outside needed attention. It was his job to *check-it-out* whenever they returned home, or visited somewhere new. Anything different—a sound, a smell—could set off his alert, and she'd rather Shadow err on the side of caution. Even if they found nothing she didn't want to discourage the dog by ignoring his concern. Training never stopped, after all. She'd learned the hard way to trust her gut, and her dog. Shadow yawned and stretched, but his tail continued to signal his agitation.

Six months ago, she'd have locked the bedroom door and called the police. No more, not after what she'd survived in the last few weeks. She'd take her dog for a walk, and check out the property, like any other normal person. *Let it be a squirrel or raccoon.*

Shadow spun and twirled, nearly running into the wall in his excitement when she slipped on her coat, and stuffed bare feet into mud-caked garden shoes. She grabbed his leash on the way to the door.

"*Sit. Wait.*" She bent to hook the leash to Shadow's collar, and unlocked the kitchen door to the back patio, keyed in the security, and switched on the outside lights. If someone intended harm, the lights would either flush them out or send them scurrying on their way. With luck, any interlopers would be kids taking a dare to trespass on the notorious property. Nobody had any legitimate business being out here so early at five-frickin' o'clock. She slammed the door shut. It had a nasty habit of unlatching and swinging open in the wind.

No stars broke through the overcast sky, and the setting moon's glow tarnished heavy clouds. She should have pulled on a pair of sweats. The down-filled coat, a remnant from her years in Chicago, made her look like the Michelin Man, but covered only her upper thighs. Despite the muggy atmosphere, her bare legs chilled in the sixty-degree temperature.

She couldn't walk too fast in the sloppy garden shoes, and the dog adjusted his gait but remained insistent. Every time he paused to sniff, she found herself dodging one of the dozens of wind chimes she'd hung from every available spot. They served as a low-tech security system. The tinkle of bells, clatter of shells, and rattle of pottery shards played a counterpoint to the clop-shuffle-clop of her awkward shoes on the brick pathway.

She stepped off bricks and into grass when they rounded the house, and the soil squished. The rain finally stopped last night, at least for a while, but the countywide flash flood warnings continued. February more often unleashed ice storms that coated trees, broke branches and downed phone and power lines, so nobody complained about the extra rain. Except maybe her garden, if the plants hadn't drowned. Maybe they'd all die, and she'd have a good excuse to get rid of the roses that had become thorny memories of past pain.

Shadow led her to the wooden ladder next to the carriage house/garage. She'd created the set up as part of his training. You never knew what a search might require of a tracking dog, even climbing a ladder. She'd never met a dog so hungry to learn new things. He sniffed the area thoroughly before moving on.

September scanned the end of the driveway. A pair of carriage lamps on each side spilled light through the bars of the closed green gate, throwing jailhouse shadows in her path. No traffic lit the county road. She started to relax. Maybe the intruder had left. Shadow hadn't alerted to anything yet. *Trust the dog.*

He slowly made his way down the drive, and stuck his nose through the gate, tasting the air. He huffed, and pulled harder, and she noticed an old car parked some distance away, half hidden beneath a live oak. Her throat tightened as Shadow delicately sniffed one side of the gate. His nose hit the ground.

*Okay then.* She squared her shoulders. "*Seek,* Shadow. *Seek!*"

He towed her quickly up the other half-circle of the drive. September could barely keep up and cursed her decision to wear the sloppy shoes. Shadow dragged her up the front steps, exploring the front door's brick landing. Her heart thumped faster.

The dog continued to track his prey. He pulled September off the side of the front steps, across the lawn and padded quickly around to the other side of the house. They'd made a full circle. The dog moved faster and faster, signaling the target was near. His head came up.

Shadow's tension traveled up the leash and she trembled in response. His bristled fur made him look half again as large when he stalked stiff legged toward the kitchen door that now stood ajar. No wind had tugged it open; she'd latched the door securely.

His deep-throated roar shattered the quiet. September grabbed the leash with both hands to contain Shadow's sudden lunge. He wasn't a Schutzhund-trained protection dog, but after what they'd gone through together, Shadow had every right to be defensive when a stranger invaded their home.

September put a hand on his ruff, and he quieted into a down position, but continued to shake and huff with tension. She had to steady her own voice, outrage as much as fear fueling her emotions.

"Who's there? I'll send in the dog." At her words Shadow lept to his feet. This time, September didn't correct him, but watched when Shadow whined and cocked his head, listening. She wished she'd collected her gun from the SUV's glove box while they'd been near the garage, or brought along her cell phone to call Combs for backup. Screw being self-sufficient, she'd welcome some help. But they were on their own. She'd have to trust Shadow to do his job.

September leaned down, stroked both sides of Shadow's face, and he wagged at her touch. She unhooked the leash but held his collar a moment longer, and whispered. "Good-dog, Shadow. You know what to do." She spoke the command full-voice. "*Check-it-out,*" and released his collar.

Shadow sprang forward, claws scrabbling on the slate floor of the kitchen. He paused, then dropped his nose and traced the scent of the stranger's tread. September edged inside, and stood in the doorway to watch him work. His tail wagged with excitement. Shadow loved hide and seek games.

He tested the edge of the table where someone must have touched before he raced from the kitchen to the adjoining dining/living room. September hurried to keep up, but he easily outran her.

She didn't bother to switch on lights. Scent lit up rooms for a dog brighter than any lamp. Shadow raced into the dark living room, sniffed past the big table and across the carpet until his claws tap-danced on the wooden entry, with September in his wake.

September nearly ran into Shadow when he stopped to nose the handle on the front door. The deadbolt and other locks remained engaged, though. His head whipped around, attention drawn to the music/office room. A split second later, September heard the soft sobbing breath, too, and tore after the sound.

Shadow blocked the doorway, lay down, and barked once, his signal of a successful find.

The soft snuffling came from the kneehole of the desk. Someone as small as a kid. They'd have to be small to have wiggled through the bars on the green gate.

"Come out. I know you're in there." September took a cautious step into the room, and finally turned on the stained glass lamp. "Good-dog, Shadow. *Wait.*"

A girl called back. A tremor in her voice. "I only want to talk. Please don't send the dog after me."

Shadow wagged and stuck his head forward, but didn't break the *wait* command. He'd gotten better about that. His attitude, more excitement than defense, bolstered September's confidence. If the dog showed no fear, she'd trust his judgment.

"Come out from under there. Shadow won't hurt you. Unless you do something stupid." She stood with elbows wide, chest out, and tried to quiet her noisy breathing. Nobody showed up at five in the morning and walked into a stranger's house.

Shadow tipped his head, looking quizzical as the stranger finally pushed the chair away from the desk, and cautiously crawled out of the hiding spot.

"Where'd you come from? Who are you?" She softened her words for Shadow's sake when his ears went down and he yawned and turned away. Despite his scary size, shepherds were sensitive and he didn't like loud voices.

"Came from Chicago. Claire O'Dell." She answered quickly, but moved with slow caution to put the chair between herself and Shadow. "I parked outside your gate, I rang the bell, and when nobody came, I walked around the house. I've called you before, but you never answered, never returned my calls." Her tone became strident. "So I had to come. Beg you to help."

Not a girl, but a petite woman stood trembling, gaze locked on Shadow. Claire's head barely came level with September's shoulders. The whites of her eyes shined in the dim light, and she held up her hands in surrender. "Is he going to bite me?" Her voice traveled up an octave.

"No, he won't bite. Sit down already." September's exasperation made Shadow slick back his ears. "But stop staring at him, no dog likes that." She waited until Claire perched on the edge of the desk chair. "I'm calling the police."

"Oh no, you can't." She wrung her hands. "If you call the police, my little girl will die." Claire sobbed.

Shadow broke his *wait* command. With an apologetic glance at September for disobeying, he trotted over to the stranger, and licked clean her tears.

# **Chapter 2**

Kelvin Quincy's dreams had come true. He'd waited ages for this and couldn't wait to rub everyone's face in his success. Not that he would. He'd act modest and classy, like the stuck up District Attorney, but he'd gloat on the inside.

Kelvin nursed two decades of professional hurt. He'd been passed over for promotions, denied raises he deserved, and relegated to the background time after time. His credentials should have put him over the top when he ran for DA, but instead, the public bought into the pretty skirt, prettier face, and Lollipop TV sound bites.

He couldn't do sweetness and light if you dunked him in syrup, even though he'd never lost his west Texas drawl. On a woman, it sounded sexy but it turned Kelvin into a backwoods hick. His acne-scarred face, balding head and geeky-good grades didn't help so he'd compensated with bodybuilding and tattoos in college and gone overboard. Now Kelvin tried to cultivate a classier appearance. Most of his extra income went toward three-piece suits (not those cheapo off the rack kind, either), silk bow ties, designer suspenders, and tailored shirts with French cuffs and signature cuff links.

Kelvin got into the law to see justice served. He'd been a team player. But he gave and gave and gave, provided the brains and behind-the-scenes support, and stayed invisible with nothing to show for his good works. Although surrounded by less qualified and talented individuals, Kelvin ran a hamster-wheel life while others received acclaim and praise. *If you ain't—aren't—the first horse over the finish line, you get real damn tired of the view.*

No more. This time, *Kelvin* would get the credit. *Kelvin* would be a hero. Sure, he'd have to bend the rules a bit, but the world celebrated shades of gray. It'd be worth stepping up to help kids, put away a bad guy, and line his pocket at the same time. This time *Kelvin* would get everything he deserved and more. Win-win, all the way around. Well, except for the nasty-ass guest he expected anytime.

The intercom buzzed. Kelvin had a tiny office space in the first floor of a converted warehouse. They hadn't yet turned on the AC, so he ran the overhead fan on high. It squealed and wobbled and he prayed it wouldn't unscrew itself from the ceiling. Part of the rent included a receptionist to serve the entire building, but she apparently had stepped away. Kelvin pressed the button to answer.

"It's me, Sunny. Open up."

He smiled, and pushed the release. "Come on in. He's not here yet."

Sunny Babcock sashayed into the tiny office, her neon orange hair in a ponytail, and pulled up one of the rolling chairs. She folded her lithe figure into it. "Tell me again why you don't have the cops staking out this place? They've searched for this guy for six months."

"Don't ask questions. That's the deal." He came around the desk and balanced his narrow butt on the edge. "I'm paying you good money to do as you're told, Sunny. Already gave you the background on this and paid up front. And there'll be a whole lot more, a huge bonus, when we pull this off. So don't second guess."

He'd been Sunny's defense attorney on some minor brush-ups with the law over the years. They'd gone to high school together, and later both got into tattoos and hunting at the same time. He'd lost his taste for hunting, but not tattoos, or Sunny. They had a history, and Kelvin had intimate knowledge of one of Sunny's illegal passions. That's why he needed her in on this. It also gave him more leverage to keep her leashed.

"Fine. You pay, I'll play." She narrowed her sky blue eyes. "I'm already on the inside, but you have to promise I walk away clean. These folks don't take kindly to informants. I need enough to disappear after."

"Sure, Sunny. I need your eyes and ears letting me know the exact time and place for the meet. We need to catch them in the act, not too early or too late. Can't be like last time, where all the witnesses protected each other. And if you hear even a hint that something could derail this, squash it flat." She'd helped him out as a freelance investigator in the past, but he'd never before had so much riding on a case. "You vouch for me, and get me on the inside." For once, his biker tats and low profile would work to his advantage. "Once the event's a go, there's no turning back. I'll call it in, give you the high sign. Get the hell out of Dodge before the cavalry arrives."

"You sure you got the stones for it? Takes more than my say, Kelvin. If you want to be more than a *spectator*, it'll take more than money. Give them something that's, shall we say, indicative of your intentions."

"Like what?"

"I'll set up intros, and as good faith, you deliver some bait." Her brows knit at his expression. "Don't ask. You know exactly what I mean. You won't keep your hands clean on this one. To catch a fish and especially monster whales, you need bait." She nodded. "That's how you play your part to prove you're serious. Sooner rather than later, too."

Damn. He smoothed his shaved head, stood and walked back around the desk so she wouldn't see his expression. Nothing for it, though. If it would put a stop to everything, then a bit of sacrifice would be necessary. The buzzer sounded again.

This time the receptionist announced the visitor. "Doctor Gerald Baumgarten to see you."

Sunny stood, and Kelvin straightened and buttoned his coat. "Yes, send him in." Kelvin walked to the door, opened it and kept his face carefully neutral.

The Doctor stood so tall he had to duck to miss the ceiling fan. He wore a floor length bat-black cowboy duster that turned his pale face and silver hair ghostly. His expression didn't change as flat gray eyes scanned the cramped space, flicking over and dismissing Sunny until finally lighting on Kelvin.

A chill raised gooseflesh, but Kelvin didn't react. He closed the door and motioned to an empty chair. "I'm Kelvin Quincy. This is

Sunny Babcock, my associate. An honor to meet you, sir. We've heard a lot about you." He stuck out his hand.

The doctor stared at the hand, and took a seat without shaking. "What?"

Kelvin glanced at Sunny. "Excuse me?" Kelvin hurried to the chair behind the desk and urged Sunny to sit. She shook her head, and instead leaned against the wall, pursing her lips and watching.

"What have you heard about me, Kelvin Quincy? You said a lot."

Sunny started to say something but the Doctor cut her off.

"I know you. From TV. Hog Heaven, episode 21 and 27, Sunny "The Babe" Babcock and her handsome hounds." He cocked his head. "Where are your handsome hounds?" He swiveled his chair to include Kelvin. "Do you have handsome hounds, too?"

His monotone voice and metallic eyes gave Kelvin the creeps. "Uhm, well I have one dog. A big guy, but he wouldn't hurt a flea."

"Dogs don't hurt fleas, fleas hurt dogs. They bite dogs, the flea saliva makes allergic dogs itch and they carry tapeworms, *ehrlichiosis, babesiosis*, Lyme disease, Rocky Mountain spotted fever, and plague." He paused. "Dogs hurt dogs, too. In fights. You know about dogfights? I need a dogfight, people who fight dogs. Bad people, but useful. You will connect me with these bad people. That's the deal we make today."

Kelvin opened his mouth, closed it, and indicated Sunny should take the lead. She stepped forward. "Gerald, I can—"

"Doctor. I am *Doctor* Baumgarten. You will show me respect, Sunny "The Babe" Babcock." His voice didn't change, but his weird silver eyes made her flinch.

It took a lot to make Sunny flinch. For the first time, Kelvin noticed the gun peeking out from beneath the Doctor's coat, and understood why he wore the duster in this decidedly off-season warm weather.

"Sure, sorry about that, Doctor." Sunny smiled.

She managed to sound pleasant, but that didn't fool Kelvin. He knew her background, knew she hid her feelings instinctively—hard lessons learned as a teen from her bastard of a father—but Kelvin knew her tells. She flexed her fingers, full lips flattened, and the muscle in her jaw twitched. She'd better keep that temper of hers in check.

"I know dogfights, Doctor," she said. "There's a convention, a really big one, in a few days."

"A few? Definition: several or many or three. A couple means two or several. You said, *a few days*. How many days, exactly?"

Before she could respond and possibly blow the deal, Kelvin interjected. "Six days. This weekend. If this damn weather holds."

"Bad words. Lazy language." The Doctor stood up, his coat flapping, and reached for the gun.

"Oh shit...I mean, shoot. Sorry, that slipped out. Please. I'm sorry." Kelvin held out his palms in a conciliatory gesture. "You're right, no cursing, that's not polite. Doctor, please sit down. My apologies."

Kelvin pulled out a handkerchief, monogrammed to match his French cuffs, and mopped his brow. This loose cannon needed to be taken off the streets, for sure. He debated abandoning the plan and calling the cops for half a second, but couldn't let go of the glory he'd gain for bringing down everything this "doctor" stood for.

"Six days." The Doctor left the gun holstered but didn't sit. "Plans made cannot be un-made. I pay you to give me the time and place. Nothing must stop this event. My associates will attend this event to prepare delivering miracle medicine for many children." He paced. "I promised Mother to continue our important work. A promise made cannot be un-made." He stopped pacing. "Promise: a declaration or assurance that one will do a particular thing or that a particular thing will happen."

Kelvin knew that the freak blizzard last November hadn't stopped the Doctor's Rebirth Gathering, either. They'd caught his mother, the brains behind the outfit, he'd always believed, but the Doctor got away. Kelvin could call the cops now but they'd take the credit. No, better to be patient and spring the trap later so they'd catch both the Doctor and his entire drug crew. That would make anyone's career, and show the bozos in Heartland they'd snubbed him for the last time. Now Kelvin had baited the trap, and he needed to lure the Doctor the rest of the way in before slamming the door.

"I'll find out the time and the place." Sunny licked her teeth. "How much?"

*Damn it, why can't she keep her mouth shut?* "I'll take care of you, Sunny. This deal is between me and the Doctor."

The tall ghost-man stuck his hands in the pockets of the long coat, and pulled out a banded stack of bills from each. "First payment." He tossed a bundle first to Kelvin and then Sunny. "Another when you give me time and place. And final payment when our work is successful and I'm far far far away."

"Holy Jes—" Sunny clamped her mouth shut before finishing the oath.

Kelvin experienced the same surprised delight. A hundred-dollar bill on each side sandwiched the inch-thick bundle. He'd finally get out of this shit-hole of an office. But he didn't dare say that aloud. "It's a deal." He stuck out his hand again.

The Doctor stared. "Germs on hands make people sick. Do you want to make me sick?"

"No, of course not." Kelvin dropped his hand.

"That's good. You now will make me a promise. That's a written or oral declaration given in exchange for something of value that binds the maker to do, or forbear from, a certain specific act and gives to the person to whom the declaration is made the right to expect and enforce performance or forbearance." The Doctor paused. "Repeat after me: *I promise, Doctor.*"

Kelvin shrugged. "Okay, I promise." Kelvin held one hand behind his back, crossing his fingers like a scared kid. He smiled, faking confidence but sweat trickled down his neck.

"That's good." The Doctor turned to Sunny. "Now you say it, Sunny "The Babe" Babcock. Say, *I promise, Doctor.*"

She didn't hesitate. "Yeah, whatever. I promise Doctor." But she didn't look up. She instead busily counted her stack.

"Promise made cannot be un-made. Make it happen." For a moment, the Doctor's face creased into a forced but practiced smile, one he clearly intended to put people at ease.

Instead, it gave Kelvin more chills than the gun's presence.

# Chapter 3

September carried the pot of coffee to the stained glass table, topped off her own "son-of-a-peach" mug, and poured Claire another cup.

The woman offered a tremulous smile, pushed black curly hair out of her blue eyes, and took a sip. Shadow nudged her with his nose, and Claire tentatively patted his head. "You'd think he's mean with that scary ragged ear, but he's actually nice." She sounded surprised.

"Shadow and I consider that a badge of honor." The gunshot that took Shadow's ear tip could have killed her instead. Shadow had every reason to be suspicious of strangers, yet he still met the world with wide-eyed puppy optimism. She shouldn't be surprised he'd responded to Claire's tears the same way he did hers. Dogs read and reacted to emotions much more strongly than people imagined. Shadow had a gift for knowing when and how to soothe distress.

"Thanks for not calling the police." Claire stopped petting Shadow, and he whined and nosed her hand.

"It's only a reprieve, until you tell me what this is all about." September took another swallow. Something told her she needed to get fully caffeinated to meet this day.

"I drove straight through the night, thank God the roads were good this time. So tired, I'm not thinking straight, or I never would've come into your home. I've never done anything like that before." Claire's swollen eyes must have cried miles of tears. She suffered from terminal bed head, endearing on a youngster but tragic on an adult. The constellation of freckles dusting her nose and cheeks stood out in stark contrast to a ghost-pale complexion born of weeks of worry. "There's a lot of things I've never done before. Things change when you have kids." The words were bittersweet.

"You got that right." September rose and crossed to Shadow's food bowl. So many things these days reminded her of Steven, her sister's autistic son. She'd first trained Shadow to be Steven's service dog. Legally, she had no kids, other than the four-legged wonders she lived with. And she liked it that way.

Shadow rose, shook himself, and eagerly headed to the filled dish September set on the floor. "Must be pretty important to drive from Chicago to break into my house. What's the deal?" She opened a drawer, took out a bottle of pills and rattled it, and Macy appeared in the stairway. "Don't mind me, I need to feed and medicate the troops."

Claire stared as the shaggy twenty-pound feline gave her a cursory once over, pointedly ignored her further, and leaped from a standing start to the top of the refrigerator. "Like I said, I tried to call you. Left a bunch of messages since last November, and never got an answer."

September froze. So, that's what this was about. "Macy, pill time. Open." The cat obligingly opened his mouth to accept the tiny pill. September made a "click" sound with her tongue, and Macy trilled with eagerness for the treat reward.

"Did that cat just. . .? Never mind." Claire turned away, swallowed a slug of coffee, and then studied the empty cup as though it held answers to the universe. "My daughter Tracy just turned six. She's autistic."

Like Steven. "I can't help you." She'd put that horror behind her, and wanted no reminders. Besides, it was a police matter now. September filled Macy's bowl with food, and set it on top of the refrigerator out of dog nose-sniffing range.

"My husband and I, we prayed for a miracle. And we got it."

"Claire, I can't help you." She stared into the sink, refused to turn around. Her sister April prayed for that same miracle for Steven, and it nearly got them both killed.

"They took all our savings; we'll lose our house. Maybe our marriage." She knuckled her eyes, and her voice turned fierce. "But it's all worth it because we got our Tracy. Our little girl."

September finally faced Claire. "But that has nothing to do with me. Don't you understand? I'm sorry, but there's nothing I can do, even if I wanted to." September resented Claire's stinging litany. "My sister pulled me into that mess. Steven got out of the hospital, the psych ward, last month, and April's still recovering from being shot." September crossed to the smaller woman, and spoke with gentle firmness. "People died, Claire. I'm sorry about your daughter, but Tracy isn't the only one hurt, and I can't go back in time and make it go away. Believe me, I wish I could. At least the people responsible are in jail." She took a breath, knowing what Claire wanted. "There's no more medicine."

"You're wrong." Claire straightened in her chair, and pushed the cup aside. "Not everyone is in jail. That's why I'm here. Those of us at the last Rebirth Gathering got a supply of the medicine, and a promise we'd get refills as needed. We get the medicine every six weeks by mail as long as we pay." She sounded bitter.

The news hit September like a gut punch. "The Ghost? Gerald Baumgarten? He's still selling that poison?"

"DOCTOR Baumgarten." Claire corrected her, still defending the lunatic. "It's not poison. He saved my daughter, and hundreds like her, from being locked inside themselves. I'll be forever grateful for that. He says the cost went up because he had to go underground." Her chin jutted out with accusation.

Shadow leaned against September's thigh, and she absently stroked the dog's neck. He could tell when her stress levels skyrocketed, and right now, Mt. Vesuvius was a sparkler in comparison.

Claire's voice shook. "Three nights ago, Tracy disappeared, and it's your fault."

September's legs turned to Jell-O. Another child lost, needing to be found? She couldn't play that emotional hide and seek game, not again.

"I can't call the police. They'd take Tracy away. They only care about catching the Doctor. They'd be like you. Prejudiced because of what happened, never mind our children's needs. I can't let that happen, not to Tracy, not to any of the kids." Claire clenched her fists, clearly struggling for control.

Shadow whined and pushed against September. "I'm sorry, I truly am. But you're wasting time. How could a six-year-old get all the way here from Chicago?" She'd escaped that city nearly a decade ago, and would never willingly return. Bad enough she visited the place in her nightmares. She'd never move forward as long as the past kept dragging her back. Her mouth turned sour, signaling an imminent flashback, and September sank to the floor and opened her arms to Shadow's insistent nudging. She grabbed him like a furry life preserver.

"Tracy came here. Where it all began." Claire sank to the floor next to September, and spoke with a mother's passion, begging for her child's life. "Soon as we discovered her gone, I called my friend Elaine. Her son Lenny also got the treatment last November, and he disappeared the same time. We think they're together."

It made no sense. "Kids on the Spectrum often wander. You can't know they're here." That's why she'd originally trained Shadow, to keep Steven safe. Shadow only became her service dog when Steven spent months in the hospital after the drug fiasco. "Just call the police. You wouldn't need to say anything about their meds."

"Lenny took Elaine's van. We know they're on the road, and we know they planned to come here." She pulled a folded piece of paper from her pocket, smoothed it, and handed it to September. "I don't know why they're here, but Lenny left this note."

September reluctantly took the page, torn none too neatly from a spiral bound notepad, and smoothed it against the slate floor. It featured a beautifully rendered drawing with a few block letters. She saw a van traveling on a road, complete with patched tires and rust spots. A boy with short brown hair sat in the driver's seat, while a pretty girl with freckles and black pigtails peered out the passenger window, holding a green dinosaur in one hand and pill bottle filled with blue and white capsules in the other. The detail amazed her.

"It says, 'No worry Tracy and me fix.' Nothing about coming here." September tried to give back the page.

Claire tapped one corner of the page at the end of the highway. "There, see that? They're both on the highway, Lenny driving and Tracy with her medication and Grooby, the dinosaur. And there at the end of the road, the destination."

September stood up. "It's a city, with the red sunset reflecting in the windows. Lenny's a talented boy, but it could be any city."

"Look closer. Lenny's art communicates both literally and symbolically. Sometimes it's hard to understand but Elaine's gotten very good at reading his messages." Claire stabbed the paper again. "There are exactly twelve pills left in Tracy's bottle, and they left three days ago so she has only two or three days left before they're gone. You know what happens when they stop taking the meds. I know you do. It happened to Steven, I read about it in all the news reports. "

September flinched. Other children, including Steven, suffered psychosis when the medicine stopped. Her nephew stole his father's antique gun, wounded the Doctor's mother, and a near miss blasted Shadow's ear. Only intensive therapy over the past several months allowed Steven to leave the Dallas hospital but he'd never be a normal child.

"Please, September. Look again. And then if you don't see what Elaine and I saw, I'll ... I'll go away and leave you alone." Her voice broke.

Reluctantly, September examined the paper. A frantic parent saw special meaning in everything, and she had no wish to deny that hope, and hurt Claire any further.

Damn Gerald Baumgarten to hell. His accomplices including his recovered mother awaited trial, but he'd escaped, disappeared despite the manhunt. She wondered if the authorities knew the lunatic's vision survived, and that he continued to devastate families with his quack drug, while sucking them dry of hope and funds. No parent deserved such anguish. Now Claire wanted to drag September back into the nightmare.

"Right there, at the city destination. In the windows. I saw it driving in over the hill into town as the sun came up over the buildings. What do you see?" Claire prompted, eyes impossibly bright.

Squinting, September held the page closer and then sucked in a breath. Rendered in intricate detail, Lenny had drawn signature buildings of Heartland, Texas in stylized but recognizable detail. To make the point irrefutable, what she'd thought to be sunlight reflection instead named the place. In the window of each building shined a tiny red heart.

Claire smiled with triumph. "You see it, don't you? You do."

September looked from the page to the woman, and Claire's expression acknowledged her triumph; gaining a reluctant ally. Even if she'd wanted to, September couldn't deny that Claire had won this round.

Hands on hips and voice fierce, Claire stood as tall as her petite frame allowed. "You're going to find my daughter."

# Chapter 4

Detective Jeff Combs took the rinsed plates from his daughter Melinda, and added them to the dishwasher. He kept an eye on her younger brother, Willie, as his son dumped clean laundry on the couch. The boy soon had sorted a small pile of his own socks and underwear. Melinda rattled silverware under the faucet, and dropped them into the dish rack.

Combs treasured these times spent with his kids, even on mundane chores. He didn't get much time with his kids since the divorce. It had been a rough few years for their family, especially Melinda, his little drama-queen.

"Hey Melinda." Willie snagged a pair of his sister's hot pink undies, wrinkled his nose, and twirled it in the air around his finger, making sure she could see. "These'd make a great sling-shot." He launched them toward her.

Her face flushed red. She'd turned thirteen, and no teenage girl wanted her brother—or her dad—to notice, let alone handle, her undies.

Combs hid a smile.

She tried to snatch them, missed, and the dog grabbed them and ran, a white streak of fluffy fur. "Dad. Make him quit." Melinda chased down Kinsler and had to play tug with the terrier mix to retrieve her underwear. The dog shook his head and sneezed, the tan saddle spot and contrasting ears striking against his snowy coat. Combs could swear the dog smiled, dark eyes twinkling through the curtain of disheveled fur.

"Quit bothering your sister. Finish folding your own laundry." He tried not to laugh. He'd been a pest to his sister at that age, too.

Willie launched another bit of lace toward the dog. "Kinsler likes them. Hey boy, go guard second base."

He'd named the dog after Ian Kinsler when he still played for the Texas Rangers. Willie wanted to change Kinsler's name when Ian deserted The Rangers to go play ball for the Detroit Tigers, but Combs convinced him that would confuse the dog.

"William Stanley Combs, stop bothering your sister and put away your laundry. I promised Rick you'd get chores done before he brings your mom home from the hospital. You may have the day off but I have to work. Detective Gonzales picks me up in fifteen minutes."

He'd never imagined such an arrangement when Cassie left him for Rick-the-Prick. Normally Combs wouldn't lift a finger to help his ex-wife and her new husband. She'd been a bitch during the divorce, and made him fight to get joint custody. Now with her inability to care for their kids, and her CPA husband's fourteen-hour tax season rush, he could sue for sole custody, but couldn't afford the court costs. Besides, he didn't want to put his kids through that tug-of-war, and his job schedule with the Heartland Police Department made time a challenge.

So, he made a deal with the devil. It gave him a guilty sense of satisfaction to know Cassie would hate being beholden to him, even if these days, Cassie wasn't aware of much.

Melinda caught the dog and retrieved her underwear. She stuck her tongue out at Willie when she thought Combs couldn't see, a gesture far younger than her teenager status. "Stupid dog. Now they need washing again, yuck." She disappeared into the laundry room.

"You need to cut your sister some slack, champ." Combs finished rinsing and loading the breakfast dishes, and closed the dishwasher.

Willie slowly folded his clothes. "Uncle Rick says you're only helping because Mom's sick and won't get better."

"That's a lie." Melinda flounced back into the room. "Tell him, Dad." She punched Willie on the arm. "Don't say things like that, it's bad luck. Besides, they can cure all kinds of things, even cancer these days. Right Dad?"

Combs pretended to wash his hands, to give himself time to form an answer. "I'm not a doctor, Melinda. I don't know if it's like treating cancer. Rick hasn't shared any details." Before her scowl melted into tears, he hurried to add, "But you're right. Lots of new medicines and treatments happen all the time."

She punched Willie again. "See, brat? And you're folding wrong."

He clutched his arm. "Bossy-pants."

"Stupid face." She squealed when the dog leaped onto the pile of laundry, splitting the pair, barking and dancing, scattering the clothes onto the floor. "Daddy. Make them stop."

"Both of you, that's enough. Melinda, pick up the clothes."

"But Dad, Willie's the one—"

"Don't want to hear it." He turned to Willie. "Take your dog outside. Keep him on the leash, or he'll try to catch every squirrel on the planet. And stay out of the mud, or I'll hose you both off. With ice-cold water. Got it?" He rubbed his eyes. Probably not a good incentive. Both Willie and the dog would relish a game of hose tag.

Willie ducked his head, and whistled for the dog. Kinsler barked— he had an extraordinarily loud bark—and the pair clambered noisily out the door into the fenced back yard. Before Willie could attach the leash, the dog dodged away. Combs sighed.

Melinda glowered. "Not fair. He's such a brat lately. Why does he always get off the hook?" She picked up the spilled laundry, and threw each piece one by one back into the basket. "Now he and Kinsler'll track all over and I'm the one who has to clean up the mess. Uncle Rick's barely here anymore." She sulked.

"Nobody said life's fair. He's your little brother, and now you're a teenager, I expect more from you. This isn't easy for any of us. I need you to take more responsibility." He crossed and pulled her into his arms. God, she was so much like Cassie, a redheaded firecracker ready to explode. She stiffened, and pulled away from his hug. That hurt but didn't surprise him.

"He won't listen to me." She turned her back, concentrating on the clothes. "How can I be responsible if Willie won't listen?"

Combs ran a hand through his hair, and then searched his pocket when his cell phone buzzed. "I'll talk to him, okay? Dump Willie's on his bed. He can fold his own stuff later. Wouldn't want you to touch boy undies."

"Oh, Dad." Melinda scooped the remaining laundry back in the basket, and carried it down the hall.

The phone call brightened his mood. Talking to September always made him smile, especially since she'd finally relaxed enough to go out with him. He couldn't wait to surprise her with his belated Valentine's Day plans. She refused to go out that day, saying it made things too serious, but that didn't mean he couldn't turn a later date into a romantic evening. She needed someone to spoil her for a change.

Melinda called from her brother's room. "Dad, it stinks in here."

"Then hold your breath." He answered the phone, still smiling. "What can I do for my favorite lady?"

"Hi Jeff, sorry to bother you at work."

He didn't correct her, and checked the clock. Gonzales should be here any minute. "No problem, the day's still young. What's up?"

"Can you recommend a private investigator?" Her voice sounded hushed, as if she didn't want someone to hear.

Combs crossed to the front door to watch for his ride. "Why? What's wrong?"

"Don't worry. It's not for me. A friend asked."

Melinda came back into the room, and checked the oven. "Your breakfast burrito is ready."

Combs mouthed 'thanks' as Melinda poured coffee into a mug and secured the lid before he answered September. "Sure I can't help?"

"For now, she wants to keep it private. I found out this morning when she dropped by the house a couple hours ago."

He checked the clock and frowned. Awfully early for someone to stop by. She sounded nervous, too, and he wondered who among their friends needed a P.I. He knew all of September's local friends. She'd not been back home in Heartland long enough to make many new connections.

"There's a guy I considered working with last year." He'd nearly left the police force when summarily demoted over a scandal. It ultimately blew over but had been the straw that broke his marriage's back. "If he's available, I'll ask him to reach out to you directly." He cleared his throat. "On another note, I want to pick your brain about an animal issue."

She laughed. "Kinsler acting up again? Or your sister's cat, Simba?"

"Kinsler's a mess. Acts demented around squirrels and keeps digging out from under the fence. But your cat tips did the trick." Simba had been Mom's cat and probably still missed her, hence the litter box indiscretions.

Melinda leaned across the counter. "Is that September? See if she'll take the mutt off our hands." She batted her eyelashes, clearly not meaning it.

Combs shook his finger at her. He knew she loved the dog as much as Willie did, if not more. "September, we're working on something up your alley and the Captain authorized you to consult on the case. We got a lead on a dogfight ring."

Her voice turned cold with outrage. "Here in Heartland? That's disgusting. What is wrong with people?" She took a beat, and he could imagine her finger combing her hair, a nervous but endearing habit. "Does this have something to do with the dogfight bust two weeks ago in Oklahoma? You know, the ASPCA has a whole division devoted to shutting down dogfights. They even have a veterinary forensics team. That's how they nailed Michael Vick."

Combs turned around when a car honked outside, and nodded at Melinda when she held out the hot burrito in a bag, with the coffee ready. "Listen September, Gonzales just got here. We can meet later, and I'll share what I can and pick your brain."

"Sure. I'm in and out today, too. Got a consult about a stray cat that ought to be a hoot. I keep waiting for the number of AWOL pets to diminish, now that the wildlife die-off has abated. And then thanks to you, I'm playing cello over at the theater." He could hear the smile in her voice, and was delighted she enjoyed the gift so much.

She'd created a unique business tracking lost pets with Shadow. Combs admired her ability to celebrate happy reunions as well as accept sad outcomes. The latter seemed to outnumber the live finds. He knew from his own experience with missing persons that finding the body, while tragic, also offered closure to loved ones. Maybe it was the same for pet owners.

"Have a good show at the theater. Do I say break a leg? Or a string?" Combs grinned when she laughed. After he disconnected the call, he quickly texted a brief note to the P.I. for September. He set his phone down beside the coffee. "Where's my coat, honey?"

Melinda retrieved it from the back of one of the kitchen chairs. "You promised to talk to Willie."

"Right, right." He hurried to the back door, cracked it open and shouted into the back yard without stepping outside. "Willie, listen to your sister. When I'm not here, she is the boss of you." He winked at Melinda, and she smiled back as he shut the door. "Melinda, you watch your brother. It's a boy rule to be obnoxious to older sisters, so you'll have to put up with it. Okay? I'm counting on you."

The horn honked again. Melinda offered the bag in one hand and coffee in the other, and once his hands were full, she held the door for him. When she got back inside, she didn't notice he'd left behind his phone.

# Chapter 5

September hated withholding details about Claire's missing daughter from Combs. She sympathized with the woman, but she couldn't help directly. Hooking her up with the private investigator salved her guilt.

Claire reentered the study that doubled as September's music room, dabbing her face with a clean hand towel. "Thanks for letting me freshen up, and for helping me find Tracy. And Lenny, too. I promised to keep Elaine updated." Her smile hinted at the attractive young woman beneath the frazzled worry.

Bracing herself for an argument, September tried to let Claire down gently. "I want to help you, I really do."

"I read all the newspaper stories about how you found Steven after he got lost in that blizzard. And how that dog saved your life." Claire watched Shadow and took a seat on the nearby piano bench. "Tracy doesn't have much time." She leaned forward, elbows on her thighs. "You know this town, know the people, and have resources that I don't have."

September had only a handful of connections and Claire's refusal to inform the police cut out Combs. It still amazed her that Combs not only forgave her involvement in his mother's death last November, but also had become one of her dearest friends. Maybe even more than that.

September took a breath, cutting off that thought. "I still think you should call the police." She raised a hand to stop Claire's protest. "Just tell them Lenny's a runaway, or it's a joyride gone on too long, or something. The police can put out a bulletin with the license plate. You have the number?"

"Sure. But I can't risk it." Claire balled her fists. "Believe me, I've thought everything through. If the police find Tracy before we do, they'll call CPS and they'll take my daughter away. You said you'd help."

"I've contacted a private investigator to help."

"Oh." Claire bit her lip. "I thought you'd do this by yourself." Her voice rose, worry the constant undertone. "I can't afford some fancy investigator."

It wasn't her problem. If she had any hope for a normal life, a future without the threat of flashbacks and panic attacks, she couldn't subject herself to constant reminders of the past.

"Claire, I appreciate your confidence in me, but I train dogs and cats, help solve behavior problems, and sometimes Shadow helps me find lost pets." September shook her head. "I don't find missing kids, that's not what I do. You need a professional for that."

"But you found Steven."

"He's my nephew. My sister begged me to help, I couldn't say no. And I got incredibly lucky." She leaned forward in the chair, elbows on her knees. "A private investigator—"

"I drove straight through the night to get here and you blow me off, won't even try?" Claire rose, a thunderous expression making her ugly. "You're a selfish, despicable person, September Day. You got called a hero, but what about Tracy and the other kids? You made the cost go up. If it wasn't for you, Tracy could still get her medicine. She'd be home safe." She breathed heavily, and impatiently swiped tears away.

September bowed her head. Claire and the other parents believed their own version of the truth. The fees would have gone up regardless, but Tracy and Lenny going missing added to the tragedy. "I'll pay for the P.I., but that's all I can do."

"That's right. You can afford to throw money at your problems. I read about your lottery winnings. Must be nice."

September hunched her shoulders. She couldn't save the world, and had enough trouble taking care of herself, despite what the public might think. The winnings had been enough to move home to Heartland, buy this house and renovate it, but medical costs—she owed it to Steven and her sister April—had depleted the balance substantially. That didn't matter, as long as she had a chance for a life now, one without drama.

She cleared her throat, fidgeting. "Do you have a place to stay?"

Claire sank back onto the piano bench, and dropped her face into her hands. "What am I going to do?"

September felt even more like a heel. "You're going to rest. Stay here. I can do that much, there's two extra bedrooms. You can't do anything until I hear from the P.I."

Claire, ready to collapse from nerves, exhaustion, and worry, could have been a lost child herself. "Thank you. I don't mean to be such a bitch; I know I'm asking a lot."

"You're a mom. I get it. And in my world, being a bitch isn't such a bad thing." September's phone ping reminded her the day's busy schedule meant leaving Claire, a virtual stranger, alone in her house, and was surprised it didn't bother her. Well, not much. In the past, the thought might have triggered a panic attack. She *was* better. Besides, with a little luck—and Claire deserved good karma—the promised help from Combs should quickly take Claire off her hands.

Claire yawned. "I am exhausted. But wired, too, you know? There must be something I can do."

"Keeping busy helps. Shadow and I have to go to a behavior consult." Before Claire got upset again, she explained. "We won't be gone long. What's your cell?" They traded phone numbers.

"Tracy took her iPad, and Lenny has a cell phone." Claire yawned again. "The voicemail is full from me and Elaine calling. I don't think it's on. Elaine said Lenny didn't take his charger so the phone may be dead. Both of them do better communicating digitally than verbally."

That sounded familiar. Steven used his iPad or computer almost constantly, a major complaint from Mom, who did the lion's share of caring for the boy these days. She wondered if that would work in Claire's favor. Maybe the P.I. could get the signal traced. She kept the thought to herself, not wanting to add false hope to Claire's already stretched nerves. She also needed to let Combs know about the pill distribution scheme without betraying Claire's confidence.

"While I grab a shower, why don't you put together information for the investigator?" September moved to her small desk and brought up the computer's word processor. "Make a list. What they're wearing, any unique habits, likes and dislikes or behaviors, the car license plate, email and phone number, online sites they frequent, anything and everything. I haven't a clue what could help, so don't leave anything out."

She left Claire busily typing away on the keyboard. Shadow followed her up the stairs and stood guard as September quickly showered and dressed. Macy made a point to apply full body rubs against her legs. "I know, you hate me washing off all your good cat smell, don't you, buddy?" He trilled, and led the way from the bathroom, pausing to nose-touch Shadow before galloping down the stairs.

The doorbell rang. Shadow raced to the front door and waited impatiently for September to join him. On the way, she peered into the nearby office to check on Claire. She had dozed off, head on the desk, and September put a finger to her lips, signaling Shadow to keep silent. That might be the only rest Claire got until they found Tracy.

A tall, lithe figure moved in front of the stained glass sidelights, but sparked no recognition. Shadow snuffled loudly at the bottom of the door, his tail an agitated metronome. His hackles rose and a low growl bubbled deep in his throat.

The bell rang again, followed by knuckles rapping on the door. "Hello?" An impatient voice called out. "Detective Combs sent me, said you need a P.I."

September's shoulders unclenched. "Hold on, let me get the locks. Shadow, *sit. Wait.*" He yawned loudly as she unlocked the several deadbolts. The door swung open, and September stared. The woman was drop-dead gorgeous, with doll-bright orange hair and a china complexion despite swollen blue eyes and runny nose.

"You must be September Day. You're surprised, I get that a lot." The woman dabbed her nose with a tissue. "My business associate got the request and passed it on to me. I'm Sunny Babcock." She noticed Shadow, and her smile widened. "Oh, what a handsome fellow. I adore dogs, have a couple of my own." She held out her gloved fist for a sniff. "What's your name, puppy?"

Shadow slicked back his ears, bared his teeth, and snarled.

# Chapter 6

Combs cracked his knuckles as he sat in the passenger seat of the unmarked car. His partner flinched. "What? This?" He cracked them again.

Detective Winston Gonzales pulled the car into the lot outside the police station. "You'll be sorry. It'll turn your knuckles huge and grotesque."

"Says who?" Combs reached for his thermos of coffee, black-no-sugar, after taking a bite from the triple-decker cheese, bacon and sausage breakfast burrito Melinda had made. He had to make up for Gonzales's health kick.

"My granny says so. Grannies always know. They'll tell you so." The smaller man took another bite of his veggie wrap, then carefully wiped his black mustache with a paper napkin as he chewed and swallowed. "September won't like you with grotesque knuckles. Besides, your knuckle cracking makes my teeth hurt as bad as scratching a blackboard."

Combs winced. "You had to say that? And never mind about September." But he smiled.

Gonzales eyed Combs's food choice. "Better than cookies and caffeine, I suppose. Eat up, we've got a meeting in ten minutes." He took another bite, sipped his drink, and balanced the O.J. on the dashboard.

Even seated, Gonzales exuded the confidence of a bantam rooster, and never hesitated to face down men twice his size. Combs could have been partnered with anyone once reinstated as a detective, and counted himself lucky this time around. They'd both been previously partnered with the same career-climbing piece of work, and ironically ended up together.

Others on the force cracked wise about the Mutt and Jeff size difference, but they'd stopped laughing when Combs and Gonzales cleared cases in record time. Because of that success, they'd been tapped to lead the local investigation of a wide-reaching drug ring, operating in a loosely connected group of small cells scattered throughout the Midwest and southern states.

"Talked to September this morning." Combs sipped his coffee.

"Late night into early morning, eh?" Gonzales lifted one eyebrow.

"Wiseass." *He wished.* "She called while I was with the kids. Wanted a favor, so I asked one of my own."

"She going to consult? Yes!" Gonzales pumped his fist, and nearly knocked over his drink.

After the recent Oklahoma bust, one of the perps angled for a reduced sentence with insider info, and connected dots between the drug ring and its distribution system. When Combs cross-matched drug busts with dogfight complaints, the pattern became clear. Now they had departments in five states involved. All they lacked was a dog expert.

It'd been Gonzales's idea to pick September's brain. Combs resisted. He wanted to protect her, and was reluctant to involve her.

"Let's keep it to consulting offsite, Gonzales. Answering questions, suggesting leads, that's enough. She's been to hell and gone." He'd let work take precedence over family in the past. He wouldn't repeat that mistake with September.

"She's stronger than you think." Gonzales held up his hands, palms out. "It's the Captain's idea, his call. And you said she said yes."

"Fine." He wadded the paper bag. Combs could run interference with the home team. Hell, they might not even need September's help, once the Chicago team weighed in.

"Sure, Combs. Whatever you say." Gonzales dabbed his mouth. "Just don't tell September you're keeping her in bubble wrap. She'll go off on your ass."

Combs grinned. True enough. She'd always had a prickly self-preservation designed to keep people at arm's length. That defensive attitude had mellowed now that she finally felt safe. She acted more confident, more relaxed, but took offense at the slightest inclination she received special treatment. Combs tried to respect that and balance it with his desire to shield her from any further hurt.

Combs gulped the rest of his coffee as Gonzales crumpled the wrapping on his own breakfast. They headed inside, Combs adjusting his tie and brushing imaginary crumbs off his coat. Gonzales's perennial spit polished appearance had no need of spiffing up.

Captain Felix Gregory stuck his head out the door of his office as soon as they entered the bullpen, and signaled them to hurry. Through the frosted glass door, Combs could see a tall silhouette.

Gonzales spoke before Combs had a chance. "Sir, we've got our dog expert on board. September Day agreed to consult."

Combs stifled a curse, and covered it with a cough. Sure, the Captain needed to know. He'd have preferred to share that info himself later, if and when they needed her expertise. "She may not be much help. But she'll refer us to resources and answer questions." He glared at Gonzales.

Before they went inside, the Captain stopped them, his voice hushed. "You will extend every courtesy and treat our guest with respect throughout this investigation. Work as a team, no grandstanding, and no keeping secrets to one-up each other. Do I make myself clear?"

Gonzales had to crane his neck upward to meet the Captain's gray eyes. "Of course." He pointedly didn't look at Combs.

Combs wondered at the caution. Neither he nor Gonzales had ever cared about the glory, only wanted justice done. Like all the other cops and detectives on the force, they worked each case with that in mind.

The Captain spoke as he led the way across the room. "We've come full circle." He opened the door, took his place behind the desk, and offered a tight nod to the visiting detective who waited. "Y'all already know each other, so skip the happy reunions for now. Detective Doty, bring us up to speed from the Chicago end."

"Yes sir." Detective Kimberlane Doty towered over Gonzales and stood eye to eye with Combs. She didn't offer to shake hands, unconcerned by the men's reaction.

Combs's stomach tightened, and a sudden sour taste paralleled his opinion of the woman. He did his best to maintain a stoic expression.

She hadn't changed. Doty still sported the white-blond flattop haircut, tailored pants and jacket, and Amazon warrior stance. Always a competent if not flashy investigator, she'd relied on subterfuge and manipulation of informants to get the inside track. It had gotten a young girl killed on Combs's watch, but Doty managed to wiggle away and leave her then-partner Combs holding the bag. The firestorm nearly destroyed his career, and Combs doubted he'd have returned to the force if Doty hadn't transferred to Chicago.

In Combs's experience, horses don't change their spots. He leaned against the wall, watchful, waiting to hear what she pitched.

Doty pulled out a stick of clove-flavored nicotine gum, noisily unwrapped it, and stuck it in her mouth. "Like the Captain said, we've got a déjà vu situation, gentlemen. That Oklahoma bust two weeks ago produced more than rumors. These drug runners are a cut above the usual scum. Or a cut below, depending on how you view the situation." She popped her gum.

"Distributing through dogfight rings, that's a new twist." Gonzales pulled out his note pad. "Drugs always have a presence, but not in such an organized way."

"True, Gonzales. But we got a sample of what they're running." Doty grinned, making them wait. "Damenia. Sound familiar?"

Combs stood away from the wall. "You're shitting me!" That's why Doty came back to Heartland.

Gonzales licked his pencil and jotted a note before looking up. "Damenia's not a recreational drug the usual suspects get a jones for. Whoever's selling has a very specialized market." He glanced at Combs.

Combs leaned forward. "Doty, that's got to be random. Damenia doesn't produce a high. Nobody's going to get rich off that."

"Give me a little credit. And somebody got rich off it." Doty crossed her arms.

"Sure, I get that." Combs looked at the Captain, and got an encouraging smile from Gonzales. "Why're we going down this old rabbit hole? It's been what, four months, for God's sake. This is the first time it's resurfaced, and the entire country from the FDA and every initial agency out there's been on high alert watching for the stuff." He cracked his knuckles. "With respect, our guest from Chicago jumped the shark on this one."

Doty opened her mouth, but Gonzales cut her off. "Even if there was a black market for Damenia, what parents attend dogfights to pick up a prescription for their autistic kid?" He seemed to enjoy the exchange, too.

Doty's lips pooched out as though she tasted a lemon, clearly unsettled by the challenge to her assumptions. Combs knew that must be a rare experience for her.

Combs kept his voice neutral. "Everybody knows drugs and dog fighting go together. But tying a few pills back to the Blizzard Murders takes us in the wrong direction. We all want to nail the one that got away, but not by ignoring the whale in the bucket. Let's concentrate on the dogfights and drugs angle, shall we?"

"Does seem you're trying to wrangle zebras, Detective Doty, when cows'll do." The Captain leaned back in his chair until it touched the wall. "I'll buy the connection with North Texas. But why now?" His chair creaked. "We've got a dogfight expert on retainer, so let's get her in here." He swiveled to face Combs. "Get the Day woman on the phone and find a time the three of you can confab."

"September Day?" Doty's lip twitched, not quite a sneer but close enough. "Talk about a reunion."

Just like that, the blonde drew blood. Combs's jaw ached with the effort to stay cool. "No need to involve her, not at this point anyway. I'm still waiting for Doty to convince us Damenia isn't her personal McGuffin."

The Captain rocked forward on his chair. "Ms. Day's expertise will be needed regardless." He motioned Doty to continue.

"Thank you, Captain." She unwrapped and stuffed another stick of gum into her mouth. "Timing is suspicious. Remember, we questioned all the families, and they clammed up about any and all details."

Gonzales still wasn't buying it. "So? We figured they got a supply that'd keep them stupid and happy for weeks, maybe even months."

Combs grudgingly put it together. "And it's been months. What would happen if all those kids ran out of Damenia at once?"

"Exactly. Crazy-time. It started about two weeks ago in Chicago. Runaway kids, lots and lots of them." Doty's cud pooched out her cheek until she could've been a cowboy dipping an entire can of Skoal at once. "When I got the tip about Damenia showing up at the dogfight bust, I started looking for more runaways."

"How many kids this time? How many dead?" Gonzales turned green, probably thinking of his own kids.

"Five kids in three different states so far. No deaths yet, but a dozen or more injuries." Doty popped her gum. "They're not attacking anyone this time. Instead, they steal cars, hitchhike, and borrow bikes, all running away from home. Most injuries result from vehicular collisions." She popped another stick of gum in her mouth. "Some are so young they can't see over the dashboard. We talked to the parents and got nowhere. Sound familiar? Five for five of the kids were in that roundup last Thanksgiving." She smiled with satisfaction. "My partner's heading up a team to debrief all the parents, and hope at least one will spill. But they're scattered across several states, so it's a jurisdictional issue. It'll take time."

Combs rubbed the back of his neck and wished for another cup of coffee. Doty assumed a lot.

Gonzales didn't buy it, either. "Pretty thin, Doty. I'll concede the timing could work for withdrawal symptoms in the kids. But why not psychosis like last time?" He chewed his mustache. "And all the kids running south at the same time? That's not coincidence. Kids that age don't plan." He tapped the pencil against his teeth. "Three states? Dios."

"Doty, do you really believe those kids are being influenced by—"

"Don't know what's going on with the kids." Doty glared. "But they're a piece of the puzzle. Think of them as one symptom of the bigger disease." She held up her hand, counting on each finger. "Drug ring connects to dogfights. The dogfight connects to Damenia. Damenia connects to these specific kids. And the kids connect to Gerald Baumgartner."

The Captain squeaked his chair, put the flat of his palms on the desk and stood. "Detective Doty, great speech. Still damn thin. What else you got?"

Gonzales snapped his notepad closed. "Dazzle us, Doty. I would love for you to dazzle us."

Doty popped her gum again, looking like the cat that ate the canary, and Combs wanted to shove the cud down her throat. She'd been playing them.

Combs leaned forward. "What haven't you told us?"

"I got someone on the inside." Doty reached out and patted Combs on the shoulder. "For over a week now, I've had an informant infiltrating the local dogfight scene. Something's going down, and soon."

"Is that so?" The Captain didn't sound any happier than Combs. "Detective, I've already made clear to Gonzales and Combs that this team shares information and holds nothing back. I expect no less from you."

"Of course, Captain, my apologies." She didn't sound sorry. "Guess we all got caught up in brainstorming, but at least now we're all on the same page. Last message from my guy said he'd get us the fight location."

"Great. That's news worth waiting for." Gonzales flipped open his notepad again.

"Who do you have on the inside?" Combs looked at Gonzales and shrugged. He had to hand it to her. Doty never stuck in a toe when she could jump in with both boots. "I still think your kid connection won't float. Someday we'll nail the Doctor, but I'm happy to slam the door on the drug distribution."

The Captain nodded. "Get us the day and time, and we can put eyeballs on the site, catch the whole slew of 'em with their britches down. When's your guy's next check-in?"

For the first time Doty looked uncertain. "Benson is supposed to check in every 48 and it's been three days now." She shrugged. "Can't count on civilians."

"Benson? Not BeeBo Benson?" Combs throat grew tight.

"Yeah, you know him? The guy from that hog hunting show. He knows the area, knows the players, and knows Pit Bulls. He said, and I quote, 'A feller who'd abuse a critter was lower than pond scum.'"

"Sonofabitch! Doty, did you ever meet the man?" Combs shook off Gonzales's hand when he tried to hold him back.

"Detective Combs. Stand down!" The Captain's command stopped Combs in his tracks, but his fingers still itched to wrap around Doty's scrawny neck.

"Never had the pleasure. We talked on the phone." Doty's face turned as expressionless as granite. "He's pure West Texas good 'ol boy." Her voice grated with temper. "He said an older cousin introduced him to dogfights when he was a kid, and he hated it so much, he decked them. At first he wanted nothing to do with the idea, so I appealed to his civic duty." She jutted her chin. "He acted particularly incensed that kids might be involved. Said it ruined his cousin for life."

Gonzales looked ready to tackle her himself. "BeeBo is a child in a man's body. And you sent him undercover? He couldn't lie to save his life."

She didn't back down. "He seemed fine to me. Insisted he wanted to help, after I explained the situation." Doty licked her lips, and reached for the pack of cigarettes she no longer carried, and then dropped her hand. "If he's slow, even better. Nobody'll consider him a threat, or believe he'd be working with the police."

"We got to check on him." Combs whirled and strode across the room.

"Combs, leave it. Benson is Detective Doty's informant." The Captain paused. "Doty, you started this operation, so finish it. I want this drug ring shut down. And for damn sure, I don't want any civilian casualty."

"Yes sir. It's under control." Doty glared at Combs.

A uniform officer knocked on the door and without waiting, stuck his head inside. "Captain, we just got a call on a missing kid—"

The Captain held up a hand to stop him, and aimed steely attention at Combs and Gonzales. "You two, take that call. See if it ties in with the other AWOL kiddoes. After that, liaise with September Day and get as much information as you can about dogfights, the people involved, and what to expect. I want a full report by shift's end. Got it?" He took a seat behind the big desk, and waited a beat, looking at all three of them. "What the hell you waiting for? Get out of here."

## Chapter 7

Kelvin shed his clothes, trading French cuffs and tailored suit for soiled and patched jeans, a Texas First tee shirt with ripped off sleeves, and scuffed steel-toed boots. He tugged a black knit cap over his bald head, hoping it wouldn't itch and drive him nuts, and pulled on a sleeveless denim vest with an assortment of badges. The patches were legit, from his crazy motorcycle club days, even though the club had long since disbanded. He hoped they'd add to his cred.

Hercules sprawled on the bed, soaking the cover with dog drool and thumping his tail each time Kelvin turned his way.

"What do you think?" He posed, flexing his biceps so the tats of snakes undulated along his arms.

The dog wagged, stood up and shook his 240-pound tan torso, black muzzle spraying drool across the room. His collar tags jangled, bed springs squealed and the headboard thumped the wall like a seedy hotel room's amorous neighbor. Kelvin smiled wistfully at the thought, knowing he'd had his last taste of Sunny. If not for her pillow talk last week, he wouldn't have connected the dots that brought the Doctor within reach.

"Only good times ahead. New apartment and better class of neighbors and clients, just you wait, Hercules. Maybe even a doggy girlfriend for you." He'd counted the wad of cash three times, and had the $10,000 stashed in a yellow sock and locked in the top desk drawer at his office. You couldn't deposit that much cash without pointed questions being asked and paperwork required. Time enough later to figure out how to manage the windfall.

To reap the full rewards, though, he had to pay in blood—not his own, but innocent blood. He walked to the bed and opened his arms to Hercules, welcoming the heavy heat against his chest when the Mastiff leaned into his embrace. They'd been together six years. He'd want to kill anyone who offered to hurt Hercules. So would anyone with half a heart. Something must be broken inside of Sunny. Now, he'd have to play a gruesome price to buy the trust needed to gain insider access to the dogfight ring.

"Not you, boy. Never you." Kelvin thumped his palms on the dog, and Hercules panted happily.

It'd only take a couple to satisfy them. Surely, he could wrangle up a couple of strays. Besides, people who let pets wander didn't deserve to have them. He told himself it'd be only a day or so before he called in the authorities, not enough time for anything bad to happen to them. Kelvin didn't know if he could live with himself otherwise.

But he had no choice.

His phone beeped, signaling an incoming call. Kelvin hurried to the adjoining bathroom vanity where it charged next to the sink, and recognized the sender.

"Got the location and the time." Sunny quickly rattled off directions, and he scribbled them down. "Here's the deal. You deliver three animals to the location today. Better hurry, before the storm hits. There's dumpsters on the property. Put 'em inside one of those."

"Dumpsters? I thought they were supposed to be alive?" His stomach tightened. "That doesn't give me much time." He unplugged the phone and carried it back into the bedroom, and sat beside his dog.

"Yes, alive. Open the lid and drop them in. You can toss some hot dogs if you want. With all this rain, there should be plenty of water to drink. It's not like they'll be in there for long."

He closed his eyes. If Sunny had been in the same room with him, he would have smacked her, never mind he'd never struck a woman in his life. He'd make an exception in her case.

She must have read his mind. "Hey, this isn't some sweet-and-fluffy Disney adventure, Kelvin. I'm the messenger. If you don't have the stones for it, my guys won't let you inside."

"Right, I know." He stroked Hercules, imagining reproach in the dog's eyes.

"This is a test. You won't see them, but they'll be watching your every move. I want the rest of my money, what's coming to me." Her voice turned fierce. "So don't mess up. That would reflect poorly on me, too."

"Yeah, whatever." This was his party, and he had the most to lose. He knew what the dog men did to fighters that disappointed, and could guess his fate, should he fail in any of myriad ways. "Maybe there's another way."

She blew out breath with exasperation, and he imagined Sunny tossing her neon locks. "Figured you'd try to weenie out on me. I need the money, Kelvin. I've got plans, gotta get the hell out of this stinking place and start over. You can't trust anyone here. It's all empty promises, lies and disappointment."

God, she'd played the victim card again. In her world, everyone was out to get her. "Sunny, hear me out. That referral I pitched your way, over to that old renovated Victorian, 205 Rabbit Run Road? I'll double your fee."

Combs's text had been insulting. *Detective* Combs now. He hadn't been so high and mighty last year after his demotion. Combs came to Kelvin begging for a job. Kelvin strung the cop along for a while, figuring Combs would still have inside connections even as a tainted ex-cop that could prove helpful with Kelvin's clientele. But once reinstated, Combs no longer had the time of day for Kelvin Quincy. Until now.

Sunny laughed. "Figured it wasn't worth much or you'd do it yourself."

He grit his teeth. He couldn't let anything distract him from nailing the Doctor's drug ring, but couldn't tell Sunny that. At the same time, Combs knew Kelvin never turned down a job. Doing so could make the detective suspicious, when Kelvin couldn't afford cop noses in his beeswax, so he'd referred the job to Sunny. "You already agreed to take the job, Sunny, I'm just sweetening the deal."

She waited a beat. "I'm playing with you. Already on the job. I never turn down a bonus."

The P.I. job would keep Sunny out of his hair until he could figure a better way to manage this whole thing. Maybe he'd send the Doctor to the designated spot, and let Combs know. The detective would owe him. He'd heard Combs was a stand-up guy willing to share credit. Kelvin wouldn't have to mention the $10K socked away, literally.

"As for this deal, Kelvin, I won't let you back out."

He laughed so hard, he shook the bed. Hercules sneezed, joining in with a doggy laugh, and his collar tags jingled again. Kelvin was many things, but he was not a dog killer. *Drop in a dumpster? Sheesh.* "Sunny, what kind of leverage could you possibly have?"

"I took care of BeeBo, like you said. Squashed him flat. So to speak."

His shoulders tightened and he stopped laughing. "What do you mean?"

She drawled, voice dripping with treacle and seeming to enjoy every word. "Got word about BeeBo asking questions, sniffing around. I did my own sniffing, and sure enough, it smelled to high heaven like bacon." The honey turned to brimstone. "BeeBo's cousin turned me on to his little game. We go way back." She giggled. "Then when BeeBo called me to help out with his undercover sting, I couldn't resist fixing our problem. The poor simple soul had a little accident with his gun."

He leaned forward, and shouted into the phone. "You *shot* him? Are you crazy?" His voice raised an octave and he leaped to his feet. "You crazy bitch. If he's undercover, a suspicious death won't help our cause." Murder had never been part of the plan. He was supposed to be one of the good guys.

"Don't take that tone with me. I'm not stupid, I quizzed him first. He hadn't reported to his handler, not yet, but was going to. I couldn't wait. He'd already been out to the site. Had a kitten he must've pulled out of there. I hate cats." She sniffed. "I'm still so stuffed up with allergies I can't breathe. If I hadn't taken care of business, you and me and the Doctor wouldn't *have* any business."

Kelvin pulled off the black stocking cap and threw it across the room. "That's dandy. That's it, Sunny. I'm out. Bad enough this deal involves murdering dogs. But you killed a *man*. They'll never buy that a gun guy like BeeBo got careless. You're on your own." He'd call Combs, come clean and the devil takes Sunny and the Doctor and the whole shitty mess.

"Before you click off, hon, you should know about my insurance."

He hesitated. She sounded positively gleeful, and he couldn't bring himself to disconnect. Not until he knew what the witch planned. "What? What insurance?"

"The police investigation will turn up a rabies tag that doesn't belong to one of BeeBo's *dawgs.*" She drawled the last word, the way BeeBo would have said it. "Now, you give that big old Hercules-boy a pat for me, y'hear? Always loved the way he jingles his collar."

# Chapter 8

His feet squished with each cautious backward step, and Larry froze and prayed the slight noise wouldn't raise an alarm. There were dogs out there, a lot of them. Pit Bulls.

Every horror story he'd ever read about the murderous beasts flashed through his mind. A single bark would alert whoever had staked them out here in the middle of nowhere. If they were guard dogs, he didn't want to find out what they protected.

A half mile back, his car hydroplaned off the pavement when he stupidly crossed a low spot covered by running water. Now that his MiniCoop sat up to its headlights in black mud, and the weather knocked out cell phone service, he'd never make track practice in time. Coach would have a cow, not to mention his dad once he found out about the new car.

Larry lifted one foot and winced at the slushy sound it made coming free of the ooze. The sticky muck turned his feet into black snowshoes that nearly tugged off his sneaks. Larry carefully scraped them against a nearby tree and lamented his Christmas track shoes, barely worn, were ruined. His eyes pricked and he silently berated himself to suck it up. After all, he'd turn seventeen next week. Maybe Mom would replace the shoes for his birthday.

Not likely. They'd been too expensive the first time and the gift was supposed to count for both Christmas and birthday combined. Ditching the car made the shoe issue pale in comparison.

Wind panted hot breath against his face. This had been a year for weird weather, and the February temperatures mimicked May, excessively warm even for Texas. The breeze swirled his curly hair into his eyes. His girlfriend was right, he needed a haircut. If he'd listened to Melinda, he'd be getting shampooed and trimmed in downtown Heartland, instead of hiding from a pack of devil dogs. Larry hoped they couldn't smell his fear. Fear smell made them crazy, or so he'd read. Even he could smell his rank sweat, like he'd already run a marathon.

He sheltered behind a stand of burl oak, but the naked limbs did little to screen his presence. The wind rattled dry-bone branches, and he shuddered, remembering the recent news accounts of bone yard dumps. Maybe the dogs belonged to hog hunters like from that reality show? At least they'd rounded up and arrested all the bad guys. Larry relaxed a bit with that thought, until lightening strobed a dark cloud, and a simultaneous BOOM! made him wince.

The dogs didn't like the thunder, either. A couple of young ones yelped. Some had empty metal barrels laid sideways on the ground, but the makeshift shelters squatted in the same muddy swill that hobbled Larry's feet. He heard the rattle of the enormous chains that tethered each dog, even the pups, collar-to-stake-in-the-ground in a scatter-shot pattern around the remote clearing. Poor dogs, they couldn't help their nature. Was it necessary to chain them up like that? Must be to keep the dogs from killing each other. Everyone knew Pit Bulls were bloodthirsty beasts eager to attack innocent bystanders. They must be something powerful if they needed huge chains to restrain even the babies.

He hoped they'd focus on each other long enough for him to get away. Hell, he'd run farther distances before, and in the rain, too. This would be a great story to tell Melinda and their friends at school. At that thought, his chest puffed out. She'd be impressed.

Larry had only plodded down this chewed up drive to find a house, homeowner and phone connection, or maybe a truck that could pull him out. When he'd seen the dogs staked in front of the cement block barn, he'd stumbled off the gravel drive to hide behind scrubby trees.

He debated whether to beat a more hasty retreat, or slog through muck to take advantage of the half-assed shelter of the trees.

An engine revved behind him. Larry crouched, heart thumping, and started to flag down the driver for help. Whoever owned those dogs, though, might not take kindly to him trespassing. Before he could make a decision, the mud-spattered truck pulled up next to him, rolled down the window and stared, pockmarked face grim. The driver's bare arm boasted snake tattoos writhing from wrist to shoulder.

A massive canine with close-cropped ears, nearly as broad as it was tall, rode in the truck bed with front paws balanced on the roof of the cab. A short chain kept the beast anchored to the truck. It stared at Larry but remained silent.

"That your yellow car back there, swamped beside the road?" In answer, the Pit Bulls leaped up and stood at the ends of their chains barking, most with lowered heads and wildly wagging tails. Both the man and his gigantic dog ignored them. "I said, is that your yellow car?" The driver raised his voice over the barking.

Larry swallowed hard, and nodded.

"Figured somebody needed help when I saw that. Glad my Hercules didn't have to get out in the mud to find you." At the name, the dog in the back wagged his tail. "Don't stand there in the rain. Hop in, I'll give you a ride. Got a rig in the back ought to yank your car back onto the road."

Larry straightened. He swallowed, but saliva had turned to dust. The big canine—Hercules?—perched in the back of the truck stared at Larry while the Pit Bulls barked.

Shifting sideways half a step, Larry scanned the area, curly hair whipping in the stiffening wind. Dogs at the barn, scary stranger beside him, the monster dog in the truck, and nowhere to hide.

"What're you waiting for? Get in the truck. Bet your folks won't be happy you got your car stuck." He smiled with sympathy when Larry flinched. "Get in the truck, kid." He put a hand out the window, and the huge dog leaned forward to sniff and lick the snake tat on his arm.

"Does he bite?" Larry wanted to kick himself for asking. What did it matter? He had to run and take the chance. He'd had a few close calls during runs, and even one butt-nip from a Toy Poodle, so embarrassing he'd told no one, not even Melinda. He imagined the bright-hot pain of Hercules's giant teeth grappling his legs.

"All dogs bite in the right circumstances."

Larry stumbled a half step backwards.

"Hell, kid, take a breath already. I'm trying to save your ass." The big man wiped his acne-scarred face with a paisley kerchief. "Hercules puts the fear of God into some of my clients. I'd never tell them this, but he wouldn't hurt a fly. He's more a wrestler. He don't—I mean, he doesn't bite. Mastiffs pin you to the ground but never leave a mark." He paused, and added impatiently, "I got things to do. And I'm trying to do you a favor. I just want to get you out of here safe and sound, and get that toy car of yours back on the road. Do we have a deal?" It wasn't really a question. "Get in the truck."

Larry gulped. "Absolutely, sir, whatever you say." He took a couple of steps toward the truck, stalling and doing his best to clean the rest of the muck off his running shoes. He'd sooner face the chained Pit Bulls than climb into this guy's truck.

The gravel drive sat above the mucky field on one side while more scrub trees blocked the other. He could be halfway back to the main road before the driver could turn around and give chase, or release good old Hercules from his tether in the truck bed. Larry consciously steadied his breathing, psyching himself the way he did at the start of any track meet.

The man leaned over and swung open the passenger door to the truck. "Don't worry about the other dogs, either. Even if unchained, they might lick you to death. Pit Bulls love people. They only hate each other, same as lots of terrier breeds that are dog-aggressive." He chuckled. "All that hoopla about being mean does give folks pause, though, so they keep their distance. But a well-bred Pittie would sooner kill itself than harm a human." He craned his neck to follow Larry's progress around the back of his truck.

The gravel drive, littered here and there with a muddy puddle, beckoned with open invitation once Larry cleared the tailgate, and he didn't hesitate. With the truck between him and the stranger, he put his head down and sprinted.

The truck's engine snarled. Shit. The guy hadn't taken the time to turn around. He'd shoved it into reverse to come after him.

The Pit Bulls had gone nuts, too, barking and snarling. Larry imagined them lunging, breaking each massive chain one after another. He tucked his chin and increased his speed.

Overhead, thunder crackled. Dark shadows dance across the road. The truck's tailgate loomed. Hercules rode the bed like a surfer, silent and watchful, and strained against his tether.

Before the tailgate smacked him, Larry vaulted off the embankment. Within two steps, mud mired his feet. Damn. He tripped and fell forward. His braced hands sank wrist deep into black soil.

The truck revved. The dog man shouted. "Kid, what the hell you doing?"

Sobbing, Larry clawed to push himself upright. His thighs and calf muscles screamed against the weight of the clay. When his feet and hands sank deeper still, the mire anchored him in place. He crouched with eyes wet and chest heaving.

The weight of Hercules hit the end of the tether at the right angle, and snapped. The dog tumbled from the tailgate, landing on the incline at the side of the gravel drive. The trucker opened his door and clambered out.

"Hercules, STAY. Come, boy. Come." The man scrambled to retrieve the tether, and hissed when it screamed through his bare hands when the beast couldn't stop his forward motion.

Hercules hit Larry high in the shoulder. Larry opened his mouth to scream, anticipating the crush of jaws, but instead the dog yelped and floundered in the sticky muck as hobbled as Larry.

"Hercules, oh God no! Kid, hang on, hang on."

The dog flailed for solid footing, and then lunged, forelegs grasping Larry's waist. Larry caught a glimpse of the man's terrified expression before Hercules pushed his face deep into the cold muck.

The Mastiff rode his shoulders, claws scrabbling for paw hold.

Larry struggled to lift himself upright. Mud filled his ears and muffled the stranger's frantic shouts and the dogs' barks. Larry flailed, kicking legs churned, and he craned his neck side to side. His mouth filled with black dirt.

For one last sane moment, Larry calmed himself enough to reach down, down, impossibly far, seeking rock, tree limb, anything solid for leverage to push up out of the soup. But his hands met no resistance.

Lungs burned. Eyes snapped open into the grit that tears couldn't wash away. Screams bubbled tar pit slow from his mouth, and he inhaled, choked on black cold death.

Larry convulsed. Sludge cooled super-heated nerves, almost a balm, until all went black.

# Chapter 9

Shadow braced himself in the back seat. The big car jolted down and up again when it lurched off the regular car-path. He stuck his nose in the window crack, making wet streaks on the glass with his nose. A low tree branch switched against the car, and he flinched back.

"Sorry, baby-dog." September reached through the metal bars that separated him from the front seat. He slurped her fingers. "Just chill. When we get there, we'll play Frisbee."

He thumped his tail to show he understood. Shadow loved fetch-games, but the happy words couldn't change his disquiet.

He'd growled at the scary woman. Oily acrid scent rolled off her gloves in waves, covering up the clean dog smell underneath. He wondered why she needed guns when she had dogs to keep her safe?

Gun stink made his lip curl. Guns made ear-hurting noises, and could reach out and bite dogs and their people from far away. He didn't like or understand guns. Teeth were better, even for show. Good-dogs don't bite, not ever, even when scary strangers deserve biting. But instead of listening to a good-dog's warning, September shushed him.

She knew best, but he remained alert until the stranger drove away with the crying lady.

Despite her rude intrusion into his house, the weeping woman hadn't worried him. When he smelled the salty wet on her face, he knew she posed no threat.

September couldn't enjoy the scent-colors that filled the world. He did his best to show her these hidden treasures, wanted to share his joy. Usually she listened to him, reading the lift of his ear or shift in his posture, but sometimes Shadow didn't know how to explain. If dogs detected smells and sounds hidden from people, then humans must know things dogs couldn't understand.

People knew names for so many things, and he loved learning new names in the *show-me* game. People made cars run faster than any dog, and he relished wind-taste that blew through car windows. Shadow half closed his eyes, licked his nose, and stuck it further out the window to catch the scent-stream. Bliss.

The car slowed, and tires crunched when they made a turn. He stared ahead, tipping his head to one side for a better view. The path unraveled in front like the paper roll Macy-cat liked to steal.

Shadow saw a small wooden-sided house, its yard messy with tall uncut brown grass all around. He stood on the seat, wagging as the car came to a stop. To one side, a chain-link fence with a cement floor enclosed half the yard, empty now, but he smelled two dogs. He wagged harder, his tail raised with excitement. He couldn't stop the small whines of anticipation when September released her car-harness to get out.

"Sorry, Shadow. *Wait.*"

He yelped in protest. He knew what *wait* meant, his least favorite word. He needed to do his job, lead the way, *check-it-out* for danger the way he always cleared their house when they returned home.

"Everything's fine. Scariest thing here is the stray kitten BeeBo rescued, and a frightened kitty won't appreciate you nosing around." September took in the empty dog yard and frowned at the mud-crusted truck parked under a nearby carport.

Shadow wagged again, and whined hopefully. He loved September talking to him, even if he didn't understand all the words. He understood the emotions and intent, so the words didn't matter.

"His truck's here. Maybe BeeBo's out with Dot and Teddy. Can't have them come back and discover you baptizing their personal space, so you have to wait. I won't be long, I promise." He panted and pawed the window. "Give me a break, you're not hot. Okay, I'll leave the blower on. How's that?" She restarted the car and flipped a switch so that wind from the front of the car ruffled his fur. September slammed the car door, and stuck one hand to the barely opened window for him to nose-touch. That made him feel better. A little.

Shadow sighed, and watched her walk up the path to the front door, climb the stairs, and knock on the door. And wait.

She knocked again and called out. "Hey BeeBo, you home?"

An eerie keening howl rose from behind the door. Shadow came to full attention with the *DANGER!* cry from the strange dog. His fur bristled when September's back stiffened. She glanced at him, and he woofed and stood up, willing her to return, let him out to protect her from *DANGER!* the dog's howling fearful threat *DANGER!* inside the house.

"BeeBo? Everything okay?" September's voice shook.

A second dog joined the first's lament. Hysterical woofs mixed with frantic yelps and mournful howls. September reached for the door handle, but before touching it, pulled her hand away as though from a flame.

Shadow added his bark to the chorus, wanting, needing to reach September. He barked louder, but she ignored him, stepped off the porch, and disappeared around the side of the house.

He whined, frustrated. She'd left him behind. He paw-slapped the window, clawed the door, frantic. Dot and Teddy's horrific howls of loss infected him with worry.

September screamed.

Shadow howled. He braced one paw on the door-ledge and wedged his nose further out the window. The glass abruptly scrolled down, and he didn't hesitate. A good-dog protected his person. Shadow vaulted from the car window, and dashed to join September.

***

She bit her fist to stop another scream. The dirty window offered only a cloudy view, but enough for September to recognize the giant shape mounded in the middle of the floor. A long gun of some kind balanced against his torso. She couldn't see his face, but a dark stain pooled beneath his bulk, and smeared paw prints surrounded him. Did his chest rise and fall? Could he be alive, with so much blood everywhere?

His dogs were inside. The white dog, Dot, peered back at her with what BeeBo called her "stare of death." She'd never seen the red dog so still, and only the duet of howls told her Teddy was alive.

Before she could unfreeze her legs, Shadow sprinted around the corner, kicking up mud when he skidded to a stop at her side. "How did you? . . . Crap, forgot the child locks again." He poised to leap up against her, and she crossed her arms and leaned into his space to back him off. "Good-boy. Sit."

She'd love to bury her face in his ruff. But BeeBo needed help. "Stay close." She welcomed his warmth pressing against her thigh as she hurried back to the front porch, pulled out her phone and dialed 911.

September shared her name, BeeBo's address, and as much information as she knew to the dispatcher. "I can see through the window, he's on the floor. There's a gun nearby, and lot of blood."

"Is he alive?"

"I don't know. Going to try the door now." She paused. "Send animal control, too. His two dogs are with him." Shadow pushed in front of her to block the door, fur bristling. "I've got my dog here, too." She had to secure Shadow. Dot and Teddy had every right to protect BeeBo from a strange human and dog entering their house.

"Shadow, car ride. Now." Her voice turned drill sergeant sharp. He hesitated, but when she moved, Shadow whirled and beat her back to the SUV. He leaped into the rear seat through the open window. "*Wait.*" September opened the driver's side, scrolled up the rear windows, punched the child-lock mechanism, and shut the door. She ignored Shadow's wail of protest and returned to the porch.

September called to the two dogs through the door, making her voice calm but cheerful. "Dottie, here pup. Teddy, good boy. Who's a good dog? I'm coming in, you remember me." Teddy had always been extra protective. She grasped the knob, cracked upon the door, and the smell hit her. Dog poop and pee. And underneath, the coppery stench of old blood that made her stomach crawl up to her throat.

The smaller white dog, Dot, crowded close to September, trying to climb up her leg as she stepped inside. Teddy, the red nose Pit Bull, crouched beside BeeBo and continued to cry. "Good dogs, that's the way. Let me see." You could never predict how a dog might react in such situations. Even though they knew September, she trod carefully. She couldn't help BeeBo if the dogs wouldn't let her.

"BeeBo, do you hear me?" She stepped around the blood as best she could. Much of it had dried in a sticky dark stain near the big man's head. September knelt beside him, and checked his neck for a pulse, but his cold flesh didn't lie.

The red dog growled. "Teddy, good boy, you're okay." She slowly withdrew, and spoke into the phone. "He's not breathing. I think he's been gone a while. The gun . . ." Her eyes filled with tears.

"Wait for the authorities. The ambulance is on the way, and the police will dispatch someone shortly. Don't touch the gun. Was he suicidal?"

September frowned. "I don't think so, but I haven't known him long. He knows...I mean, he knew a lot about guns. I can't imagine he'd be careless with one." She wondered why the dogs were inside, when BeeBo's phone message made such a point about keeping them away from the rescued kitten. So far, she'd seen no sign of the cat.

"Don't touch anything. Leave the house, and wait outside, can you do that for me?"

"Sure." It broke her heart to see the dogs' grief. They knew. Dot huddled and shivered against the door, while Teddy interspersed whimpers with low growls, still intent on protecting his master. September clicked off the phone, stuck it in her pocket. The dispatcher couldn't mean for her to leave the dogs in here. It would take time for animal control to arrive, and she didn't want the police delayed by upset dogs.

Especially with anything that looked like a Pit Bull. Like most APBTs, Dot and Teddy fell all over themselves to please people, but still suffered the bad reputation media often fostered. September couldn't do anything now for BeeBo, except protect his dogs. She'd get both dogs to their kennel, and settle them safely away from the police circus that would only stress them further.

"Dottie, c'mon good girl, let's get you out of here." Teddy might calm a bit once Dot left the building. The girl dog dropped to the ground and dramatically rolled over. The right side of her face was brown, with a black dot giving her a jaunty make-believe black eye, and the rest of her face white like her body. BeeBo always pointed out Dot's eye shadow smudge over her left eye, and lipstick dark lips, saying they made her a glamour dog. September blinked hard, and wondered what would happen to the pair with him gone.

She had extra leashes in the back of the SUV and various other dog and cat consulting paraphernalia. BeeBo trained his dogs to respond to voice and hand signals unique as himself. She'd only seen him work his dogs once, and hoped she'd remember and they'd respond.

September fumbled with the drawstring on her sweatpants, and pulled it free. She half crouched, turned sideways toward Dot, and called. "Yoo-hoo, comy-yup-pup." She patted her leg at the same time, and Dot put her head down and wiggled toward her, flailing her tail as she bared teeth in a classic submissive grin. "Comy-yup-pup, good girl, Dot." Quickly, she threaded the drawstring cord beneath Dot's collar, stood up, and moved toward the door. "Who's a good girl? Dottie's a good girl." The dog pressed hard against September's leg, waited patiently until the door opened and followed with unmistakable relief to the kennel gate. "Kennel-up, good girl, Dot."

September latched the gate behind Dot, and trotted to her SUV to get a sturdier leash. Teddy was bigger, stronger, and probably less willing. She also grabbed a couple of bandannas, and liberally sprayed them with a commercial analogue of a dog pheromone. She stuffed one in her waistband and carried the other with the leash back to the house. At least Shadow remained quiet. Having him near kept her calm, able to focus on getting the dogs out. She'd need a Shadow-fix after this, once the authorities came.

Before opening the door, she called again to Teddy to warn him. Nothing worse than a startled, hyper-vigilant dog. "It's me again, Teddy. Want to see the handsome fellow." She moved inside and latched the door, avoiding direct eye contact with the stressed dog. "Comy-yup-pup, Teddy." She stood sideways, a few feet away from the entry, crouched down and patted her leg again. "Comy-yup-pup." September wadded up the treated bandanna, and tossed it halfway to the dog.

The dog whined and stretched his neck toward the cloth, sniffing. Mother dogs produced the pheromone while nursing puppies, and it soothed fear even in adult dogs. September hoped the chemical signal would take the edge off Teddy's fear-aggression. Luring Teddy away from BeeBo also reduced the chance the dog would want to guard. "Comy-up-pup, let's go see Dot."

Teddy sniffed BeeBo's face, nose nudged him, and when he gave no response, the dog stood and shook himself. That released the invisible cord tying Teddy to his body, and he rushed to meet September. The big red dog nearly bowled her over trying to get into her lap.

"Good-boy, such a good doggy, sweet baby, I'm so sorry, honey." September babbled, but the words meant less than the emotion. Teddy wriggled as the leash clipped to his collar. September pulled the bandanna from her waistband and knotted it through the collar like a bow tie. The other one she'd attach to Dot's collar.

She kicked the wadded bandanna on her way to the door. Before she could retrieve it, a streak of fur sprinted from beneath a nearby chair, grappled the cloth with tiny claws, and skidded into September's ankle.

Teddy immediately stuck his nose into the kitten's face and got a snout full of claws for his trouble. It must be Fuzzit, the rescue cat that BeeBo mentioned. Before September could scoop him up, the tiny kitten shimmied up her pant leg and chest to reach her chin. She tucked the trembling baby under her shirt to contain it on the trip outside, tugged Teddy's leash, and led the dog to join Dot in the fenced yard.

Shadow woofed from the car, and she hurried to meet him. "I promised you fetch-time, didn't I?" She'd never felt less like playing a game, but it would be therapeutic, reduce her stress, ward off the panic attack clawing the back of her mind. She couldn't leave until the police arrived and took her statement. But first, she needed to situate the kitten.

September popped the SUV's rear hatch, and snagged the small fabric duffel-shaped cat carrier in the rear of the compartment. After she zippered the tiny kitten inside, she collected the stack of dog toys, stowed the carrier on the front seat, and opened Shadow's door.

As soon as his paws hit the dirt, Shadow nosed the scent path to the front porch, hackles raised. "Shadow, no. Wanna play fetch?" She sing-songed the magic words, knowing that the happy association could change a dog's attitude.

Shadow's head whipped around at her words. When she waved one of the disks in the air and then wrist-flicked it away from the house into the next field, he flew after the sailing toy. September's shoulders relaxed as he snatched one after another from the air, and raced back to drop them at her feet. He paw-danced with impatience, urging her to toss the next.

Cars appeared at the end of the narrow lane, quickly closing the distance. A black and white led the way, followed by an unmarked vehicle September recognized. Her shoulders tightened. Not Combs, anyone but Combs. There must be other detectives in Heartland.

"Shadow, that's enough. Bring." She watched as he gathered up the Frisbees, neatly stacked them, and returned to her carrying all six of the toys. September deposited them in the SUV and got Shadow into the back seat, rolled the window partway down, and waited.

Officers from the black and white disembarked, but she only had eyes for the tall lean detective climbing out of the unmarked car. Her studied composure began to crumble. She wanted to run to him, hide her face against his broad chest, and feel the warmth of his arms.

Before she could say a word, Combs stomped across the gravel drive to join her. White tension marked the corners of his mouth, deepening the cleft in his chin, and she flinched in surprise at the fury in his tone.

"What the hell are you doing, playing games in the middle of my crime scene?"

# **Chapter 10**

Combs turned away from September, fuming. He motioned to the uniform officers. "Secure the scene. Let me know when the coroner arrives." He glared at September, and then turned from her hurt expression. He'd been on the way to interview the missing boy's parents when they got the call about BeeBo. So much for Doty handling things.

He couldn't believe September had discovered the body. Again. Media would gnaw that bone like a starving dog.

Gonzales offered quietly, "You want me to talk to her?"

He grunted, not trusting himself to speak but shook his head and waved Gonzales toward the house. When the smaller man took the hint and walked away, Combs strode so quickly toward September, she shrank against the car and Shadow offered a warning bark. That took him aback. Combs tried to soften his tone but the words still sounded accusing. "You found the body?"

September's catlike green eyes narrowed, and she crossed her arms, her tone equally defensive. "BeeBo called for a consult." She gestured toward the dogs in the pen beside the house. "They were inside with him, already contaminated the scene. Didn't want emergency folks to be delayed waiting for animal control." She spoke so fast the words barely made sense. "Took me a while to get them out. The animals, I mean."

"You know better than to disturb a crime scene." She'd let her concern for the animals rule her actions but Combs acknowledged she had a point. They couldn't process until someone removed the dogs.

"I couldn't leave them in there. It was heartbreaking." Her voice caught, then steadied and she pushed mahogany hair out of her eyes. "They tracked blood everywhere, and Teddy—he's the red one— wouldn't let me close enough to see if BeeBo was alive. I had to try."

Combs rubbed his eyes. "Okay, yeah, I get that." He offered a conciliatory smile. "Seeing you here surprised me, that's all. Dispatch didn't say who found the body. Can't quite wrap my head around you being here. "

"Neither can I." She hugged herself again.

He noticed the dogs had retreated to an igloo-style house and huddled so tightly together they could have been a two-headed dog. "They're calm enough." He strained to see. "Is that blood? Were the dogs injured?" Something dark stained the white one's lower flank. "BeeBo was a dog guy. What he didn't know about his dogs you could fit in a thimble. Never figured he'd need your advice."

Her arms tightened across her chest.

"That didn't come out right." Combs mentally kicked himself. September didn't know Doty recruited BeeBo to infiltrate the dogfight ring, but that wasn't his info to share. Combs wanted September as far away from this case as possible. "Okay, tell me top to bottom what happened, what did you see, you know the drill."

"Don't you want to read me my rights? Or record my statement? So you can check later to see if I change my story?" The sarcasm didn't suit her but he probably had it coming.

He put out a hand, wanting to pull her into his arms, and knew he couldn't. Not here. He'd make it up to her later. Right now, they both had to keep a professional distance. "Let's start over, okay? Finding a dead body doesn't do great things for my personality."

She finally offered a tentative smile. "Me either. The sooner we get this over, the quicker I can get out of your hair."

He leaned against the car door, and absently scratched Shadow when he stuck his big head out the window. "Gonzales has the recorder, and sure, you'll have to tell it three ways to Sunday. I need a general time line for now." She played with the zipper on her coat, avoiding his eyes. "I'm not mad at you." He wanted to throttle Doty, though. "I'm angry you had to discover another victim. Now tell me—"

"Victim?" Shocked, September stuck her hands in her pockets and shivered. "You haven't even been inside. BeeBo was shot, yes, with that fancy gun he inherited. I figured he wasn't used to it and it went off or something."

Combs caught her arm. "Walk with me." She started to follow him away from the car, and Shadow yelped. When September raised her eyebrows, Combs sighed. The pair was a team virtually joined at the hip. "Sure, bring the mutt, he's already trampled all over the field." Shadow hopped out, leaned briefly against September's leg to get his head stroked, and then raced ahead at her signal. "Now, tell me what happened."

She spoke in a rush, walking so quickly he barely kept up with her long legs. "BeeBo called about Fuzzit, the stray kitten he found." She told him the rest. "The kitten is in a carrier in my car."

That made more sense. Dogfights used all sorts of "bait" to train the bloody sport, and if BeeBo got close enough to rescue the kitten, he also could have learned about Damenia. The Doctor had killed before to protect his mission. "Animal control will take it."

She made a face. "But the kitten is so young. The city shelter will expose it to all kinds of things. Let me handle it?" She put a hand on his arm. "What difference can it make?"

He hesitated. They'd need to have someone examine the dogs and the kitten for evidence. He couldn't forget that September's cat Macy provided evidence last Christmas. Blood from beneath Macy's claws matched her stalker. Juries loved that kind of evidence. "Okay, no shelter for the cat. But you can't take it home either." Cats weren't his thing, and he'd been grateful his sister agreed to take Mom's old cat Simba.

"I'll give Doc Eugene a call, he's got a quarantine room."

"Perfect. I'll sign off on any fees incurred. Tell him we'll try to get the cat seen in the next 48, sooner if possible. I don't know how long evidence can be preserved on a cat. They're self-cleaning, right?"

She rolled her eyes. "Right. Like an oven. Now it's your turn. Why do you say murder?"

"I didn't say murder, I said victim."

"Don't play that game with me, Combs. You said I disturbed a crime scene." The contrasting white strand of hair nested among sable tresses blew across September's lips, and she impatiently smoothed it behind her ear. "You've got uniforms out here, so why do you need two of Heartland's detectives? You suspect it's more than an accident." Shadow raced back to her, carrying a stick he'd found and pressed it into her hand to throw. She tossed it and they watched him bound away. "BeeBo grew up with guns, and I don't buy him being careless." She wiped her eyes. "His dogs were the world to him. But it did seem weird Dot and Teddy were inside."

"Weird? I figured BeeBo slept with them." The joke fell flat. He knew September slept with Shadow, but that was different. He couldn't help a bit of jealousy, of a dog, no less. "No offense." Hell, he kept eating his foot today.

"Lots of owners share their pillow with their pets, not only us PTSD folks." She answered softly, but her fists clenched.

"Truce, okay? We're both on edge." Hair blew across her face again. Combs reached to push it aside, and she jerked away, and then relented. He cupped her face, started to say something else, and then pulled back when the coroner arrived.

Combs, September and Shadow walked back to her car. He caught her arm. "What was weird about the dogs being in the house?"

"BeeBo didn't trust them with the kitten. He'd kept Dot and Teddy in the kennel, so it strikes a sour note they were all in the house."

Combs pointed the coroner to the house as Gonzales came out the door, snapping off disposable gloves. The small man ducked his head in greeting to September, and she offered a tight smile in return.

"It's a mess in there." Gonzales's mustache twitched. "Dogs tracked blood everywhere, but the prints are dry and the blood pool under the body congealed. The coroner will give us a timeframe." He pulled out his digital recorder. "I know you already told Combs, but give me the Cliff's Notes version and we'll get you out of here." He winked at Combs. "He knows where to find you for details."

She quickly recapped what Combs already knew.

"Wish you hadn't moved the dogs." Gonzales clicked off the recorder. "We've got shoe prints, one set is probably BeeBo but the other's too small. To cross all the t's we need to eliminate you from the trace."

She shifted her weight as if her feet had betrayed her. "I have a change of clothes in the back of my SUV." She stroked Shadow's face. "Do you need Shadow's paw prints, too?"

"And the cat," said Combs drily. "Dealing with a Noah's Ark."

Gonzales didn't hide his disgust. "Not the way the Captain wanted us to liaise with you. We can do the consult here, or head downtown."

Combs made a "zip it" gesture with his fingers.

September frowned. "Consult? In this investigation?" She turned to Combs with surprise. "What does all this," she waved a hand toward BeeBo's house, "have to do with dogfights?"

Gonzales kept the recorder going.

"Tell me." Her jaw tightened.

Combs cracked his knuckles and stretched his neck, but the tension wouldn't leave. "Several departments, including Heartland, are on alert." He hesitated.

Gonzales picked up the narrative. "The fights move around. Every time the investigation gets close enough to shut it down, it disappears. Oklahoma, Louisiana, even Kansas. Now we got word they're here. Somewhere in North Texas."

Her mouth gaped. "You think BeeBo was involved in dogfights?" She laughed, and then choked off the garbled sound.

"I didn't say that." Combs glared at Gonzales, and the smaller man took the hint. The less anyone, including September, knew about the operation, the better. She was an outside consultant, period. Although after this, she might refuse to help at all.

September connected the dots anyway. "BeeBo couldn't hurt a fly. I watched him melt into a blubbery mess when one of his dogs got sick. He'd have nothing to do with that abomination." Her brow smoothed and she took a staggered step backwards, and caught herself against the car. "Did you get him to snoop for you?" She breathed heavily, outraged.

Combs reached out for her, but September danced out of his way.

"That's perfect, just perfect. Just because BeeBo has Pit Bulls." She fought tears. "I can imagine all the arguments." She knuckled her eyes. "You encouraged that gentle soul to cozy up to dog abusers, put himself at risk." Her eyes widened. "They did this! How could you?"

Combs flinched. She'd pretty much nailed Doty's argument, and his suspicions. To his mind, Doty might as well have pulled the trigger. He pinched his lips white with the effort to stay silent. Right now, the best he could do for September and the case was to shut his mouth and let her rage.

"I'm not a simpleton. I know dogfights attract gambling, illegal guns, drugs and who knows what else." September whirled, her lightening-streaked dark hair a storm cloud spilling over her shoulders. "BeeBo never would have agreed, unless you told him it would save dogs."

Gonzales interrupted her tirade. "You're making assumptions not in evidence." He gestured with the recorder. "We don't know that BeeBo's death had anything to do with the dogfight ring. You'd agreed to consult on the case."

She leaned against her SUV as though fearful she'd fall to the ground. September ignored Gonzales, refusing to break eye contact with Combs. "Tell me you didn't ask BeeBo to sniff around the dogfight ring."

"I didn't." He kept his eyes steady. "Neither did Gonzales."

She didn't back down. "Someone did."

He hesitated, but couldn't lie to her. "You know we can't share everything about investigations, and sometimes we don't agree with every decision . . ."

"Oh God." Her voice broke. Color drained from her face until her complexion matched the moon mark streak in her hair. She pushed past Combs and yanked open her car door, and searched for her keys. It took three tries to find the ignition. Shadow whined from his perch in the back seat and yawned.

Gonzales held up a hand. "Hey, you can't leave yet—"

September ignored Gonzales but stared up at Combs with brimming eyes. She slipped off her shoes, thrust them at him without a word, slammed the car door, and drove away.

# Chapter 11

September knuckled her eyes with one hand, driving as fast as she dared with the other. Hard-to-miss potholes turned the car into a bronco ride. Shadow bounced once too often and yelped when his nose banged the bars separating him from the front seats.

"Sorry. I'll slow down." She stuck her hand between the seats, and he nosed and licked her palm. The contact helped, as always.

The lump in her throat wouldn't go away, though, and she hiccupped a muted sob. Poor BeeBo. She didn't know which hurt worse: his senseless death, or Combs's investigation putting BeeBo in harm's way. She blinked hard when Shadow again licked her hand.

She'd planned to thank him for sending the private investigator, and let him know about Damenia's reappearance without betraying her promise to Claire. But BeeBo's murder left her reeling.

September knew cops made tough choices. That didn't make it any easier to accept. During her short marriage to Detective Chris Day, she'd seen him agonize over cases. He'd always protected her and refused to discuss details. Chris rescued her, kept her safe, and introduced her to the joy of tracking dogs. After Chris's murder, she'd run home to barricaded herself behind dozens of deadbolts, and kept everyone at a distance, even her family. Shadow broke through, insisted they belonged together and convinced her that chosen family was every bit as important as birthright. September dared to hope she'd have a future, maybe even with Combs.

"Stupid, stupid, stupid." She pounded the steering wheel in rhythm with her words. She hadn't considered if she could live with the tough, unsavory choices of a detective. What did it say about him? She'd never thought much about it with Chris, but at that point, in her life, she'd been in hibernation mode.

She wanted the dogfight ring shut down, too. Combs wouldn't confirm it, but he didn't deny BeeBo's involvement, either. There had to be a better way, without risking innocent lives.

Maybe Mom was right after all. She kept trying to set September up with men that were more "appropriate." Wouldn't that be a laugh? She pressed hard on the muddy gas pedal, icy sock feet as bruised as her heart.

"Who needs him, right Shadow? You're my best boy anyway." She checked the mirror, and smiled when the black dog laid his ears back. She could hear his tail thwacking against the seat cushion. "Want to go see Doc Eugene?" He barked, and wagged faster, and that tickled her.

Doc Eugene had treated Shadow for several injuries, yet instead of associating the clinic with scary pain, Shadow adored the veterinarian and his staff. Most of them, anyway.

Pulling into the parking lot, September noticed the new office manager's car parked in the only handicapped spot right next to the front door. Typical. Robin Gillette probably didn't want to get her hair wet in this rainy weather. While efficient and thorough, something bothered Shadow about the woman and as a result, September treated Robin with respectful caution.

"You didn't like Sunny Babcock, either." Shepherds typically acted reticent around strangers, and September worked hard to counter Shadow's natural suspicion. As a service dog, he needed to be calm and nonthreatening in public, as much to counter her own PTSD as to be welcome wherever she might go. He acted more comfortable around kids, probably because of his training with Steven.

Dog savvy folks like Doc Eugene usually turned Shadow into a fuzzy puddle of wags, so September wondered why he'd taken such an instant dislike to Babcock. The woman had worked on the same reality TV show with BeeBo, and had her own brace of hog hunting dogs.

But people sometimes took an instant hate-at-first-sight dislike toward each other. So could dogs.

She plugged her cell phone in the charger and left it in the car. Shadow jigged and whined in the back seat when September grabbed the cat carrier and juggled it out of the car before releasing him. He immediately scoped out the best places to baptize with a blissful expression as he sniffed up all the juicy Pee-mail messages left by clinic visitors.

Her sock feet squished despite avoiding puddles. September scrubbed her face with the cuff of both sleeves. She'd only recently begun wearing a bit of makeup again. What a waste. Now, tears had turned her into a clown. She could blame it on the pouring rain. She stopped for the moment to stare at the glowering sky. Grabbing the armful of dry clothes and boots from the back of the SUV, she balanced them atop the carrier and slammed the hatchback shut.

"Shadow, let's go. Take your leash." He bounded to her, took the leash in his mouth, and she followed him to the clinic doorway. After elbowing open the lever handle she pushed the door closed, and left a dirty sock print on the kick plate. September made a mental note to clean it off before Robin noticed and complained.

Shadow paw danced around the empty waiting room, claws ticking like tap shoes on the tile. He ran to the front counter, jumped up to peer over the edge, ears forward and tail waving. His ears fell and he hopped down and dropped his leash when Robin stood up and glowered.

"I told you before, he should be on a leash. Carrying it doesn't count." Her disapproval extended to the muddy footprints, both dog and human.

September didn't bother to acknowledge the old argument. "Is Doc Eugene around? Need to talk with him about this kitten." She set the carrier on the counter and the baby stuck a paw through the grill. "And I need to change clothes."

"Another charity case, I bet." Robin said something under her breath and started to take the carrier. "All these freebies cost the clinic money. The Good Samaritan Fund is nearly depleted."

"It's a rescue, yes, but a special case." September shifted the carrier out of reach. She gave in to temptation. "Please tell your *boss* I'm here. I'll wait."

Robin stepped away, her back stiff. "I just mopped the floor, you know, and appointments could come in at any time. Why don't you

wait in the dog room—number three—and stop dripping all over."
She flipped her hair as she whirled, and this time September caught the
muttered, "Cheapskate."

Shadow leaned against September's thigh and whined, so she
stroked his ears. "Don't let her get to you. She wants to be in charge,
and gets pissed when reminded she's not." Robin knew about her
lottery winnings and thought, like much of Heartland, that September
had money to burn. She didn't know and probably wouldn't care that
most of the money was gone. Robin would be equally surprised to
learn September funded the Good Sam program that paid fifty percent
of care costs for un-owned critters, if the rescuer agreed to pay the
other half.

September heard arguing voices. Crap. Robin probably redirected
her aggravation toward someone else. People did that with spouses and
kids after a bad day at work where they couldn't talk back to the boss.
Even pets did it, lashing out against other pets or owners when they
couldn't reach the preferred target.

Reading her disquiet, Shadow nudged her and picked up his leash.
He tried to push it into her hands, implication clear.

She laughed. "We'll go soon." She gathered the carrier and clothes,
and led the way down the narrow hallway to the examining room
Robin indicated. If the woman hadn't acted like a jerk, she'd have
mopped up the mess herself.

The kitten stuck paws out of the carrier front once more. "Poor
baby, this has been quite an ordeal for you." She crooned and touched
the little paw, encouraged when it didn't withdraw. The kitten flinched
and yowled when she touched the other bloody paw. "What a brave
little cat." It clearly had suckered BeeBo, a confirmed dog guy, into
championing its cause. She wondered where he'd found the tiny thing.

A soft knock on the connecting door made Shadow alert. He
cocked his head as the door opened and a young girl peeked around.
"September? Hi Shadow." Nikki fell to her knees and opened her arms,
and Shadow turned into a blithering idiot dog. He fell on his back, legs
splayed and tail waving, making blissful noises in his throat as Nikki
rubbed his chest. "Robin said to tell you Doc Eugene's busy, and that
I should help. And she said to blame you that I get to mop again."
Nikki smoothed her white-blond hair behind each ear, and giggled. "I'd
rather mop than muck out the kennels any old day."

September grinned. "When you work with animals, crappiocca
happens." She motioned to her clothes. "I'd give you a hug, but you'd

get soaked, too. Can you babysit Shadow and the kitten for me while I get changed?"

Nikki nodded, and at mention of the cat, left Shadow waving his paws in the air to peer in the carrier. "Aw, what a cutie."

"That's Fuzzit. Don't let him out, and don't touch him, not until I talk to Doc Eugene, okay? It's sort of a quarantine situation."

"It's sick?" Nikki peered closer. "He's got a torn claw. Poor baby."

September gathered up the clothes. "Shadow, *wait*. Be right back, I'll bring some treats." He stood and shook himself, and whined a soft protest, but didn't argue.

She rushed to the small bathroom in the rear of the clinic, in a hurry to get inside before Robin interrupted again. Quickly she shucked out of her outerwear, and peeled off wet socks. The dry jeans and old but clean sweatshirt warmed her chilled skin, and a paper towel dried her feet. The work boots would fit loose and probably rub on bare feet but she didn't have a dry pair of socks. She wouldn't have to wear them for long, though, and could change once she got home. September checked the mirror. That explained Robin's expression when she'd showed up. She washed away streaked makeup. She couldn't do much with her rat's nest hair, though.

She bundled the wet clothes and carried them back to the exam room, surprised to see Nikki playing the *show-me* game with Shadow.

Nikki held a cat magazine in one hand and the leash in the other. "This is *magazine*." She held it out. "This is *leash*." Shadow cocked his head, and panted happily as she held each an equal distance from her body. "Shadow, *show-me* LEASH."

He leaped forward, and nose-poked the leash.

"Good-boy." Nikki preened. "He did it for me, too."

"Yes, he's a good boy. By the way, he knows the word *book* for magazines, books, anything like that, so it's less confusing. Short names work best." She stroked his head. "He's smart, but we have to give him a little help."

"Can we teach him new words?" Nikki searched the exam room for something else to name.

"His head will explode soon, he knows so much." The game taught Shadow names of objects. September used *show-me* more as a way to practice their communication and keep his attention sharp. But people delighted in seeing the trick demonstrated. In practical terms, a service dog learned the names of many objects in order to partner with the human. Although she'd never planned it, more than once the lessons learned in the *show-me* game had saved her life.

"I tried to play with my cat Hope, but she won't pay attention long enough. Unless there's food involved."

September dumped the clothes on a nearby wooden chair. "I've not taught the game to Macy. Cats have shorter attention spans than dogs, and different motivations. And not every dog has the focus or interest, either. All pets are individuals, Nikki."

"That's for sure." Nikki crossed to the cabinet and pulled open drawers for a likely pair of objects. "Maybe he already knows everything."

"He likes to play the game anyway. We can use things he already knows." September rummaged in her damp clothes and found the car keys, and drew the dog's attention to her. "Shadow, this is *light*." She thumbed on the laser light that Macy adored chasing. "And this is *sock*." She dangled one of the wet socks she'd shed. "*Show-me* SOCK."

Shadow pounced forward, and grabbed the soaked material, and then shook it and tossed it in the air. It landed with a soft "splat" on the tile, and Nikki giggled again.

"Wait, I know." Nikki pulled out a small tablet. "How about this?"

September took the device, frowning, and tried to think how it appeared to Shadow, and what other objects he already knew might correspond. "Hand me that, too." She pointed, and Nikki passed her the coffee mug from the sink with lettering that spelled, "Real Doctor." She'd bet it had been a joke-gift from the veterinarian's late wife.

Shadow watched with interest. He already knew that she called all drink containers "cup" so that made it simple. "Shadow, this is *cup*." She held out the mug and he sniffed it. "This is...*tablet*." September held the objects, one in each hand, out to her sides. "*Show-me* CUP." He nose poked the mug, and she didn't move either object. "Good boy. Now, *show-me* TABLET." He happily touched the tablet, and tried to take it from her.

"Ew, dog drool." Nikki, delighted, took back her tablet and wiped the surface with her sleeve. She scrounged for something else, opened another drawer, and pulled out a pair of shiny bandage scissors and held them up with a question in her eyes.

September pointed to a jar of treats on the counter. After all, she'd promised him treats. This would be a real test for him, something new compared to something he wanted. Shadow licked his lips when the treat jar lid clinked, but sat patiently.

"Shadow. This is *treat.*" September held one in the palm of her right hand. She took the scissors from Nikki in her other hand, and held it carefully, pointed away from the dog. She hesitated, and decided on a name. "This is *knife.*" He glanced quickly at it, and then back to the treat hand. "Shadow, *show-me* KNIFE."

He bounced forward, and nose-bumped the scissors and then scooped the treat out of her other hand. Nikki gasped as the scissors took flight and rebounded against the opening door.

Doc Eugene entered. "Sounds like a party in here." He bent and picked up the scissors.

"*Show-me* game." September shrugged an apology.

"You mean, the show-off game, right, big fellow?" Shadow slicked his ears down and rubbed against the big man, happy with the attention. "Nikki, could you put these away, please? Oh, and these, too." He handed her the bandage scissors along with a pair of bolt cutters. "Thanks, dear. I'll call you if I need you." He watched as the girl scurried out the room. "I should have so much energy."

"You use bolt cutters in a cardiac practice?" Doc Eugene served as both a general practitioner for dogs and cats, and a veterinary heart specialist. He'd diagnosed Macy's hypertrophic cardiomyopathy.

"Yep. And sadly, not the first time I've needed to use them." He rubbed the back of his neck. "Newly adopted dog came in, only been with the owners a week or so, and he suddenly turned vicious. Snapped at their kids. They were heartbroken, but wanted him euthanized, said they couldn't risk giving him to somebody else."

September's heart constricted. "Extra furry, right?"

Voice grim, he added, "We sedated him, and shaved his neck. Found exactly what you'd expect. A puppy size chain collar digging into his skin. Somebody put it on him months ago and didn't bother to remove it when he got big. Had to use bolt cutters to get it off. We cleaned him up, and physically he'll recover. He even wagged his tail, licked my hand after it came off." He pulled off his glasses, polished them. "Amazing the resiliency of pets."

"So the owners? . . ."

"They're willing to try. My bet is on the dog. Sweet little guy." He cleared his throat, and adjusted his glasses. "Now, Robin said you have another charity case." His smiled at her expression. "Don't let her get to you. She's trying to show me how to turn more of a profit. Is this the kitty? What's the problem?"

Quickly she told him, and watched his expression darken. "BeeBo was a good man. Who has his dogs?"

"Animal Control was on the way. I left before they arrived."

"So the police need a safe place for this kitten until they can collect any evidence?" He frowned. "The isolation room is empty; we can quarantine there."

"I was told it wouldn't be more than a day, two at the most. Tell Robin the city will pay. And if it's longer, I'll take care of it." September knew BeeBo would have done the same for her.

"Never mind about the payment." Doc Eugene's expression changed. "Are you all right?"

At the kind words, her eyes filled with no warning. "No. I am not all right." She grabbed a tissue from the nearby dispenser, and blew her nose. "I found a man dead."

He patted her shoulder. "Of course you're upset. Don't worry about the kitten. You take Shadow home and play some Frisbee, why don't you?"

At the F-word, Shadow tipped his head, and woofed as if in agreement.

September collected her clothing, Shadow's leash and the car keys, and returned to her car. Her feet slid up and down in the boots. But before she could start the car, her phone rang.

She saw two missed calls and a text, all from Mom. None were from Combs, and she choked back disappointment. She told herself she didn't want to talk to him anyway. Besides, he had his hands full with the dogfight ring.

"Yes Mom, sorry I missed your calls."

"Where are you? The curtain goes up in twenty minutes. I told the director how professional you are, and now you've embarrassed me, and—"

"Wait? There's a performance today? You said rehearsal."

"They changed it from a brush up to a performance after the run sold out. The entire cast, orchestra, and crew, not to mention the theater board of directors, are all here. You know how important this is for Steven, too, and for me. I'm the hostess for the after party." Her voice went up a notch. "If I tell them, they can hold curtain for maybe ten minutes. Are you coming or not?"

Crap. She'd let her family down too many times already. Besides, she didn't have anything better to do. Not like she had a date or anything. "I'll be there."

# Chapter 12

Nikki crooned to the cat and put her hand against the front of the stainless steel cage. The kitty cheek rubbed and clutched her hand through the bars. "Let's get you a clean spot, okay?" She'd already spread fresh newspaper in the adjacent cage, and quickly opened the door to move the patient away from its soiled temporary home. "Don't be embarrassed, kitty. It's the anesthesia makes you wet the bed, it's not your fault. And your mommy will come pick you up soon, so you can go home."

She briefly cuddled the cat, but carefully avoided the spay stitches on the sore tummy. Nikki loved volunteering at the clinic on weekends, and had learned bunches from Doc Eugene. Mostly she kept the kennels and cages clean, walked the dogs and played with the cats.

Ever since Daddy came home from deployment right on time for Christmas, Mommy smiled more and Nikki and her older brother Hank got to do more stuff on their own. Hank wasn't so bossy anymore, either. After all, she'd finally turned ten years old, a very responsible age. Daddy said so.

For Christmas, she got to keep her rescued kitty, Hope, even though Mommy got sneeze-attacks around cats. And for her birthday a week later, Doc Eugene invited her to come learn how to take care of Hope and other animals on weekends. Today school closed for teacher business or something, so she got the day off and extra time at the clinic. For the first time ever, she got to watch a surgery.

Mommy thought it'd be gross and didn't want to let her. But Daddy called her his "littlest hero" because of how brave she'd been during the fire. He told Mommy that if she wanted to be an animal doctor, they had better find out now.

Turned out, it wasn't near as ooky as she expected. Blue paper covered up the prepped pets, with a little open spot for the surgical site. The opening centered on the tummy for the girls, or what Doc Eugene called "nether regions" for the boys. She loved seeing their upside-down kitty faces, so cute under the paper. Doc Eugene showed how to put ointment in the eyes, to help protect them.

Nikki gathered up urine-soaked paper, wrinkling her nose as she dumped it into the trash. Then she sprayed the cage with a cleaner, wiped it out good, and added more clean newspaper to the bottom.

"All set in here?" Doc Eugene stuck his head in the door. "Any problems? Everybody waking up okay?"

"Just finished. Tuxie sure is a stinker, though."

He walked down the bank of cages, checking each of the five recovering felines. "Remember what I told you about boy cat urine?"

"Yep. The girl cats think it's kitty cologne." She walked to the sink and used a bunch of liquid soap to get rid of the smell. "But when they get neutered, the smell goes away."

"Well, it's not as pungent anyway. Cat pee still smells like cat pee." The black and white Tuxie reached out and hooked Doc Eugene's sleeve with his claws, until he stopped and gave the cat some attention. "What did you think of the surgery?"

"Kind of neat. Hank said I'd pass out from all the blood. But there wasn't hardly any." She'd had worse nosebleeds.

"I sure didn't want you to pass out."

"It's way more complicated than I thought." Nikki smoothed her special veterinary assistant smock, powder blue with cartoon cats, dogs and bunnies on it. "You got to weigh them, figure out how much sedation to put in the shot, then get them ready."

"What else?"

"Put on a heart monitor and...put that tube thingy down their neck."

"Intubate, right. And?"

"Hook up the gas anesthesia. Put them on a heating pad. Then you got to scrub in." She ticked each item off on her fingers. "Can I do that sometime? Wash really good and put on gloves and gown and mask and all?"

"You think you'd like that? Help with surgeries someday?"

"Not only help. I want to DO the surgeries and be a vet."

Doc Eugene walked to the door. "You keep that focus, Nikki, and it'll happen."

She fairly glowed. Nikki pulled her tablet out and activated her favorite app, and quickly posted an update to the private Show And Tell group of a bunch of kids from all over. Somehow, it was easier showing and telling stuff to strangers than people you saw every day. Nikki shared everything with the group, especially happy stuff. Almost immediately she got several "likes" and started to post a picture of Tuxie when Robin stuck her head in the door.

"Nikki, stop messing around and go walk the dogs." Robin spoke with a broad West Texas drawl that got on Nikki's nerves.

"I just got finished." Nikki hunched her shoulders and stuck the device back in her backpack. She liked the dogs well enough, but Robin always made sure Nikki got the truly nasty kennels to clean. As much as she admired Doc Eugene, she disliked the new office manager he'd hired. She was all cotton candy sweet in front of the veterinarian, batting her heavily made up eyes and swinging her hips, but morphed into a tyrant dishing out scut jobs as soon as he turned his back. Nikki ducked past the big woman who nearly blocked the doorway, and turned toward the dog kennels on the other side of the building.

Nikki nearly reached the far door before Robin stopped her again. "Have you soaked the instruments? I showed you how to get them ready for the autoclave. If I have to tell you every single thing, I might as well do it myself."

*Then why don't you?* But Nikki didn't dare voice the words. She suspected Robin tried to get Nikki fired. She didn't know why Robin hated her. "Do you want me to walk dogs, clean kennels, or do instruments?" She tried to make her voice soothing the way she talked to her skittish cat Hope.

"Don't take that tone with me, young lady." Robin's eyebrow piercing bobbed up and down. "You smart mouth me, and I don't care how much Eugene likes you, your narrow little butt is gone, charity case and all."

"What do you mean? I'm a volunteer. I just want to learn stuff."

"I just want to learn stuff." Robin mimicked her with baby talk. "Give me a break. I work my butt off, and take any overtime I can get to cover rent and make car payments, buy groceries, pay off loans. You waltz in here, spend a couple hours a week petting puppies and kitties—"

"Well duh. I'm a kid. My parents don't make me pay for food, except special snacks I get from my allowance." Nikki covered her mouth, tickled at the thought. "And I can't drive, so why would I want a car?" She couldn't help rolling her eyes.

"I wanted tickets to that sold out musical, but you whined and cajoled and Eugene gave his tickets to you. It's your day to volunteer, but I have to work." She stomped down the hallway toward her, and it was all Nikki could do to hold her ground. Robin stuck her face close, and her fierce whispers smelled of beef jerky and Dr. Pepper. "When you work for free he doesn't have to pay me overtime. And on top of that, he gives you all your cat food and meds and even the spay surgery for free. *For free.*"

Nikki started to deny it. She'd seen Daddy give Doc Eugene money for Hope's care. But she also remembered her parents argued over the cost. Was it true? Had she embarrassed Daddy? But that meant she needed to work even harder to pay and make it up to Doc Eugene, never mind what Robin-the-Rat said. She drew up her chest and stood tall and proud, the way Daddy said soldiers stood, and never took any guff. "We're not a charity case either."

"Just go clean up the dog poop. That's all you're good for." Robin stalked away, opened the door to the front reception area, and closed the door.

Blinking furiously, Nikki whirled and banged through the door to the dog room. A Chihuahua yelped in surprise, and a big black mutt recovering from anesthesia lifted his head, tried to stagger to his feet, and instead banged his tail against the floor.

Nikki retrieved her tablet and let the hurt flow in an impetuous burst of misspelled words to the Show And Tell group. Nobody knew who Nikki-Kitty was anyway, so what could it hurt?

Before she could stow it away and begin to muck out the poopy kennels, the "bing" announced a message reply. Her eyes widened. She got more than a simple "like" this time. It came from Kid Kewl himself, the owner of the whole super-secret group.

*"Hush little Nikki, don't be mad.*
*I'm gonna fix, turn your sad to glad."*

## Chapter 13

Singers on the stage moved with practiced ease as they awaited their musical cues. Seated above the actors toward the rear of the orchestra loft, September counted the measures silently, attention divided between the conductor at the front of the orchestra and soloist poised on the balcony across the way. The baton raised, cue given, and September's extended right arm danced her bow across the strings in a syncopated drumbeat of sound while her left hand fingered the strings. The eerie driving rhythm, echoed in the rest of the string section, built the desired tension and had the attentive matinee audience on the edge of their seats until all fell silent save for the celesta's single delicate music box chord.

"How...could I ever know," sang Lily-the-Ghost.

With a smile, September leaned forward, long hair spilling over her shoulders only a few shades darker than her cello. She embraced the cello she'd named Harmony like a mother comforting her child. Musical tension released along with her shoulders with the audience's collective sigh. Harmony's tenor strains blended molasses-rich to complement the actor's mint-fresh soprano soon joined by the tragic hero's tenor.

The lyrics cut too close to home. Guilt, shameful secrets, lives destroyed, all remained too fresh and September funneled the pain into each bow-stroke until music washed clean and transformed emotion into pure bliss. Music saved her sanity once before, and she'd only recently dared to play again after a year's long hiatus. She had no reason to hide anymore. Music wouldn't betray her and might even complete the healing.

Playing might give Mom reason to be proud of her, for a change. Her parents, Rose and Lysle January, sat in the front row in the audience to cheer their grandson in the children's chorus. This was eight-year-old Steven's theatrical debut.

Steven still didn't talk, but when Grandma Rose discovered he communicated most easily with rhymes and singing, she arm-twisted the theater director to include him in the children's chorus. September doubted how much Steven enjoyed being around so many people, but one didn't question Rose January. Especially about her grandbabies. She was always right. She'd tell you so, herself.

Thunder shook the theater, real thunder, not the electronic sound effects already used several times during the show. The actor playing Lily hit a high note, the shimmery tone pure, true and clear. Archibald strained to hit his high tenor part of the duet. His voice cracked into an unfortunate squeak, but quickly recovered. Shadow, positioned next to September, added a soft baritone moan of complaint, turning the duet into a trio.

September gave the "shush" signal, but Shadow continued to moan-sing along with the actors. When the tenor's voice again failed to reach the appropriate note, Shadow's arrroooo climbed the scale in a two-octave arpeggio that rivaled the singers' ranges.

Her face warmed at the orchestra director's dirty look, but she kept playing. How could she stop? September could imagine Mom's reaction and risked a quick peek over the railing to the audience below. Dad hid a smile with his program, but Mom sat stiff and unyielding, ignoring the doggy trumpet-blat.

At least the rest of the audience didn't realize it was a dog. The first act had struggled with feedback from the mics, after all. The actor playing Archibald turned red-faced but sang with renewed vigor, determined to out-sing Shadow's enthusiastic counterpoint.

A rest came in the music, and September again signaled Shadow to shush, but he thought it was a game. Other musicians giggled, some outright laughing with delight. September mouthed a silent "sorry" to the director but his expression forgave nothing. His nostrils flared while the baton beat the air.

The duet came to a close and Shadow's commentary quieted. She whispered to him, still aware the director watched. "Good-dog, Shadow, good shush." Praise the good, ignore the bad while gritting your teeth. That took practice, but the effort worked much better than the alternatives. "Here, take care of Bear. Bear is lonely." She nudged the dog's stuffed toy with one foot, giving him something legal to do with his mouth other than howl. He grabbed it, propped one paw over it, and began to nurse on its misshapen head.

She readied herself for the finale, grateful for the end of the performance but dreading the after-party. Mom planned the shindig for the entire cast and crew, more to showcase herself as a donor and her grandson Steven. After Shadow's impromptu solo, September knew she'd be the target of hurt and angry glares from actors, the directors and most especially, Mom-the-perfectionist.

The rest of the performance finished note-perfect both onstage and off. The applause faded, and September cleaned her bow, wiped rosin from the strings and closed the cello score. The rest of the players put away their instruments, most smiling at her on their way downstairs. A few spoke to Shadow, but none offered to pet him. They were locals. They knew her history, and respected his working dog status despite his lapse in etiquette.

Dr. Parker Belk, the orchestra director, weaved through the chair obstacle course until he loomed above her, and September flushed again. They'd only met briefly two hours ago, when he'd introduced her as the substitute cellist.

She forced herself to meet his storm-cloud-gray eyes. "I'm so sorry." She put one hand on Shadow's head, and the dog wagged but didn't release his toy. "It's my fault, I need time to prep him to the singers." Shadow had never been around singers. He'd probably considered singing to be a human howl.

"Your mother told me you were a professional, and I appreciate you sitting in at the last minute. Sight-reading the score, that's impressive. But Rose said nothing about your pet wolf attending the performance." Parker straightened his red bow tie, and smoothed the black tuxedo jacket, making September feel even frumpier in the old jeans and tracking boots she'd not had time to change.

"He's a service dog." She turned off the stand light and rose to face him. He stood a head taller than her five-feet six inches, but not as tall as Combs.

"A service dog should have better manners. Don't you have to take a test to get a license or something? Why doesn't he wear a vest?"

"You're right, he shouldn't have howled. Beyond that, you're misinformed." There was no test, license or identification required of service dogs. In fact, under ADA guidelines, even business owners were only allowed to ask if a dog provided a service, and what the dog was trained to do.

September accepted the cello case he handed to her. She expected him to march off in a huff.

He was right. But he didn't have to be a jerk. "I said I'm sorry, Professor Belk." She kept her voice low, but Shadow immediately dropped his Bear-toy with a whine.

"Call me Parker." He smiled, the first time she remembered seeing anything but a scowl, and it transformed his stormy expression and took years off his age. "I hate this monkey suit but can't change until after the meet-and-greet with donors. You're coming, too." He gestured at Shadow. "Bring the wolf, so they know it wasn't me this time criticizing the performance."

The turn-about caught her by surprise. The vertical scowl lines framing his wide mouth smoothed, replaced by a dimple at one corner of his crooked smile. She smiled back, but she couldn't quell disquiet. "Okay, sure. There's a week until the next performance, plenty of time to work with Shadow before then. He won't howl again."

"Oh, that's right. Rose said you trained him yourself. Everyone's doing that now." He rubbed his chin. "My sister-in-law got one of those Internet certifications so she could take her little poufy dog on planes for free."

She stiffened. "Excuse me?" She hated fake services gaming the system. It just made it harder for those with legitimate animal partnerships. September put a hand on Shadow's brow, and steadied her breathing.

Parker didn't seem to notice he'd offended her. "Thanks for filling in on such short notice. You saved my bacon."

At the *bacon* word, Shadow cocked his head and licked his lips. September made eye contact with the dog and shook her head and his ears drooped with disappointment. She sheathed her bow into the front-case slot, and noticed the other musicians had already left.

When her phone pinged, she checked the display and noted three missed calls, all from Combs. She quickly pocketed the phone, and her music-induced high drained away quicker than a toilet's flush.

"You have to come to the party." Parker's request held a note of pleading. "I hate these things, but it's expected. Everybody knows everyone, but I'm a newbie to the theater like you. Besides," he leaned forward and whispered, "Rose made me promise to get you there."

That explained a lot. Rose never did anything without a reason. She wondered if Parker was Mom's latest matchmaking target. September took a moment, appraising him. Heck, why not? They at least had music in common. That was a hell of a lot less stressful than dead bodies.

Shadow pressed against her. "I'm okay, baby-dog." She touched his ruff and her breathing steadied. Mom would have a cow if September had a panic attack here, in front of the folks Rose wanted to impress.

Her phone buzzed in her pocket. September pulled it back out to check. Combs again. She declined the call, and pocketed the phone.

"Let me carry your ax?" Parker didn't wait for her answer. He grabbed the cello's backpack straps, slung Harmony onto his shoulders, and headed for the stairs. "You coming?"

What choice did she have? "Shadow, let's go. Bring Bear."

Shadow thundered down the cement stairs and waited for her impatiently at the bottom. September kept one hand on the railing, habit after her knee repair surgery. This could be good, reconnecting with fellow musicians, people she understood and with whom she shared common interests. She'd make a ten-minute appearance at the party and be polite to Parker. At least she had a good excuse to dodge Mom.

Thunder boomed again, and the lights flickered off and back on. "What fun, it's a thunder party, right Shadow?" She joined the dog at the foot of the stairs, jollying him with her happy voice as she reattached his leash.

He offered a muffled woof, the Bear-toy still clenched tight in his jaws, and shook the stuffed toy hard while his tail flagged high. The sight of his bullet notched ear was a stark reminder of past danger they had faced. Better to focus on music. Anyone with half a brain would choose rim shots over gunshots.

Parker stopped, eyebrows raised. "Thunder party?"

"Some dogs fear loud noises, especially thunder. So ever since Shadow was a baby, we've had thunder parties with fun games and treats when it got noisy." That probably had helped Shadow get through his close calls, although she hadn't planned it that way.

She followed Parker from the backstage to the floor of the stage. Actors mingled with fans, mostly family, and accepted bouquets, hugs, posed for pictures and signed programs. Most of the musicians stood in an awkward group to one side. September moved to join them, until she saw Parker dodging between bodies to cross the stage. He still carried Harmony over his shoulder.

"Parker, wait." He made a beeline to her parents. Crap. Into the lion's den. Now she had to explain Shadow's disruption with the whole world listening.

The play director stood chatting with Mom and Dad, and Rose gave Parker a brief hug and then searched the room for September. Parker bent to greet Steven, and the child turned away, his green eyes stabbing September from across the room.

She hadn't seen Steven since that horrible day last November. He'd grown since then. And he acted so formal, not like a child at all, despite his frail frame. Steven stood military straight, but when Mom reached to stroke his white-blond hair, he shifted away like a skittish cat. Mom urgently beckoned September to join them.

Shadow whined, leaning back against her legs. September smoothed the dog's black brow, unconsciously mirroring Mom's comforting gesture. Far from dodging away like Steven, though, Shadow leaned into her palm wanting more. He dropped Bear-toy and shivered a bit, and then pulled back on the leash not wanting to move. "What's wrong, baby-dog? You've never been scared of thunder before."

*** 

Shadow stared at all the strangers milling about and talking with loud voices. He only recognized a few. Nikki saw him and smiled, and he wondered if Doc Eugene might be there, too. Shadow's tail stirred until she turned away to talk to Steven. His tail fell.

Steven had grown taller, thinner, and somehow *sharper* than before. Shadow shivered when Steven stared into his eyes. His-boy had never done that before, and Shadow slid his eyes aside, the way a polite dog should.

All around him, strangers laughed and talked so loudly it hurt a good-dog's ears. He felt unsettled by Steven's odd behavior. He trusted September, but she acted distressed, too. That made Shadow worry. Her smell always changed before she had a scary-gone time, when her heart hammered and she panted like something chased her, and she fell into a deaf-blind-screaming fit. In those times, she couldn't hear him, or see him. Shadow warned her before a scary-gone time happened, and sometimes September kept it at bay. When she couldn't, Shadow protected September until she knew him again.

Her smell hadn't changed. But it might. September tried to be brave, but he could always tell when she struggled. So, Shadow pressed close to her side to keep her safe. Nobody told him he should. Shadow figured that out all by himself. He was smart that way.

In the before, a lifetime ago when Steven had been his-boy, Shadow kept Steven safe. September showed him how. He stayed close beside Steven so his-boy didn't wander away, and barked loud to warn adult humans when Steven needed help. Shadow learned how to understand what September wanted him to do when she told him to *sit* and *down* and *wait*. He learned not to pull too hard or lag behind on the leash, especially when Steven grabbed hold of the leash, and that he should always stay with his-boy.

September played games that made him think hard and wag harder when he finally figured out what she wanted. September made a "click" noise with her mouth and gave him a treat when he guessed right, until he didn't have to guess anymore. He knew many words, like "phone" and "cello" and "Macy-cat." He'd learned some things all by himself, too, including "car ride" and "Frisbee" and "bacon." He really liked bacon.

Steven never talked but sometimes he screamed. Shadow wondered why. He yawned, and peeked quickly at Steven again, relieved that his-boy no longer stared. Staring made his skin prickle.

Long ago, Shadow decided he should teach Steven the joys of playing tug and fetch, tummy rubs and running fast-fast-fast. Instead, Steven stacked rocks, or made things spin, boring games for Shadow. Before, his-boy never looked at him, not directly. And Steven never ever petted him, even though Shadow ached to be petted. Maybe if he knew how to make the click-mouth-sound, Steven would understand.

Shadow nudged September with his nose, and her hand dropped to smooth his brow. That made him feel better. She'd been a constant in his life even in the before-time when Shadow lived at Steven's house.

She understood Shadow even when he couldn't make click-noises to explain. She petted him—BLISS—and scratched his hard-to-reach spots. September never yelled if he made mistakes. When he did something right, she called him "good-dog" until he thought he'd melt with delight. He liked pleasing September and being called "good-dog" even more than getting a treat. Unless it was bacon.

He didn't *try* to love September. It simply happened. And now they belonged to each other.

Seeing Steven made his heart jump with concern. Fur stood off his shoulders at the memory of Steven pointing the gun, the scary-pop sound and acrid smell when it bit his ear. Ever since that day, he'd lived with September and been a good-dog for her, keeping her safe from bad dreams and bad men. He didn't want to get close to Steven ever again.

Shadow whined, and nudged September's thigh again with his nose. He wanted to go home, take a car ride back to their house. Macy waited for him there. His Frisbees were in their car. His life belonged with September.

"What's wrong, baby-dog?" He could tell she didn't want to talk to Steven or the people around him. But her voice made everything better, and he licked her hand to tell her so. He jumped up, surprising her. He wasn't supposed to, but needed her arms around him. She scolded him with a laugh that said she didn't mean it.

Shadow didn't object when she scooped up Bear-toy where he'd dropped it, and tucked it under her arm. When she tugged his leash, Shadow reluctantly followed, but he kept his eyes down, away from Steven. His tail tucked.

She wouldn't, would she? Hand his leash to Steven? His tail tucked tighter at the thought and he whimpered. Humans did things that made no dog-sense sometimes. Shadow wanted to please September, but not if it meant going away from her. He'd do anything to stay with her. She belonged to him, they belonged together.

Why had Steven come back, unless he meant to take Shadow away? That would hurt worse than the gun-bite.

His whimper became a steady whine. He debated digging his feet into the rough floor. Shadow had chosen to disobey September before, when he knew—knew for certain—that she was wrong. This time he wasn't sure, and the confusion and worry made his head hurt and heart ache. Before he could decide, September's phone made a funny sound and she stopped to talk.

Her scent changed and then her voice. Alarm fluttered his stomach when she asked, "Who is this? Why do you have Detective Combs's phone?"

Shadow didn't recognize the young voice on the other end of the device. Only that the girl sounded terrified.

"Melinda?" September stiffened when she said the word, and Shadow nose poked her thigh, but she ignored him. "Willie's gone? Oh my God."

Cocking his head, Shadow studied her face. The whites of her eyes and wrinkled brow matched her words, and her scent became brittle with the rush of energy. September waved at the adults across the room, and pointed to her phone. He couldn't help his paw-dance of relief when she did an about face.

"Let's go, Shadow."

They hurried back through the crowds to the rear door of the building. Together. A team. Away from Steven.

# Chapter 14

September ran from the crowded stage. A lost child trumped anything Mom had planned. No time to discuss or explain, especially with Steven within earshot. She couldn't guess how much her nephew remembered about his ordeal. No need to remind him.

"Let's go, Shadow, time for car ride." He woofed and pranced and she let him off the leash. Thunder rattled the building again, but this time he didn't react. His earlier fearful behavior she ascribed to the strange place and crowd. September regretted leaving Harmony behind, but trusted Parker would lock the cello in the box office until she could collect her.

As they left the building, the sky dumped buckets of rain. Heavy winds pushed water into waves skittering across the pavement and sheets lashed her tangled hair. Crap. It had been cloudy and warm when she arrived, so she'd left her coat in the car. With no other choice, the pair ducked and ran to September's SUV parked half a block away. She thumbed the key-lock, waited for Shadow to leap into the back seat, slammed his door and then dove into the front.

Wicked gusts caught the driver's door and it took two tries to slam it shut. Cold water poured down September's neck, and she swiped her face with a drenched sleeve. In the back seat, Shadow shook, splattering the inside of the car.

"Gee thanks, baby-dog." In response, he wagged, slicked back his ears and poked his nose through the metal grill that kept him from claiming the driver's seat. September reached back, and smoothed his soaked face. Her sweatshirt stuck to her skin. She gathered her soaked hair to one side to wring it out on the passenger side floor. *At least it's not a blizzard.*

The slate-color clouds churned, black edges tattered flags streaming with the wind. Occasional lightening strobed the area into an eerie stop-action movie.

After she started the car, September crept from the parking lot, leaning forward to peer through windshield wipers that snick-snacked but still couldn't clear her view. The deluge cut visibility to nil, but they couldn't wait. Shadow could track Willie's dog, and with luck, they'd be together. Any hope for a successful search ticked away with every minute delayed, and rain diluted scent while wind chased it away and made it harder for Shadow to track. But they had to try.

Before she'd gone half a block, a dashboard light alerted her to an unlatched door. She must have keyed open the rear hatch of the SUV. She pulled to the side of the road, and Shadow watched with interest when September caped her down-filled coat above her head to run and slam shut the rear door. The piles of blankets and tracking equipment stored in the back would need drying out later.

Although she knew the address, September had no reason or desire to visit the Harrison residence before today. Combs's kids lived with his ex-wife Cassie and her new husband Rick Harrison in a two-and-a-half story brick monstrosity designed to shout their elevated social status to the world.

After fifteen minutes, the overhead faucet shut off. Gutters on each side of the street overflowed, creating whitewater the overtaxed drain system couldn't handle and leaving only the crown of the street free of runoff. September un-crunched her shoulders and sat back in the seat, steering toward the middle of the road to stay clear of the flood swell. After so much recent precipitation, North Texas had been under flash flood warnings all week. Weird weather for February. September worried the temperature would drop and create a statewide skating rink.

Ten minutes later, with no traffic to speak of, September pulled into the Harrison's drive. Shadow stood and made concentric nose prints on the window. His tail thwapped against the back seat.

"Shadow, *wait*."

He yawned, and muttered his opinion, then turned away and pawed at the back seat. He woofed, and pricked his ears. Maybe he wanted his tracking gear she'd stowed in the back of the SUV. Shadow sometimes read her mind, and September liked to think she also tuned in to his thoughts.

She preferred Shadow with her, but better to question Melinda first. She left the keys in the car, hit the window child locks, and switched on the radio to her favorite classical station.

Cold gusts turned September's wet hair to a chilly mop that trailed over her shoulders nearly to her butt. Quickly she snugged tight the zipper on her oversize coat, the poufy padding more suited to snowstorms than rain. Even the damp cover helped cut the wind.

Before she could ring the bell, Melinda swung open the massive double doors. Red wavy hair framed her heart-shaped face. "You came." She peered past September toward the car. "You brought him? The tracking dog?" She swiped her palm against one eye.

September pushed into the foyer, and wrinkled her nose when her sodden clothes dripped on the spotless white marble. Who in their right mind designed an entry with white marble? "Where's your stepdad? Did you call him?"

Melinda hugged herself. "He's with Mom. Getting more tests." She pushed the door closed, and crossed her arms. "He couldn't do anything anyway. It's all about Mom. They don't have time for us." Her bitter tone spoke volumes.

Cassie suffered from a rare brain disorder that mimicked Alzheimer's, one of half a dozen or so in the region affected. September personally knew of two others.

"I'm sure that's not true." She had to say that, although Melinda probably was right. Rick naturally focused on his wife over his stepchildren. September understood the girl's resentment being saddled with Willie, and unable to hang out with friends. "Don't you have the number for Detective Gonzales? He's with your dad."

"I didn't want to get Dad in trouble leaving his phone and all." She looked away.

"Uh huh. Yes, I'm sure that wouldn't go over well." September couldn't resist the dry jab. Far more likely, Melinda lost track of time and knew she'd be in trouble when found out she'd let Willie out of her sight.

"Dad's busy. He's told me before I shouldn't call him during shift." Her voice rose. "You're supposed to be some dog tracking expert or something, so I called you." She jutted her jaw.

"Show me where your brother left the house. And could you loan me a towel?"

September gingerly tiptoed across light tan carpet to avoid leaving footprints. Once she reached the ceramic tile of the kitchen, she gratefully wiped her face with the hand towel Melinda offered.

The girl gestured to the hallway, voice defensive. "I was on the computer in my room. Doing homework. I heard Willie yell something about the dog. He's always trying to get me to take Kinsler out, especially when I'm in the middle of something. It was his turn, and besides, I didn't want to get my new leggings all muddy."

"That's the least of your worries." September walked to the kitchen door to check out the window. The back of the house boasted a good half acre of lush grass contained by a privacy fence painted to match the shutter's white trim. Standing water pooled in two corners of the yard, slowly draining beneath the wooden barrier. "He went out here, and through the gate? It's still ajar." She could see a narrow alley that divided this property from the neighboring house.

"Why anyone would want that dog is beyond me. He poops in the house, chewed up my fav boots. But Willie loves him." She wiped her eyes on the hem of her shirt. "Willie plays make believe with bad guys and stuff, pretending to be a super-cop and Kinsler's his partner."

Pretending to be his father.

"I heard the door open and Willie yelling and screaming. By the time I got in here, the back yard was empty."

"Why didn't you go after him?"

"I did. I'm not totally horrible, he *is* my brother." Melinda indicated her splattered leggings. "Ruined them chasing after Willie. He knows I'll get in trouble if he gets hurt." At the last word, she deflated. "I got to the gate in time to see this ginormous baby-poop-brown truck zoom away. And Willie wasn't there."

"You checked with the neighbors?"

"Yes. Yes, I checked. I'm not an idiot." She tossed her hair. "Sorry. But we're wasting time. For a while, I thought Willie hid to get back at me? But when it started storming, I knew he wasn't fooling." She grabbed a lock of wavy red hair and twisted it, a nervous habit that had left one side shorter than the other. "I tried to call Dad first. That's how I knew he left his phone when it went to voice mail and I heard it beeping on the table. Yours was the first name listed, and the first time I dialed sort of by accident. And then I thought, why not?" She took a breath. "So what about tracking Willie? We have to find him. Dad will kill me." Her chin trembled. "Willie thinks he's so grown up but he's only ten. Only a little boy."

September awkwardly embraced the girl. "It'll be okay." She'd bet anything Willie took shelter with a neighbor, and, like many little brothers, relished getting payback for being dismissed. Melinda hadn't mentioned the truck before, though, and that worried her. "I'll take a quick look, okay? But you have to call your dad. No arguments. Give me his phone."

Reluctantly, Melinda handed it over and September quickly scrolled through the contacts to find Winston Gonzales. "You know his partner, Detective Gonzales, right? Call him, explain who it is and ask to talk to your father. And you tell him what's going on."

Melinda's shoulders tightened but she nodded. "Don't you need your dog?"

"Shadow's trained to track other pets. So unless Kinsler is with your brother, Shadow probably wouldn't be much help." Besides, she still expected to see Willie trudge sheepishly out of the shrubbery once an adult ordered him inside. "Make that call. Now." She turned to the door.

Her wet tracking boots squeaked on the tile, and bare feet chaffed inside without socks. September dreaded going back out into the wind, and took a moment to pull up the hood on her coat. At least her feet wouldn't freeze. She hurried out the kitchen door, and trotted across the yard.

Sod squelched beneath her feet, and the atmosphere smelled of ozone. Her skin prickled with goose bumps that had nothing to do with the sudden temperature drop. September almost turned back to get Shadow.

She reached the wooden gate, and paused once she stepped through. The alley, more of a sandy pathway, served as shortcut through a field that separated two halves of the subdivision. The Harrison's home perched on a slight incline with the back yard leading downward to a natural runoff, dry most of the year, but now a raging torrent. Willie would have had to cross the water, and she prayed he'd not taken the chance. Too easy for a small child to be swept away. Heck, she wouldn't attempt crossing, either.

Heavy rain hadn't erased deep tire ruts that supported Melinda's account of a big truck. It had spun out to escape the mire. The drive foundation might be solid, but anything off the road hadn't a chance. She saw nothing as fine as a child's footprint, or dog's pad mark.

Lots of scrubby burl oak, cedar elm and mountain ash lined both sides of the drive, all barren of leaves, and offering no shelter to hide a small child. "Willie? William Combs, if you hear my voice, come home right now." She yelled as loud as she could, and paused to listen for a reply.

Nothing.

"Will-eeeeeeeeeeeeeeee!"

Something fluttered in a nearby tree. September cautiously stepped off the roadway, slaloming down the muddy incline, and grabbed a branch to steady herself. She plucked the blue and white scarf from the limb, each end festooned with the Dallas Cowboys star, something a little boy would love.

Lightening crackled and September jumped when a fingernail of light scratched the blackboard clouds. Rain pattered around her, the storm ready to reprise its assault.

She wheeled, and ran back the way she'd come, slipping and sliding in the muck as she cornered through the gate. September clutched the scarf close, as if shielding the fabric would extend protection to the child. She burst through the kitchen door, and nearly ran headlong into a wild-eyed woman.

"Who the hell are you?" A whip-thin lady with sharp features and flyaway red hair stalked her, brandishing a butcher knife. "And what are you doing with Willie's scarf?"

# Chapter 15

The truck lurched, and the dog in the back of the truck yelped again. Kelvin forced himself to ignore the cries of the "bait." Their sacrifice would put an end to a much larger horror, but that didn't assuage his guilt. At least the cats had stopped yowling. He needed all his attention for the uneven road.

He'd snagged the cats from the "free to good home" parking lot give-away next to the Wal-Mart. The woman's worry changed to grateful relief when he agreed to adopt them all. That moment would haunt him, and he damned Sunny for forcing his hand.

Sunny mocked his "humanization" of his dog Hercules. She treated her own dogs well, in the same way she cared for her guns and truck, but considered them replaceable tools. She treated people the same way, as either assets or expendable. Loyalty had a price, and emotion had no part in Sunny's life. The fires of childhood abuse forged her, so Kelvin didn't blame her brokenness, any more than he blamed a copperhead for its nature.

She demanded he get his hands dirty, too, as insurance he wouldn't hang her out to dry. Kelvin needed Sunny's unsavory contacts to spring the trap and be a hero. That would absolve him. Hell, if he hadn't taken the kittens, they'd be dumped somewhere else, and die anyway. This way, their sacrifice made a difference.

But compared to the high school kid, stealing a few animals barely rated. In this part of the country, anyone with half a brain knew what chained Pit Bulls meant, so it didn't surprise him when the kid ran. Hercules hadn't meant to kill the kid. Hell, the dog had been hysterical when Kelvin finally got him back to the truck. Nobody could know, not even Sunny. That'd give her insurance he'd never be able to pay off.

Kelvin couldn't have the cops bust the fight ring and disrupt the Doctor's plans before Kelvin could spring the trap.

If he hadn't got so rattled, Kelvin would've jacked the kid's car out of the muck and dumped it somewhere before running Hercules home. On his way back to address that little detail, the muddy stray dashed in front of his truck like a belated Christmas present. Kelvin slid to a stop, it waited for him, wriggling and wagging, and even slurped him across the face when he scooped it up. He slammed the kennel grate in the dog's face and tried to ignore the betrayal he imagined in its eyes.

The rain came down in sheets and he needed all his attention to keep the truck on the narrow lane, grateful when he could increase the turtle pace on the narrow drive. Kelvin slowed to a near stop, turned, and punched the gas and the truck jackrabbited onto the road. But he couldn't outrun the pungent wet-dog odor of the stolen dog that clung to his clothes.

He squinted at the dark clouds that turned day to twilight. The wipers flailed in an effort to keep the windshield clear, and the inside of the glass fogged despite the dashboard blower. Kelvin cracked opened his window to help clear the steamed glass. A prickly sensation tickled and raised hairs on the back of his neck and the rain abruptly stopped. The hum of tires on wet pavement changed when the truck slowed for the final turn.

He pulled onto the narrow pathway and rolled the window the rest of the way down. The ditch now rushed with water, and the kid's tinker-toy yellow car was gone.

Kelvin continued slowly down the drive, puzzling what that meant. Good that the car no longer flagged this turnoff like a hazard warning. If the flood took the Mini Cooper away, he must be living right.

But Sunny's friends had eyeballs on the area. If one of her cohorts saw what happened to the kid, and moved the car for the leverage,

Kelvin figured he'd just bit into a shit sandwich. He needed to pick Sunny's brain without giving her more ammo to screw him.

He pulled out his phone, and tried to get a dial tone. The weather played havoc with reception out here. Kelvin climbed out of the truck, and walked toward the rear of the vehicle before a couple of bars appeared on the phone promising better connection. Sunny answered on the first ring.

"Sunny, I picked up some bait like you said. Something happened, though, got to change plans."

Her voice crackled through static on the line. "I get paid anyway, whatever happens. That's the deal." The wind picked up so much Kelvin had trouble hearing Sunny's response.

He covered one ear and ducked his head, leaning against the truck bed to use as a windbreak. "A car got stuck in the mud, right off the road." He felt more than heard the hiccup in his voice and hoped Sunny didn't recognize the emotion.

"Did you go all Good Samaritan and help 'em out?" Sunny dropped the mocking inflection. "Keep him away from the barn, that's the main thing."

"I never found the driver." The lie came easily on the heels of relief. "I hope he caught a ride. If your friends caught him snooping, he wouldn't live to tell about it."

"True enough. Only reason they let you get close was my recommendation. It's a payday for them, too, if we don't screw it up."

"Right, that's what I figured. Anyway, now the car disappeared, and I didn't touch it." He kept his tone neutral. "Your friends again?"

Sunny paused. "Not that I heard. Whoever gave him a ride must've collected the car, too."

Kelvin half smiled. She didn't know. That didn't mean her friends didn't have him on video, though. "Maybe flood waters moved it. But you said they monitored the area. Is it cameras or what?" Lightening cracked and Kelvin jumped when a chorus of yowls erupted from the twin kennels in the truck's bed. "Could your, uhm, associates have moved it?"

Her answer again mixed with static proved too garbled to understand except for the last word: payday. Leave it to Sunny to have her priorities straight.

"I got to go, Sunny, it's fixing to storm something fierce. Don't worry, you'll get your money."

Her final jab came crystal clear. "Deliver your end of the bargain, Kelvin, and get those animals over to the barn or you'll have more than hail to worry about."

Kelvin disconnected without answering. Lightening crackled again, and rain rejoined its dance with the wind. Time had run out for the cats and stray dog in the back. He'd thought the price steep enough in terms of innocent lives, until BeeBo and the unnamed kid tipped the balance further into the red zone. He'd make sure their lives counted for something.

The truck lurched as Kelvin climbed back inside. In another day or two, it wouldn't matter if Sunny's associates knew anything or not. Once rounded up along with the Doctor, the cops would dismiss any fantastic claims they spouted as desperate fabrications.

He shoved the truck into gear, and drove slowly toward the hidden barn, already planning how to get the animals from the truck into the dumpsters. It'd take three or maybe four trips. He didn't have a carrier, so he'd have to tote one by one while dodging a path through the chained Pit Bulls. They wouldn't bother him, but probably considered smaller pets as prey. The truck hit a pothole, and the bucking movement jarred something loose in the truck's bed.

One of the kennel doors sprang open. It slapped to and fro in the growing wind. Kelvin took his foot off the gas when the three cats spilled out. The littlest one, the color of dark honey and probably just as sweet, climbed up something dark that moved. Kelvin twisted in his seat to stare, as the truck continued to coast.

The dark shape became a youngster. The boy tucked the small orange cat inside his coat and scooted on his butt to the passenger side of the truck bed. Kelvin cursed when the muddy white stray dog followed him. The boy boosted the pooch up and over the side of the truck. It yelped when it landed.

Kelvin watched with disbelief as the stolen "bait" escaped. The boy turned back, maybe to gather up the last two cats, saw him, and yelled. Kelvin slammed on the brakes.

"Run! Kinsler, run run run!" The boy vaulted over the side of the truck to follow the dog.

Kelvin leaped from the truck, cursing, but didn't attempt to stop the boy. He stood and watched him pelt down the muddy trail, never once looking back. He waited until the boy disappeared from sight and then Kelvin collected the remaining cats, and delivered them to their destiny. They'd have to be enough.

# Chapter 16

The fire in his lungs finally made Willie stop, but he still couldn't catch his breath. He stumbled off the side of the road to hunch beneath sheltering limbs of a live oak, leaves sparse but still green despite the weather they'd had. He propped himself against the tree before his noodle-weak knees gave out. The little cat inside his jacket shivered and mewed, and its tail slipped out. He tucked it back inside, thinking the waffle-colored tabby had the longest tail he'd ever seen.

Willie peered around the tree, and breathed easier at the empty road. He'd lucked out. Either the nefarious bad guy couldn't turn his truck around quick enough to chase, or he had more important stuff to do. Like maybe steal more kids' dogs and cats.

"Kinsler? Where are you?" Willie thought the dog was right behind him. "Kin....sler. Come here, boy, come on, let's go home."

Waffles shivered and yowled in answer. "Hey, it's okay, little guy. Kinsler probably caught a whiff of squirrel and took off again. Dang dog lets his nose talk him into trouble. That's what Melinda says."

Melinda would know what to do. For a girl, she was pretty smart. At least Kinsler got away from the dog thief. Maybe he'd sniff his way home.

Willie's teeth chattered. It'd be cool if he had a fur coat and could sniff his way home like Kinsler, but he couldn't see three feet before him through the curtain of rain. He winced when something stung his cheek. He looked at the sky. Pea-size beads of ice peppered the ground and shredded leaves for thirty seconds, and then stopped. His soaked jeans stuck to his legs, and when lightening crackled, he scrambled from beneath the tree. Trees attract lightening. He learned that at the school safety assembly about tornadoes.

Tornadoes were awesome. Not when they hurt people. But the combo of wind and hail and lightening played out like video games where superheroes fought above the clouds, and thundering artillery drove evil doers away. He bet the dark fluff in the south-west sky was a wall cloud. Willie always thought it'd be cool to be a storm chaser.

But storm chasers only talked about the excitement. Nothing, not even hugging the cat in his arms, relieved the feeling of *aloneness*. He looked up, as if from the bottom of a dark, enormous pit with no way out. Clouds pushed down, down, down until he couldn't breathe, and his stomach clenched the same way a roller coaster flip-flopped your insides. Daddy would know what to do. Melinda would get mad. But Mom wouldn't even know he was lost, or care if he never got home. That sucked the worst of all.

"Don't be a stupid-head." He said it out loud, to buck up his courage, and the cat purred. "Wasn't talking to you, Waffles. But guess we're in this together."

Willie's wet clothes chaffed and itched his legs when he cautiously climbed back onto the road's crest. His shoes slipped every third step but he took care to dodge channels cut in the bank as water sluiced down. Hair dripped into his eyes, making it hard to see. The ditch on both sides of the road collected brown water that churned and nibbled and swallowed whole chocolate-color chunks from the bank. As he watched, the water level rose so fast it lapped nearly to the spot he'd previously stood.

Lightening zippered across the sky, and Willie picked up his pace down the middle of the road heading toward town. Rain took a breather and the wind didn't push quite so hard, but the spider web itch on the back of his neck never let up. Creepy.

Distant headlights drove Willie to the brushy growth off the road. Only the truck guy and his creepy minions dared to be out...and stupid-head kids. He figured these minions wouldn't be cute cartoons, neither.

One step off the solid pavement sent him sliding toward stinky ditch water. Willie wrapped his arms tighter around the purring Waffles, squared his shoulders, and slowed to a determined walk in the opposite lane. Dad said attitude got you through tough situations, so he'd be tough.

The van—it was a van, not the brown truck, he saw with relief— slowed to a crawl. "Drive on, drive on, drive on," he whispered to himself, and kept his eyes averted, sure if he made eye contact, his head would explode.

But the van pulled alongside him, stopped, and the driver cranked down the window. A kid maybe his sister's age stuck his head out the window. A girl younger than Willie with black braids rode in the passenger seat clutching a stuffed purple dinosaur.

"Storm coming, bad storm. Get in, get safe. Bad storm, high winds predicted. Based on Fujita-Pearson Scale, storm will cause considerable to severe damage. Very dangerous situation. Golf ball size hail which is ice falling from sky, and F2 or F3 tornadoes. Fascinating tornadoes but deadly, too. Why outside? Get in." The boy cocked his head when Willie's rescued cat meowed. "Storm bad for cat, too."

Willie grinned. "Tornadoes are cool. I'm sort of a storm chaser. Want to be one, anyway." Rain began to spit again so he hurried to the rear door, levered it open and climbed inside. "I'm Willie. Sure glad you showed up, it's a long walk back to town." He opened his jacket and the orange cat spilled out, took a couple of unsteady steps, and then shook wet from its fur.

The little girl squealed and clutched her toy. "Grooby hates wet." She turned around in her seat, as much as the belt would allow. "Sixty-seven percent chance tornadoes hit Heartland."

The driver nodded. "Tracy knows numbers. Lenny knows tornadoes. And maps. I'm Lenny. She's Tracy." His gaze slid away.

Kinsler did that with his eyes, too. Willie hoped Kinsler found a safe spot out of the storm, or sniffed his way home. Dogs were supposed to have some sort of homing instinct. He read about that in The Incredible Journey book.

The boy behind the wheel shoved the stick shift and gears grated before the van shook and began to move.

Willie studied the two kids. They talked weird, but he didn't doubt they were smart about numbers and storms. "We're not going back to town? We could go to my house." He wanted to go home, but at least he was out of the rain. Mom always said beggars can't be choosers, so he couldn't complain.

"Basement?" Lenny kept both hands on the wheel, his knuckles white when sudden wind shook the van. When Willie shook his head, Lenny sped up the van.

What if a tornado hit his house? Melinda was there by herself. "One time we all huddled up in the bathroom. Hail took out the front window but everything else was okay." Ground shifted too much in North Texas to have a basement. He didn't know anyone who had a storm shelter, either. Most times, bad storms magically moved around or turned away from Heartland, and only hit the outskirts.

Tracy fiddled with a tablet, then held it up. Willie could see a multicolored schematic of weather radar moving in real time across a digital map.

Lenny tapped the screen. "Safe spot, there." He slowed the van, peered through the windshield past the flack-flack-flack of wipers, and turned off onto a hidden gravel pathway.

Crowding tree limbs scraped and pushed against the van like witch fingers guarding secrets. Willie yelped when a particularly large limb thumped the windshield. A star-shaped crack appeared. He remembered the drainage ditch on both sides of the road, and hoped the narrow road wouldn't wash out before they got to Lenny's safe spot. And that it truly was safe.

Dad would call the road a pig path. Willie wondered where feral hogs hid when tornadoes threatened.

The three remained silent, bracing themselves as the van struggled up a slight incline to higher ground. Lenny slowed the van, and pointed. "Down there is safe. Tornado jumps over low land."

Willie checked out windows on both sides of the van. The road straddled a man-made dam. A livestock tank on the right gave way to a steep dirt slope on the other, where a cement barn squatted halfway down screened by an army of massive bois d'arc trees. The building seemed solid, all right.

The overgrown drive veered to the left and downward, and Lenny drove slowly, babying the van. But almost immediately, the tires lost traction in the saturated ground. The van skied sideways, crabbing downward until earth completely gave way.

Tracy shrieked, Willie yelled. The van slammed the rear wall of the barn. Waffle's percussive spit-hiss morphed into banshee yowls after Lenny's head made a melon-like "thonk" on the windshield. Silence.

Then a pack of dogs howled.

# Chapter 17

Shadow wondered why September ignored the stowaways in the back of the SUV. When they jumped in the car at the theater, he'd noticed right away. Maybe it was a game, hiding under blankets. Shadow liked games. The kids only came out after September left the car to go into the house without him.

"Good-boy, Shadow." Nikki reached to scratch him. "Thanks for not giving us away." She turned to speak to Steven. "Now what? September left the keys, but I don't know how to drive. Do you?" The hitch in her voice, and rising inflection, partnered with her wrinkled brow, spoke of worry and concern.

Shadow still fretted what Steven wanted. But he liked Nikki. She gave him treats, played the *show-me* game, and scratched his chin the way he liked it. And she smelled like cats. Shadow liked cat smell.

The squeal of wet tires stopped right behind their car and made the two kids squeak and dive back under the blankets. Shadow arched his neck and pricked ears at the strange man who got out, followed by an odd lady moving with strange twitches. She had flyaway fluffy hair even longer than September's. He poked his nose out the window crack, tasting the air when they walked by.

The lady's smell mixed sweat and perfume, medicine and fever. It reminded him of the vet clinic, only without the companionable animal smells. The man's breathing hurried fast as his feet, while his shoulders hunched against the rain. Wind tossed the lady's mane over her face, and then away, and when Shadow glimpsed her wild eyes, his ears went flat. He muttered a growled caution to himself.

What to do? September was inside. Strangers near his person, without Shadow to protect, made his heart race faster than Macy chasing a toy.

His suspicion and frustration grew when the pair reached the door. The man fiddled with the handle to make it open, jingling keys— Shadow knew that word from the *show-me* game—while the woman made high pitched whines that hurt a good-dog's ears.

Shadow furrowed his brow and ran to the other side of the car to see better as the man opened the door. The sick-smelling lady scuttled inside. He whined and pawed the window. He should be with his person, to protect September and warn about sick-smelling people and strange men opening doors.

Sometimes when he pawed car doors, the window scrolled down. Shadow didn't know why this didn't happen every time. The fact it happened at all offered enough incentive for him to try every time, especially when a good-dog needed to be with his person.

People knew many things that dogs didn't. September told him to *wait* and good-dogs did what they were told. But dogs knew many things, too, sometimes more than people did.

He pawed the door, scratching the window and the side of the panel, while anxious whines spilled from his throat. Maybe Nikki would open the car door for him? Shadow checked, but the two kids still huddled under a pile of blankets, not even a twitch to betray their presence. They smelled scared, the acrid scent laser bright. He heard muted sounds that must be the whiny lady's voice even through the closed door of the house.

"Willieeeeee!"

Shadow ran to the other side of the car when he heard September's worried cry. From somewhere behind the house. He relaxed a bit. The strangers inside weren't near her after all.

He didn't know what the "willieeee" word meant, but it had the same tone as when she called Shadow to come. Was September calling another dog? He only liked to come when treats or toys were involved. But he came anyway, because he wanted to be a good-dog for September.

Would she give that willieeee-dog a treat? He listened hard, past the sizzling-bacon-sound of rain on the roof, and paw-swiped the door again.

This time, the window opened. Delighted, Shadow hopped out and stood on the pavement for a moment, sniffing the foot treads of the strangers while rain pelted his black fur.

The door to the house opened again, and Shadow's head came up. The strange man left the door ajar, and called over his shoulder. "Watch your mother, my phone's in my car."

Shadow dashed away when the man jogged toward him, and redoubled his pace at the man's startled cry. He bounded to the rear of the house, nose up to seek September and the willieee-dog she'd called. Running feet slapped a sodden drumbeat, and Shadow recognized September's quiet gasps for breath. No longer worried, now she sounded scared.

He barked as he ran so she'd hear him and know not to be afraid. He'd protect her, just as she protected him. That's what family did for each other.

Shadow found the fence, and followed it around the backyard border, barking again and again until he reached the open gate. He quickly scanned the large yard, and found September in the open doorway of the house. Her tight posture, both palms up in a warding off gesture, screamed danger.

Each splashing leap brought him closer. At first, he ignored September's voice, intent on reaching her as quickly as possible.

"Shadow, *wait*." She didn't turn, just held her palm toward him, to reinforce the command.

He skidded to a stop shy of the cement paving stones. Shadow whined, and took two slow steps closer to within nose-touch reach.

"Good-dog, Shadow. *Wait*." September backed up a step, too

Peering around her leg, Shadow saw the wild-eyed woman in the middle of the room, waving her hands around. Something silver-bright glinted in one of her fists. A young girl stood at one side, mouth a silent "o."

"Where's my son? Where's Willie, what have you done with Willie, he's not here, where's Willie?"

Shadow recognized the "where" word. September often prefaced a *seek* command with this word. He looked around, wondering what she'd lost, waiting to be told what to find.

September offered the woman a length of fabric, the sort of thing people wore around their neck because they didn't have enough fur to stay warm. September spoke with calm, but Shadow read the underlying emotion. He tensed, prepared to throw himself at the threat.

"Mom?" The young girl found her voice. "Put down the knife. Please?"

Knife? Shadow knew that word, too. He watched the lady's hand. There were no treats in her other fist.

"Who are you? Where is my son?" The words came fast and loud, jumbled together so Shadow couldn't pick them apart. The sick-smelling lady moved erratically, her head whipping back and forth so her mane-like hair covered her face. She stalked toward the young girl, jabbing the knife in the air. Shadow took a stiff-legged paw step closer, putting himself between September and the knife.

"Melinda, go!" September jerked her head and the girl sidled sideways and then turned and ran. Her footsteps thumped away to the front door, and Shadow heard it swing open. His ears rang when she screamed for help.

Shadow sidled closer. He leaned hard against September's knees, using his weight to push her back. He snarled silently when the strange man rushed into the room. Shadow showed his teeth, not wanting to bite, merely to warn away the danger.

September put a hand on Shadow's head. At the unspoken request, he lowered his lips but divided his attention between the man and the distraught woman.

"Go 'way go 'way go 'way." She jabbed the knife at the man, too, and he backed up without saying anything. "Where's Willie? My husband is a cop, go 'way go 'way go 'way."

Shadow knew the words meant bad things because September flinched like she'd been hit. Shadow nose-poked her thigh, and she finally made eye contact. Her posture changed. His tail lifted with anticipation, knowing she'd made a decision. Her hand on his head stroked with purpose, and she whispered for him only. "Good-dog, Shadow, wanna play *show-me*?"

He wagged, but remained silent. Shadow watched her face, confident now she'd taken charge and could tell him what to do. How to fix this. Together they could do anything.

"Back, back." Shadow took a step backwards, and cocked his head when both the man and girl retreated, too. The wild stabbing motions subsided. September kept her voice conversational, but the command in the tone made people as well as good-dogs pay attention and obey.

The lady started to cry, an ugly sound that made Shadow's ears fall flat. Her hands dropped to her sides like fluttery birds falling from the sky.

"*Show-me* KNIFE." September's voice cracked.

Shadow rocketed forward, and nose-punched the back of the lady's hand. She screamed. But the knife spun away, shiny and bright. It clattered against the floor.

"Shadow, BRING KNIFE."

Without hesitation, he dove for the object, and gingerly grasped the widest part. He ignored the man who had rushed to embrace the sobbing lady. Shadow triumphantly carried the prize to September.

"Good-dog, what a brave boy." With relief in her voice, September pocketed the knife and welcomed Shadow into her arms. "I must have unlocked instead of locked the windows, thank goodness."

Across the room, the young girl's angry voice made Shadow's ears hurt. "Nice trick. But can he find my brother?"

# Chapter 18

Kelvin opened his office door and waited, shifting his weight from boot to boot. He'd not had time to change, and the black clay that stained his dingy clothes chilled him to the bone. The Doctor strode toward him, open coat flapping so much Kelvin expected him to shed feathers and caw.

Water stained the calf-length duster from the shoulders halfway down the man's back. He carried no umbrella, and wore no hat. Rain tarnished his long silver hair, making the stalk of his neck appear too thin to support his head. His hair dripped, running down both cheeks, mimicking tears Kelvin doubted the man had ever shed.

"You have the place. The time." The Doctor didn't bother to wipe his face, only stood in the doorway and dripped.

"Come in, we need to talk. Yes, I've got the location and time." Kelvin crossed to his desk and pulled out a map. Sunny had refused to give him anything in writing, and it took him forever to find the site based on her directions. He had too much riding on this to risk the Doctor claiming the directions weren't clear.

He used a red Sharpie marker, wrote a #1 on their location, a #2 at the barn, and drew a line along appropriate roadways to connect the two. "Paved road most of the way. This last bit here," he poked the map with the marker, "dirt drive that follows along a levy. Narrow, my truck barely cleared the trees. Probably better for you to send in a few small vehicles than a double-wide that'd get stuck." He offered the map. "There's dogs staked out front, but they won't bother you. Just stick to the path leading into the barn. You'll want to store your—uhm, product—on the second floor, in the loft. Fights are in the pit down below, so you can do your business privately. It's not fancy, but you get what you asked for."

The Doctor tipped his head, peered at the map, but didn't take it. "What time tomorrow?"

"About that." Kelvin dropped the map on the desk and moved to put distance and solid oak furniture between them. "Sunny said her guys won't pit the dogs in bad weather."

The Doctor straightened. "Dogs don't fight in rain?"

"That's not it." Kelvin figured the dogs fought anytime, anywhere, as commanded and offered welcome respite from boredom. He figured the times between fights, chained up alone and without hope, must hurt like hell on earth.

"Rain makes dogs sick?" The Doctor stared. "Mother's Pomeranian hated rain. Made him sick. Neptune died." The man's silver eyes nearly disappeared with saucer-size pupils.

*He's on the same shit he pedals to the kids. No wonder he's antsy.* "No, rain doesn't make them sick. But it keeps customers away."

"Doesn't keep my team away. We mail medicine. Neither rain nor snow nor—"

"Not talking about your customers, Doctor. These dogfight guys, they've got their own clientele, some of them moneyed thrill seekers who bet huge numbers. They don't want to get their cufflinks wet."

"Wet cufflinks? Why—"

"Never mind the jewelry, it's a figure of speech. They don't want to get out in bad weather, okay? So it doesn't make financial sense for the fight to happen if nobody comes out to play."

"Current weather report posted a flash flood watch for this county. Possible destructive winds." He sounded like a computerized weather announcement.

"Right. That's right, Doctor. And they're talking possible tornado watch that's likely to last through the weekend." He didn't mask his frustration. Bad enough he had to deal with these scumbags and dirty his hands. If it weren't for Sunny's threats, he'd call the whole thing off and make tracks out of town. "Doctor, these fellows like to watch other creatures get bloody, but don't want to risk the wind mussing their hair."

"You made a promise."

"Yes, I made a p-promise." Kelvin took a breath. Hell, he hadn't stuttered since high school. "Sunny says they already canceled tomorrow's show."

"She promised, too." The Doctor put both hands to his face, wiping the wet upwards from cheeks to forehead, and smoothing hair from his brow. He left his big hands on his head, manicured nails grasped fists full of hair, tugging, tugging. "Promise is a contract." Tug. "Promises to Mother can't be un-done." Tug-tug. "You," tug-yank, "promised." Yank!

A tendril of wet hair fell to the floor. It made a red stain.

"Hey, stop. What're you doing?" Kelvin winced, reached out and immediately pulled back. If the guy wanted to snatch himself bald, so be it. "They canceled tomorrow, and moved up the time. Same place, but happens tonight, to beat the weather."

"Tonight?" The Doctor dropped his hands, one still clutching a hank of hair. "You promised. Sunny promised." The hand, hair still clinging, reached for his gun. "Broken promises reap punishment. You will keep your promise."

"You bet, Sunny and I have every intention to keep our promise." Kelvin rubbed his own bald head. "Those guys that set up the dogfights, though. They didn't promise. It's on them, not on me or Sunny, don't you see?" The Doctor blinked slowly, and Kelvin halfway expected those lizard eyes to shutter above a flicked forked tongue tasting the air.

When his hand moved away from the gun to a phone, Kelvin breathed again. The Doctor punched in a single number, listened, and spoke quickly with what must be latitude and longitude designations. "You have current batches addressed, ready to mail. Move them to the event site now. Yes, immediately. Call me to confirm delivery. We distribute tonight." He disconnected, dropped the phone in his pocket, and smoothed his mussed hair with the other.

"There, see? All fixed." Kelvin smiled, silently congratulating himself the meeting hadn't gone completely south. "Just means we finish our business that much faster." *And stop your money-grubbing kid-*

*destroying plot.* He had the cops on speed-dial, once Sunny left town with her crazy-ass threat.

The Doctor pulled a stack of bound bills from his pocket and tossed it on the desk. "I keep my promise. Last payment tonight, after distribution." Another creepy slow blink. "When you keep your promise." He whirled, coat furling like a comic strip bad guy as he started for the door.

"Wait. Are you forgetting?" Sunny would throw a fit. Hell, she'd play her "insurance" card if she didn't get her share. "What about Sunny? I'm supposed to collect for her."

The Doctor whirled, and the coat flared outward again. "Already paid Sunny "The Babe" Babcock when she shared vital news that you killed BeeBo."

Kelvin sat down so hard, his teeth jarred.

"Sunny cried and cried and cried. She liked BeeBo. I liked BeeBo, too. But I understand you tried to help me, tried to keep your promise." The Doctor donned one of his fake smiles. "I never cry. Mother says real men don't cry, so I never cry." He took three long strides toward Kelvin, and stood above him, a lean black wraith. A thin trickle of crimson ran from his torn scalp down his forehead to the corner of his eye, a ruby tear that grew and grew. "Do you keep your promises?"

"Promises are sacred. You bet." Kelvin stared, waiting for that red drop to fall.

"That's good." He strode to the door, but instead of leaving, the Doctor shut and locked it, and pulled out a chair and sat down. "I'm good at keeping promises. And secrets. I'll help you keep yours as long as you keep mine." The red droplet trickled into the man's pale eye, creating bloody tears that spilled from his slow lizard blink.

# **Chapter 19**

Combs flinched when the hail, now marble size, continued to hammer his car, sounding like a B-movie gunfight. Gonzales tipped his head toward the house. Combs hunched his shoulders and swung open the passenger door at the same time as his partner. "We'd better make a run for it before it gets worse."

The two men sprinted to the front porch, Combs with a forearm sheltering his face. The hail shredded the umbrella Gonzales wielded, and he dropped it with a disgusted sound. "Dammit. My kids got that for me for Christmas."

"All umbrellas are alike. Get another one." Gonzales had twin four-year-old daughters, and his son had just turned nine.

Gonzales shook his head. "I tried swapping something once when Finnegan B. Goldfish went belly up, and the kids caught me. Mercedes said they would. Moms always know. Nope, I'll have to 'fess up and tell the truth." He smoothed his mustache. "The umbrella saved my life in a battle with the Ice King."

Combs laughed. The front door swung open, so he turned it into a cough instead.

A balding thin man with a portly woman stood in the entry. She twisted a sodden tissue, dabbed her eyes, and spoke in a choked voice. "Come on in out of the mess. You the police, right? Here about Larry?"

"Mr. and Mrs. Samson? I'm Detective Combs, and this is Detective Gonzales. You've still not heard from your son?" Combs followed the woman into the house, Gonzales following closely behind. They took seats around a plain kitchen table.

"He's a typical teenager, sometimes forgetful, but a good boy. He's seventeen, almost. His birthday is next week." Mrs. Samson rubbed swollen eyes, and sniffled. "Larry never came home last night. And he didn't call."

Gonzales set a digital recorder on the table and thumbed it on, but also scribbled on a tiny notepad. "Forgive me for asking, but is your son autistic?"

"Autistic?" Mr. Samson rocked backwards. "No." He shared a confused glance with his wife.

Combs gave a slight shrug when Gonzales looked at him. Doty's missing kids were much younger, but they had to ask.

"Has he ever stayed out all night before? Without telling you?" Gonzales continued the rhythm of the questions.

"Never." Mr. Samson took off thick glasses and cleaned them on his shirttail. He cleared his throat. "He had track practice yesterday after school, but never showed up." He turned to his wife. "You have his latest school picture?"

She produced a large color image of a clean cut beanpole thin young man. His smile shone bright with braces. A few bright pimples blushed his cheeks.

"Friends?" Combs leaned forward on the table to accept the picture. Mrs. Samson gestured at the coffeepot, and he shook his head with a tight smile.

"His girlfriend called here last night." Mr. Sampson took his wife's hand. "Otherwise, we wouldn't have known he missed practice. They were supposed to meet after, and she said he was a no show, and not answering his texts."

"She's too young for him. I worry about that." Mrs. Samson crossed her arms. "She's only fifteen, way too young. Larry should date girls his own age."

"She's a good kid, she can't help if she looks older. I was older than you, and we turned out okay."

"That's different." She sniffed.

Combs figured the sore subject could have something to do with Larry's disappearance. Once Melinda turned sixteen, the age they'd agreed she could formally date, he'd be a wreck. She already pestered relentlessly to drive. He'd given in since the skill could help her disabled mother in case of an emergency. "My daughter is a newly minted teenager, and I love her to death. But Melinda wants to grow up too fast, and keeps secrets. Kids that age do. Are you sure the girlfriend isn't protecting your son? Is he in trouble?"

"Melinda? Your daughter is Melinda Combs?" She turned to her husband. "See? He says she's *thirteen*, I told you she's too young."

That knocked the wind out of him.

Mrs. Samson grabbed another tissue and blew her nose. "Larry would never worry us like this. You should have let me talk to Melinda when she called."

"Are you saying Larry's girlfriend is my daughter? Dating a seventeen-year-old?" Secrets, indeed.

Gonzales rapped on the table to get everyone's attention. "Focus. We'll worry about Melinda later. When did you last see or hear from your son?"

The couple spoke at the same time, words overlapping. "Yesterday morning..." and "Breakfast." Mr. Sampson grabbed his wife's hand again. "Go ahead, honey."

She gathered her thoughts, and repeated. "Breakfast yesterday morning." Her words spilled faster. "We make a point to have family time every day. Larry's school and extracurricular stuff make it hard to have dinner together, except Sundays after church. So, breakfast is family time, every day, without fail. Yesterday we had oatmeal and OJ but Larry was in a rush, because he convinced his dad," her eyes raked him with disapproval, "to borrow the new car. He wanted to show his friends and take them to Sonic after track practice. Except it turns out, he meant to meet up with that—I mean, your daughter." She spat the last words at Combs.

Mr. Samson took up the story. "Apparently, Melinda headed over to track after school and he wasn't there. Coach was pissed he was a no show, but his buddies swore he'd been in school."

Combs cracked his knuckles, regretting he only saw Melinda on weekends. She hadn't said a word to him this morning about the boy. "Buddies? We'll need names." Combs clearly read the terror in the couple's faces. He struggled to keep his face neutral, be the detective and not the dad. Nothing could be worse than a missing child.

Thunder cracked, and Gonzales jumped and swore, then smoothed his tie as if that would also calm his nerves. Hail turned windows into snare drums. "Maybe he got caught in the storm. It rained heavily last night. What kind of car does he drive?"

"Mini Cooper, black over yellow. Larry picked the color to match the school mascot, The Hornets." Mr. Samson rubbed his face. "He's a good driver, extremely responsible like we said. I'll get you the license number, but I shouldn't think there are too many that color."

Someone's cell phone pinged, and reflexively, Combs reached for his and only then realized that pocket was empty. How'd that happen? He never went anywhere without it.

Mrs. Samson's sour voice interjected. "He used to hang out with Zeke somebody, and a Henry or Hank, I think. But ever since he started dating Melinda, I don't know how much time they've spent together."

Mr. Sampson cleared his throat, struggling to keep it together. "I spoke to Melinda last night about 7:30 or so, and then tried to reach Larry. His phone kept going to voice mail. I even tried texting. He told me once that phone calls are *so yesterday*." He tried to smile, but his lips trembled and the expression wouldn't stay in place.

Mrs. Sampson tore tiny pieces from the tissue and rolled each into tiny balls as she spoke. "I called Zeke, and he hemmed and hawed and finally said Larry mentioned staying with Hank for the night. So I tried to reach Hank but got no answer there so I left messages. Wanted to drive over to check on him, but he wouldn't let me."

Her husband looked stricken. "Boys that age, they don't want their mom checking up on them in front of their friends. Larry has never given us reason not to trust him. I wanted to give him a pass this once, you know, and then kick his butt later if he screwed up. You have to let kids learn from mistakes." He wouldn't meet his wife's glare. "I was wrong."

Combs seethed, understanding Larry probably spent the night with Melinda. Before he could respond, Gonzales gripped his shoulder and shook his head.

"He didn't stay with Hank?" Gonzales's phone pinged again. He scribbled on his pad with one hand, and pulled out his phone with the other.

The woman shook her head. "Like you said, kids cover for each other. I spoke to Hank's mother an hour ago. She put him on the phone and made him explain, and then we called you." Her voice trembled. "Last night after I talked to Zeke, he texted Hank not to answer his phone. They thought Larry and Melinda had a whatdyacallit, 'hook up' and didn't want to get them in trouble. The two of them had it all figured out, except Larry didn't show up, and Melinda got worried and called us." Grudgingly, she added, "At least she did call."

Combs took a breath, wondering how often the pair had "hook ups?" He'd talk to Melinda later, and do more than talk to Rick-the-Prick. Cassie wasn't responsible.

Right now, the missing boy had to be his focus. "Larry left class at what time? About 3:30 or so?" He checked his watch. "So he's been missing about 18 hours."

Gonzales stared from his phone to Combs, and nudged him. "Says the call is from you. Somebody have your phone?" He answered, listened, and mouthed, "It's Melinda," and held it out to Combs.

Puzzled, Combs took the phone from his partner. "Must have left my phone this morning." He walked into another room, out of sight of the concerned parents, before he spoke. "We'll talk later, Melinda. I know about Larry. I'm so disappointed in you." He struggled to keep his cool, more hurt than angry. "I'm with his parents now. I'll call after shift."

"Daddy? I'm sorry. Please don't hang up." The girl's voice quavered, nothing like the usual brash know-it-all. "This isn't about Larry. I mean, I'm worried about him, too, but…"

His smile faded. "Is it your mother again? Sorry, honey, but Rick needs to deal with her." *Rick needs to step it up if he wants to keep custody.*

"Daddy, Willie's gone." She told him the rest. His face drained of color.

He ended the call and he rushed back into the kitchen. Out the windows, a weird twilight gloom painted the afternoon sky a sickly green that mirrored the expression on both parents' faces, and now on his own.

# Chapter 20

September stumbled and caught herself on a tree but Shadow bulldozed on, towing her in his wake. Head down and nose tasting the ground, the German Shepherd acted impervious to the brambles that hobbled her own progress. September frowned when she recognized the ring tone—Combs phone. *Melinda again.* She started to thumb it off before answering, then quickly answered without breaking stride.

"Have you found him? Where are you?" Panic in Comb's voice sounded barely under control. "Melinda says you've been gone nearly forty minutes."

She stiffened. He must have rushed home to retrieve his phone. "No sign yet, but Shadow picked up a scent that could be Kinsler."

"Forget the damn dog. Find my son." His cop's cool cracked along with his voice.

She kept her own temper. "Shadow tracks pets, you know that. If they're still together, tracking Kinsler is the best bet." The black dog flicked his ears at the sound of his name, impatient to continue the trail. "Shadow's hot after something, and I don't want to discourage him."

Combs took a steadying breath, but his clipped tone remained frosty. She could hear a weird staccato clattering in the background. "Weather guys upgraded the tornado watch to a warning. I've got pea-size hail. Where are you?"

She peered at the dark sky. Wind blew a nose-wrinkling smell of ozone, and lightening carved zigzags across the clouds but the rain had taken an intermission. "We're off FM 680 heading northwest. On foot with Shadow about midway across the field. Rain will muddy the trail, literally, but we can't stop until we find Willie or the trail goes stale."

The hail sound grew louder over the phone. "You're in the path. It's traveling about 30 miles per hour so it'll hit you in less than twenty minutes, maybe sooner. I'm on my way." His voice cracked again, clearly struggling with mixed emotions. "You need to find Willie quick, and take cover. I don't want to think about him out in this weather." He paused. "Or you."

The afterthought hurt, and shame followed. Willie was his son. She was merely some woman he'd known for a few months. "I know about tornadoes, remember, I grew up here. Even Chicago and South Bend had their share of bad weather." She brushed hair out of her eyes, and wished she had tied it back. "We've got no hail, not even rain at the moment but the window's fast closing. Got to run."

"You are the most stubborn, infuriating woman."

She said nothing. This wasn't the time or place. With tornadoes added to the mix, a little boy's life was at stake.

His tone softened. "Don't want to be scraping you off the pavement, either." The noise increased. "Dammit, the hail is getting bigger. I'll be there soon as I can. September, I don't want to lose either of you."

He disconnected before she could say anything, thank goodness. She wiped her wet face. Rain, only rain, she told herself, but her throat ached. Better to make a clean break now than hang on and hope the situation would change. People couldn't hide their true selves forever. They could lie to others, or even themselves . . . She needed to decide who she was, and what she wanted. "Dogs never lie, right Shadow?"

He cocked his head, questioning.

"Never mind. We've more important stuff, right?" She squared her shoulders. "*Seek,* Shadow, *seek.*"

He wagged again, and yelped before turning to sniff at the beckoning trail. Shadow knew what to do. This time, it wasn't about a wildlife die-off spilling into the pet population.

Melinda said her brother saw someone snatch Kinsler. Why steal a dog, when the city shelter offered near give-away adoptable animals? Kinsler was priceless to Willie, but the dognapping made no sense. Unless it had been about luring the boy away, and hurting Combs. As a detective, he certainly had enemies.

For now, the reason didn't matter, only finding the boy. September pushed with renewed determination through brambles that clawed her passing. Gloves offered protection more from the stickers and branches than the cold. Shadow ducked beneath branches and weaved through clotted overgrowth. She clutched the tracking line in one fist, keeping it taut without dragging too much on Shadow's harness, and used the other to push aside errant branches that threatened to whip back and slash her face.

The sun played hide and seek with billowing clouds, snarling September's coffee-colored mane until it appeared spun from the storm. It had already rained more—snowed more, too—this past winter than she could remember. The area's flash flood warning worried her more than the threat of distant hail or potential tornado. Thankfully, the scent trail followed higher ground. So far, anyway.

September studied the clouds with worry. If the sky broke with another downpour, rain would dilute or erase the trail. Shadow was good, but he wasn't a Bloodhound.

Shadow increased his speed, tail waving with excitement and breath huffing as the scent became fresher, drawing him ever faster along the invisible path only a tracking dog could detect. His eagerness made her hopes soar. He rarely got this excited anymore. Finding remains (or nothing at all) depressed Shadow as much as her.

Dogs needed success and hope, and finding the living rewarded Shadow as much as the relieved pet owner. They'd followed the highway in the direction of the brown truck, and then Shadow veered from the road. She didn't want to give Combs false hope, but if Willie remained with his dog, the fresh trail increased the chance of a happy reunion.

Her jeans caught and hung on a fallen branch and she had to stop to untangle the fabric. Shadow pulled and hesitated when she didn't immediately follow. He huffed impatiently.

"Give me a minute. Close, are you?" He woofed as she straightened. "Okay, baby-dog, I'm ready." He still hesitated, so she repeated the command. "Shadow, *seek.*"

He whirled, and eagerly ran into the thickest overgrowth. That would be the trail a squirrel would take, and tease Kinsler to follow. She shielded her face, turned sideways and scrambled through the stand of scrubby saplings. Some of them had already begun to bud in response to the unseasonal warming trend. Ducking under a massive branch, she stepped onto pavement, one of the many farm-to-market roads that crisscrossed the rural regions of North Texas. September sighed, her shoulders sagging. She expected Shadow to cast back and forth and lose the trail, as he had so many times in the recent past. She guessed the missing dog got loaded into a vehicle and whisked away.

But Shadow kept tugging. If anything, his urgency increased until she had to trot to keep up with him. They ran, following the highway. Maybe the dog gave up on the critter chase and headed back toward home. Wouldn't that be wonderful, to find Kinsler and Willie hiking back to Heartland?

Veering across the pavement to the other side of the road, Shadow dove off the embankment, dashing her hopes. *Please, don't let him be hit by a car—either one of them.* Shadow slid on his haunches and finally put on the furry brakes at the bottom where more of the scrubby undergrowth sprouted.

"Shadow, *wait.*" She didn't need him yanking her headfirst into a tree. While he impatiently watched, September carefully climbed down, one gloved hand grasping thick hanks of Johnson grass to brace her descent and avoid turning an ankle or worse.

When she joined Shadow, September smoothed his brow while she took in the plowed, open field. Black waves of sludge resembled cold grease on a griddle, left behind after flood waters receded. It smelled spoiled, like rotting road kill, and made her wonder what sort of wildlife drowned in the deluge.

Water carved a trench down the middle of the field where a narrow bright ribbon of water still ran. Sooty banks of mud flanked each side, the smooth surface marred here and there by detritus washed up and left stranded. The glassy flats invited the unwary to tread the surface, but she knew better.

Shadow learned the hard way. He sprinted toward a dark object situated perhaps ten feet off the road. Almost immediately, he recoiled and tried to backpedal but his front legs sank into black muck nearly to his shoulders.

He yelped and strained backwards, churning the mud. September made an effort to speak with calm authority. "Steady, baby-dog. *Wait.*

*Wait,* good-dog." He settled, but she could see his chest heave and the whites of his eyes roll. "I'll get you out, you're fine." The black mud was more annoying than dangerous, but Shadow didn't know that. He could hurt himself trying to clamber out.

September grasped the tracking line with both gloved hands, and pulled with steady pressure against the harness. "Okay, Shadow, let's go. C'mon, baby-dog. Back, back." He strained his haunches again, and with a sucking sound, the mud let go. Shadow scrambled backwards, lifting each paw in turn with a nearly comical expression of distaste. The black clay-filled soil coated each foreleg, and she knew the clammy sensation wouldn't be pleasant. "You need a bath." He found a somewhat level spot on the embankment and shook himself, hard, and September laughed when mud spattered her face. "Yeah, guess I deserved that."

He sniffed one paw and then lifted his head, tasting the wind. Shadow's tail stirred the air and he woofed low in his throat and then barked again, louder. He took a step toward the dark figure, but immediately retreated when one paw again encountered the mud. Shadow made eye contact with September, barked and deliberately lay down.

September peered toward the object. At first glance, it appeared to be nothing more than a pile of debris, coughed up by the recent rains sluicing down the side of the road embankment. Shadow barked again and a dark figure stirred, and lifted its furry head.

"Good-dog, Shadow. Good find." He'd located the missing Kinsler. Maybe Willie was with him, she had to check. Shadow beat his tail against the ground.

"Willie? Willie Combs, are you there?" No answer, but the boy could be unconscious.

Lightening flashed, and the wind sprayed rain against September's cheeks. The terrier mix barked and began to yodel. He stood, perched precariously on the mounded island he'd found, tail flagged high with excitement but not daring to leave the secure footing. Mud stained his white fur gray, clear up to his neck. A good head shorter than Shadow, Kinsler was lucky he'd found a perch before the mud dried like cement and encased him in a permanent trap.

She searched for something to reach the small dog. A tree branch tossed atop the mud might offer him enough incentive to scramble within reach.

Any loose limbs, though, had already washed along the small tributary in the wrong direction to offer any help. She needed a few two-by-fours or plywood flats that, once tossed across the mud, would support her weight. She had some at home in the garage. That would mean leaving Kinsler, trudging back through the thickets, driving home and coming back, with fingers crossed the dog would wait. Not likely, especially when the storm broke. And she couldn't risk the wait if Willie was there.

As if to confirm her fears, the little dog leaped from his perch and promptly shrieked and floundered. Within seconds, he'd managed to mire himself up to his chin in the mess. Shadow jumped up and added his own barks to the chorus. "Shadow, *wait.* Settle, good-dog." She squinted against the rain, and sighed. Wishes got nothing done. She had no choice. Time to get dirty.

September searched one of her coat's enormous pockets to find Shadow's short six-foot leash and tethered him to a burl oak. "You *wait,* baby-dog. *Wait.*" The leash served more as a reminder than anything, and she didn't want to worry about him trying to come to her rescue.

She unhooked Shadow's tracking line and looped one end around the base of the same tree. Next, she stripped off her boots, rolled up her jeans, and shucked out of the jacket as well. Good thing she hadn't replaced her socks, they'd simply weigh her down. She'd count on luck that her bare feet would only get dirty, not cut.

Stepping forward, September winced at the icy mud. She'd better do this quickly, or her feet would go numb. Keeping one hand wrapped around the tracking tether, she slowly and methodically worked her way toward Kinsler.

"You're okay, boy, I'm coming." She crooned a singsong chant to the small dog, as much to keep Shadow calm as to halt Kinsler's struggles. She had to drag each foot high and step forward before repeating with the other foot. Taking too wide a step threatened to make her slip or trip (or both) and topple her into the mess. She moved the wrong way, and her recovering knee protested with a sharp burst of pain.

The closer she came to the dog, the deeper grew the mud until it reached above her knees. The dog had to be perched on something, or would have sunk to his neck or deeper. He wriggled and barked repeatedly at her, his tail stirring the mud, but he'd learned his lesson and refused to move. Cautiously she drew abreast Kinsler, and saw nothing resembling the boy. Crap. She moved slowly, not wanting to bruise her feet on whatever stump or felled tree supported him.

"Good-dog, you're a good boy, here we go now." September dropped the tracking line onto the surface of the mud. She'd use it to pull them back to the road, once she had the dog in her arms.

September grasped Kinsler by his collar and shoved her other arm into the mud beneath his belly, ready to flex her legs to pull against the grip of the sludge. "Poor puppy, I've got you now, going to get you home." Lightning and thunder made her jump. The clouds stopped teasing and rain poured in earnest.

The mud held on for an endless moment, pulling off one of September's gloves before it let go with a weird lip-smacking sound. The dog squirmed happily in September's arms, reaching up to slurp her face. Her sweatshirt as well as her jeans turned stiff with plastered muck. She stripped off the other ruined glove and dropped it, tucking the dog under one arm and caught up the tracking line with her other hand. She half turned, wrenching free of a tree branch that had temporarily hitched a ride on the dog up out of the muck.

It let go and fell back with a splat, most still sunk beneath the muck but the near end resting on the muddy surface. As September watched, the rain washed it clean revealing not a tree branch after all, but a clenched human hand.

## Chapter 21

Beneath the blanket in the back of September's car, the air became stale but neither of them made a move. Nikki jumped when September's car door opened again. She turned her head to meet Steven's eyes, but his expression didn't change. It never did.

Someone hopped in the driver's seat, and turned the key to start the car. Had September come back? What about Shadow? She'd seen the dog jump out the window—how smart, she'd never known a dog could open windows like that—but he'd been gone when she peeked out. Soon after that, another car zoomed up and Nikki hid again, but not before she recognized Detective Combs.

He was Willie and Melinda's dad. Nikki and Willie went to the same school, but Melinda was popular, older and very glamorous with a track star boyfriend in high school. Nikki wished she could be more like Melinda, with long cheerleader legs, copper hair and a cute figure that looked so grownup. Not like Nikki's mousy straight hair, stick figure and dowdy Goodwill clothes.

But Kid Kewl's plan would change all that. Otherwise, Nikki never would have risked hiding in September's car, or convincing Steven to come, too. Steven was weird, but okay for a little kid. She worried what she'd got them into, and for the first time doubted Kid Kewl's plan.

Nikki thought for sure Detective Combs would discover them in September's car. She'd practiced what to say, but wasn't a good liar. For sure, she'd keep the Show And Tell site secret or she'd never be part of the cool kids. Besides, the awesome plan would help her family. And a bunch of other kids, too.

Thank goodness, she didn't have to make up a story. Detective Combs went inside and out again, quick as you please.

The SUV jerked into gear, and peeled out of the driveway. Nikki heard soft sobbing. She pulled aside the blanket, and sneaked a peek over the back seat.

The driver tossed red hair over her shoulder, and pounded the steering wheel, talking to herself. "I'm sorry, so sorry, Daddy, I'll find him. I'll make it up to you, promise I will."

Nikki popped all the way up. "Hey Melinda? You okay?"

The girl shrieked, eyes wide in the mirror, and nearly drove off the road.

Hanging on to the back of the seat, Nikki braced herself and pulled the blanket off Steven. "Sorry, didn't mean to scare you."

The car stopped. Today, Melinda wasn't glamorous at all, not with black smears under her eyes from runny mascara. "What the hell are you doing back there?" She rubbed her nose on one sleeve. Gross.

Steven sang an answer in the same tune from the Secret Garden part he'd performed:

*Mister Scary, quite contrary,*
*Now it's your turn to know*
*Shivery yells, and shotgun shells,*
*For pretty pills all in a row.*

Melinda's eyes grew large. "What does that mean?"

Nikki flexed her shoulders and her backpack shifted. "He's weird. Steven won't talk, he sings. No offense," she turned to Steven. "You got a nice voice and all."

"I don't have time for baby riddles. I've got to find my brother." Melinda turned around in the seat, hands shaking on the steering wheel. "I let my brother get lost, my boyfriend stood me up, and now my dad thinks I'm a slut." Her chin trembled.

She didn't sound like the cocky, popular Melinda Combs anymore. Nikki squirmed up and over the rear barrier into the back seat, talking as she came. "That's not true. Your dad is a hero, and heroes don't think stuff like that. Not about their kids. You aren't, are you? A slut, I mean?" Nikki stared at the older girl. Her clothes weren't slutty at all.

"It's not being a slut when you're in love." Melinda spoke with conviction, and then in a smaller voice. "Besides, we never did anything. Larry got scared and didn't meet me. Maybe he doesn't really love me." Her eyes welled. "And now Willie chased off after his stupid dog, so I had to call Dad's girlfriend to find them, and—"

Steven tap-tap-tapped on the hatchback window, and hummed the music over and over.

Melinda said nothing, but reached down and released the lock. The two girls waited as Steven carefully hopped out of the back, folded up the blankets, smoothed them back into the stack, shut the hatch and walked to the front passenger door. He slipped inside, fastened his seatbelt and shut the door, and silently held out his hand to Nikki. She sloughed off her backpack to dig out his tablet. The backpack held supplies Kid Kewl said they might need for their adventure.

"September Day is your dad's girlfriend?" Nikki leaned forward, the dog bars a barrier between the two front seats. "She's nice. Knows all about animals."

"Well, she can have that dumb old dog of ours; he's liable to get Willie hurt or even killed. And then Dad will never forgive me."

*Dogs are scary, not ordinary,*
*When forced to fight, you know.*
*To be the cure, save a wag or purr—*
*When you tell and show.*

Melinda stared at Steven, but he focused on his tablet as he finished singing. "What is he talking about?"

Nikki grimaced. "There's a very bad man, he's hurt a lot of kids. He hurt Steven, and hurt Steven's mom, and who knows how many other kids. Steven is autistic. That means—"

The boy ducked his head, but kept on working on his tablet.

"I know what autistic means." Melinda huffed. "Wait. Isn't he September's nephew? The kid she had to find last Thanksgiving during that blizzard?"

Nikki nodded. "The bad man who got away? He's back. Now he's hurting pets, too. Stealing pets."

"Stealing pets? Did he take our dog?" Melinda scowled. "You can't possibly know that."

Nikki turned to Steven, but he was no help. Kid Kewl's online forum was secret, so she couldn't explain. And as a cop's kid, Melinda might let something slip and get the forum shut down, what Kid Kewl called *the hive brain* where everyone pooled his or her special talents for important projects. She wasn't sure why they invited her into the group, when all the other kids knew about complicated things like math and computers and weather.

Melinda was closer to a grownup than to the kids in the forum and grownups were funny and always suspicious. "Never mind how we know. There's a bunch of us working together to catch this bad man, get the medicine all the kids need and take back the money he stole from their parents."

Melinda flipped her hair. "What, you're going to catch that Doctor guy when even my dad can't find him?" She sniffed. "My dad caught his mother."

*Mister Gerry, no more scary,*
*Now it's your turn to go—"*

"Shut up, already." Melinda cut him off. "That's creeping me out." She turned to Nikki. "I've got to find my brother. You two can come or get out, but I'm not in the mood to play babysitter."

Nikki smiled. "But you're part of the plan. That's why Kid Ke...I mean, that's why we decided to hide in September's car."

"You two are seriously creepers. I can't go home, my Uncle Rick will have fits because I took off in September's car. Hell, she may be back already with Willie." She hesitated, clearly debating what to do.

*...time to tell and show.*

Nikki explained. "When we left the theater, we sneaked into September's car because we knew she'd go to your house, to search for your brother. We know why Kinsler got stole. Why all the pets got took."

"How do you know my dog's name? I never said." Melinda sneaked a peek at Steven's tablet, and he covered it with a hand. "What's going on? How do you know stuff?"

"The dog thief works for the Doctor. We know where he took Kinsler." Nikki leaned forward, needing to convince the older girl to stay with them, to be the driver. That was key to Kid Kewl's plan. "You want to make it up to your dad? Drive us to the dog place. That's where you'll find Willie, too."

# Chapter 22

Dime-size hail grew to nickel and then quarter size and dimpled the mud flat all around September, increasing in velocity as she stared at the hand for an endless moment. Kinsler yelped when ice pinged off his head. Startled, September ducked her head and slogged back toward solid ground. Combs's storm arrived right on schedule.

*A body. Or at least and arm and hand. Adult size. So, it's not Willie.*

"Thank you, God." She breathed out in a rush, the relief palpable, but then guilt furrowed her brow. What kind of awful person gave thanks for a stranger's death? Somebody missed him, or maybe her. She couldn't tell the gender. She wouldn't dare try to move the body. The poor soul got caught in a flash flood. She had to call Combs.

Shadow woofed when September clambered up the embankment and set the smaller dog on the ground. The two dogs circled and jockeyed for position, each trying to sniff without being sniffed. September managed to attach each dog's collar to either end of the doubled up tracking line. That left one hand free while keeping the pair under control, or so she hoped.

"Ouch!" Hail pummeled her back, and September searched for any sort of shelter while fumbling in her pocket for the phone. A dark wall cloud threatened, classic preamble to funnel cloud activity, so she prepared herself for ditch-diving if something swooped out of the sky.

To the left, the dirt road led back to the highway, with no shelter in sight. September swung right. She scraped off as much muck as she could and put on her coat and boots, hating the clammy gritty sensation but needing the protection. "This way. Come on, let's go." She jollied the dogs into a trot, grateful when the size of the hail decreased but worried the lull in wind signaled worse to come. At least the drive canted downward. A low position in relation to the elevated highway should prove protective. They ran, and she fumbled for her phone to call Combs. He picked up on the first ring.

"You find Willie? Is he all right?"

She could hear the thunk and ping of hail from his end of the phone connection, but it had abated around her. "No. I found his dog, but not Willie. But there's a body."

He said something, but the words garbled. "...breaking up. Say again. What about Willie?" He barked the last words.

"Combs, I can't understand you. Have to take cover, it's bad here. Found a body but it's NOT your son."

She disconnected and pocketed the phone. Ahead, the narrow road dipped down toward a cement barn that clung to the side of a steep embankment. Three large green dumpsters butted against the near wall, while a cleared dirt space in front of the storage building held a dozen or more rusty metal barrels turned on their side as shelters, with a dog chained next to each.

September stopped short, recognizing the Pit Bulls and what that meant. She took half a step backwards when a couple of dogs noticed her and roused from their enforced boredom. Shadow barked, tail flagging, and pulled against the tether, eager to meet-and-greet all the potential canine friends.

"Shadow, no. *Wait.*" Her voice whip-cracked the command. The Pit Bulls, none in good health, leaped or in some cases staggered to their feet. She noticed young ones also dragged logging chains they could barely lift.

She'd wager the rest of her lottery winnings they figured in the dogfight ring. Kinsler tugged at the leash, and another puzzle piece clicked into place, betting BeeBo's rescued kitten came from here. Dog men used small pets to teach gladiator dogs to fight and kill. Or be killed.

Bile burned her throat. Her knees gave way, and she sat down, hard, in the middle of the road, rain no longer an issue. Shadow pushed himself into her arms, licking her face, and she buried her face in his black ruff.

September tried to call Combs again, but couldn't get a signal. Sadly, animal abuse often wasn't enough to involve the police, but the attendant guns and gambling made dogfights worth their attention. Shutting down dogfights cast a wide net.

And drugs. She reeled with sudden insight. What a brilliant, twisted notion, to distribute the Doctor's poisonous autism "cure" under the protection from a dogfight ring.

She pocketed the useless phone, and scrambled to her feet. Wind had died, hail had stopped, and a yellow-green sky colored the chained dogs in a hellish glow. Static crackled her hair into a Medusa's crown, and all the dogs howled in sudden concert as if cued by a conductor's baton.

She couldn't see it, but the freight train sound signified a funnel cloud. She needed shelter, had to drop below the tree and road level. Inside the cement barn offered the best shelter.

The dogs strained against their chains, staked between her and sanctuary. Shadow and Kinsler couldn't pass without risking a bloody war they couldn't win.

"Good-dog, Shadow, stay with me." They were dead if they stayed on the road, if not from the twister, then from wind-tossed debris bulleted with enough strength to penetrate cement.

The roar increased. No more time. She had to risk threading a path past the Pit Bulls. They'd all die without shelter. September ran in a fast limp, sore knee hobbling her progress. She scooped Kinsler into her arms and shortened Shadow's leash to keep him close to her side.

A horn honked behind September. Startled, she whirled. Her own SUV hurtled down the dirt path straight toward her.

## Chapter 23

He stared at his phone. Combs forced himself to relax before he crushed it—he wanted to throw it—and took a deep breath before hitting re-dial. He pressed the phone hard to his ear, plugging the other ear to mute the thunder and wind that shook his car.

"What'd she say?" Gonzales flinched when simultaneous lightning strobed and thunder boomed. "Dammit, Combs, get us to cover. We're no help to your son or to September if we get blown to Oz."

Combs shook his head. He ground his teeth to keep from cursing. Fury mounted when the connection failed. Failure all around. The connection had been bad, but he'd heard enough. He'd ask if she'd found Willie. Her answer broke his heart.

"*. . . found Willie. . . It's bad...a body...*" And the phone went dead. He closed his eyes, willing her to answer, for the call to go through. Damn the storm, damn the dog, damn September, she promised to find him. Alive. ALIVE, dammit.

Gonzales raised his eyebrows, silently asking again. Combs lowered his phone. He couldn't repeat what September had said. That would make it—*NO! Not his little boy!*—a reality.

Wind pummeled the car. Tornado sirens raged, coyotes answering in an eerie chorus. They'd only traveled a mile or so out of town. Combs knew the general vicinity of September's search but the storm meant no chance in hell of finding them. He slumped against the steering wheel. *Too late anyway, what does it matter. God, make this a bad dream. Let me wake up.*

"Son of a bitch." Gonzales never swore.

Combs recoiled as if splashed with ice water by the vision out Gonzales's passenger window. Snakes of black spun earthward from the distant wall cloud, lightening etched gashes in the dark sky. *Holy shit.*

"It's coming, Combs, it's coming. Get us out of here. How about, uhm, now? Now would be a good time. Vete de aqui, ve rapido, Go-go-go-go!"

A muffled Niagara Falls roar filled his ears. A sudden adrenalin spike transformed Combs from apathy to flight. He shoved the car into gear. Tires squealed, the U-turn barely held the road, and he floored the gas. "Where?"

"Don't care, just go, ve rapido, fast fast fast." Gonzales half turned in his seat. "Man, I need a raise." He turned back around. "First solid building we find, we get inside. Cars are deathtraps in a tornado."

Combs knew that. "If they don't want to let us in?"

"They will. We're the cops. People love us." Gonzales smiled.

He ignored the lame joke. He owed it to his partner to get them to safety. But how could he care about being alive, staying safe, when his son... Willie hadn't had a chance. *Don't think, just go.*

The engine screamed into town, the car rabbiting and swerving as the twister rode their bumper like a hound sniffing blood. He had to drive perpendicular to the storm path. Combs took a hard right, almost nailed a lamppost, and sped halfway up the block before he recognized a familiar business. A brick building. Glass on the front but as he recalled, the place had a storm cellar, rare in this part of the world.

"Hold fast." He fishtailed into the parking lot. Both men vaulted out before the car engine stopped and raced to the door of Doc Eugene's veterinary clinic.

The vacant waiting room, normally bustling this time of day, offered no shelter. Floor to ceiling windows offered a great view of the parking lot and death by glass should the storm punch through.

"This way." Combs loped down the hallway, and dodged through the door to the first examining room, into the treatment area. "Hey

Doc? Where are you?" Gonzales reflexively ducked and cursed again when something thumped the roof of the building.

"Who's there?" Doc Eugene's muffled voice came from behind another closed door. Gonzales and Combs hurried to join him.

"Detective Combs? Detective Gonzales, too? What're you doing here? Don't you know there's a tornado?" The small room, not much bigger than a walk-in closet, served as storage for the vet clinic's pharmacy and other supplies. Doc Eugene and a flamboyant heavy younger woman huddled on the floor beneath a shelf, in the far corner. She appeared peeved to see them.

Combs and Gonzales pushed inside and closed the door. The overhead light flickered in concert with thunder. All four gasped when another clatter-thump buffalo stampede crossed the roof.

"You said he had a storm shelter." His quivering mustache belied Gonzales's steady voice. The man might have been asking for a veggie wrap, extra hot sauce.

Doc Eugene snorted, but made room for the two detectives. "A lot of good it does me. Flooded last week, and still a foot of water and God knows what else swimming around in the sludge." He pushed his glasses up his nose. "No way to get the animals in here, but we've only a few including BeeBo's kitten that September dropped off earlier. This is the next best thing to a storm cellar: an interior room with no windows. And plenty of pain meds, pet food and fluids." He laughed, and then nudged the woman beside him. "Robin, these are the detectives I told you about. They're going to find the sick bastard who killed my Pam."

Robin ignored the detectives. She put an arm around Doc Eugene's shoulder as if to comfort him. When he shrugged it off, Robin's nostrils flared and she stared at her hands.

Doc Eugene's wife, Pam, had been Shadow's breeder. She'd died during the Blizzard Murders last November, along with Combs's mother.

Gonzales answered the unspoken question on the veterinarian's face. "We had to outrun the storm. The funnel hadn't touched down yet, but was snapping at our heels." He turned to Combs. "Hope we still have a car when we get out of here." He pulled out his phone. "I've got no bars."

Combs sank to the floor, and slapped Gonzales's leg. "Get down. We'll worry about the car later." He pushed against the wall, knees bent and arms circling them. Now they'd escaped the tornado, he couldn't stop thinking about September's call.

Gonzales checked the shelves filled with various medications, shampoos and other pet products. He picked up one of the pet collar tracking devices. "Sell many of these? Sure saved us a ton of time, when September went missing."

Doc Eugene took off and polished his glasses. "After all the news stories, I can barely keep the collars on the shelves. The company even gave September the technology and all upgrades for life."

The building shook, and Gonzales braced himself. "Damn. Didn't know I'd think back on the drought with nostalgia." The lights went out. The overhead stampede became constant.

Combs closed his eyes, and let tears run unchecked. How had Melinda let this happen? What would he tell Willie's mother? Would Cassie even understand? He was helpless, hopeless and angry, and oh, so much alone.

# Chapter 24

Claire gasped and jumped when lightening crackled, and banged her head on the passenger side window of Sunny's big green truck. She prayed Tracy and Lenny were inside somewhere, and not out in Elaine's old rickety van. Weather alerts and warnings continually beeped and buzzed on Sunny's phone.

"Now what? We've been driving in circles for hours." Her initial hope after meeting the striking P.I had faded. Sunny hadn't done anything, except drive around and text.

Sunny didn't answer. Every once in a while, she got a text that made her eyes flash with temper. As if on cue, the "ping" of her phone announced another message. "Hold the wheel." She turned her full attention to the phone.

Claire wrinkled her pug nose, but leaned over to steer the truck while Sunny texted her reply. "What's it say? Is it about Tracy? Have they found the van?" Sunny said she'd sent the van's license to her connections, and promised quick results.

"Not everything is about you."

Sunny's terse reply hit below the belt. Claire's hand on the wheel jerked, and she over-corrected, nearly driving them off the road.

"Son of a bitch. What is wrong with you?" Sunny grabbed the steering wheel, and steadied the truck. "I took on this case as a favor. Now you want to wreck my truck? That's a custom rig in the back, special made by friends in South Texas." She pulled into a mini-mart gas station, shoved the truck in park, and half turned in her seat. "Did you ever think maybe these kids don't want to be found? I ran away a dozen times, for good reasons."

Claire sniffed. "Don't be ridiculous. What a horrible thing to say. They're children, they're scared. You said you could find them, easy-peasy you said."

"I may have overstated. One of my guys saw a van matching the description in an area—" Her smooth brow furrowed. "No, couldn't be your kids. Never mind."

"Let's go!"

"It's a stretch. Trust me on this. Don't want to waste time."

"And driving around the past several hours has been so productive? Sunny, we have to do something. My little girl is out there." Thunder rattled the windows. Although the rain had abated, the threat remained. "She's out in this storm, scared, alone." Claire leaned toward the taller woman. "Do you have kids?" She had to make Sunny understand the urgency. The woman acted like Tracy and Lenny were a couple of lost pets, or something.

Sunny shuddered. "Nope. No kids for this one."

*Probably a good thing.* "That old van isn't reliable. They could be stranded somewhere. If you know where they were last seen, we should go check."

When Sunny's phone "pinged" again, and the woman focused on the message, Claire lashed out. "If you can't or won't go after them, tell me where to go and I'll find Tracy myself."

"I've got to make a call. It's private. Sit tight." Sunny exited the car, taking the keys with her as if she feared Claire might take off without her.

Claire flushed. "You're being paid to help. September said she'd pay you. Tracy's only six, Lenny barely sixteen. They're children, for God's sake." She pounded a fist against the window. Sunny waved but headed into the store, phone pressed to her ear.

Now what? Claire threw back her head, and stared at the roof of the truck, then unbuckled her seat belt. She might have taken the car if Sunny had left the keys. She'd already broken into a house. If she didn't know better, she'd think Sunny meant to stall or even prevent Claire from finding the kids. Wind shuddered the car, and splashed a new deluge against the windshield.

What had September told the P.I.? Maybe Sunny was a cop. Her stomach tightened. Claire only knew what she'd seen on television shows, but the woman's actions hit a sour note.

Worry tainted everything with suspicion. Claire sighed, and gave herself a pep talk. "Can't do this alone, you have to trust somebody." She had to give Sunny the benefit of the doubt. She could be frustrated, too, just doing the best she could.

Claire thumped her head against the headrest two or three times, as if the action would reset her brain. Then she sighed, considered the brightly lit store, and opened the door. Might as well make a potty stop while she could.

Claire hurried to the toilet. She heard someone in the wheelchair accessible stall, and when she recognized Sunny's boots under the door, Claire silently entered the next stall and quietly closed the door.

Sunny's hushed, angry voice echoed. "...Because I know you, Kelvin, I knew you'd get cold feet. And I can't let you screw this up for me. Damn straight, I threw you under the bus." She laughed quietly. "Do unto others before they do unto you. I've been a step ahead of you all the way. Yes, twenty thousand is a nice nest egg, but nothing compared to an additional ten thousand coming." Venom filled her voice. "Admit it. You planned to get me out of your nonexistent hair with this missing kid stuff, and it didn't work. Lucky for us both."

Claire clamped a hand over her mouth to stifle her surprised gasp. Claire prayed Sunny hadn't noticed her.

She guessed not, because Sunny kept talking, tone increasingly sarcastic. "I'll tell you exactly what I mean. The kids you sent me to find? They're autistic." She paused. "Yeah, right, one hell of a coincidence. And get this. My guys saw the kiddo's van in the vicinity of tonight's show." She paused. "No, we're fine. The mom's clueless, but the kids know something. It's creepy-strange, as if they're on a mission. They drove themselves all the way from Chicago, for God's sake."

Dropping her face into her hands, Claire breathed slowly through her open mouth while black sparkles danced before her eyes. She carefully sat down on the toilet, being extra careful to make no sound, afraid she'd faint if she didn't. Her pulse drummed so hot and loud in her temple she worried Sunny would hear.

"Kids complicate things, but I got us covered." Sunny's anger had cooled to practicality. "I'll ditch the mom. No, I won't shoot her unless I have to. Miss Clueless can't hurt us."

Claire's teeth began to chatter, and she clamped her jaw tight.

"Why don't you do it?" She paused. "Oh, you're with the Doctor right now? Doesn't want to get his hands dirty, I guess." She snickered. "Sure, I'll drop off the mom, and reconnoiter the barn, secure the product and make sure the kids don't get in the way." Sunny paused. "Hell, they're kids, six and sixteen, and autistic besides. What can they do? You worry too much, Kelvin."

Before she could change her mind, Claire slipped out of the stall and ran. The door banged open and closed, and she nearly knocked down the clerk on her way outside. She couldn't tell the store clerk any more than she could call the police. It hadn't sounded like a joke. Claire couldn't make Sunny suspicious by calling a cab. Besides, Sunny knew where Tracy was.

Claire dashed through the pouring rain and climbed back inside Sunny's truck. She calmed her breathing, and practiced an innocent smile for when Sunny returned.

"Didn't mean to take so long. You need to pee?" Sunny showed her teeth but the expression raised the hairs on the back of Claire's neck. The truck pulled out of the parking spot.

"I'm fine. Too worried about the kids, I guess." Claire cleared her throat when it squeaked. Water dripped from her coat, and she stammered. "I mean, I started to go in but saw you leaving. So I hurried back to the car." She forced a laugh. "Guess I got a little wet."

Sunny stared, her face expressionless. She turned away, pressed the accelerator, and the car skidded as it peeled out of the lot.

# Chapter 25

Shadow howled. His ears hurt. He shook his head to relieve the fullness, but stayed pressed next to September. He'd stay near even if she didn't have the leash so short he could barely move.

A sudden burst of wind came from all directions at once. His whiskers tingled, and he flinched at the booming overhead noise. He tucked his tail, shivered, fighting the urge to squat and pee. Shadow shook his head again and his ears popped.

Wind wailed, and tree limbs tore free to skitter across the ground like wingless beetles. He pushed against September, willed her to acknowledge him and maybe stroke his face. She always knew what to do.

But she didn't touch him. Her arms cradled the other dog that smelled of black mud and sour terror.

"Good-dog, Shadow, stay with me." Her voice jittered, squeaky and shrill, and made him shake in sympathy. She pulled him toward the distant stone house, beyond the chained dogs with distant hopeless eyes.

All around, the roar increased while sky flashes made his skin tingle and fur crackle. September ran toward the chained dogs, tripped and caught herself, and galloped on, her hand tight on his leash. Shadow leaped by her side, eager to get inside.

A familiar-sounding car engine roared and Shadow slowed, tugging against the leash. The horn beeped, cutting through the wind's howl, and September stumbled to a stop. They turned. A car headed toward them. September yanked his leash and he darted with her as she dove to the side of the road. September ran up to the car when it skidded to a stop. She had to yell over the roar of the storm. "Melinda, shove over."

The driver's and rear doors swung open at the same time. September dumped the small dirty white dog into the front and took her place behind the wheel. Shadow leaped into his back seat. He wagged and slurped his friend Nikki across the face as the girl removed his leash, but dropped his ears when he noticed Steven. His-boy ignored him, though.

The wind rocked the car, pushing it sideways on the road. September screamed. A gust hit the open door, and it peeled off the car. She screamed again, and then the car raced down the road, fast, and faster still, toward the stone house.

A limb slapped the car, and the small dog yelped. Speeding, bucking, shuddering, the car shook Shadow back and forth like Bear-toy. Nikki and Steven screamed too, and clung to each other.

"Hurry!" Melinda wailed from the front seat, and hugged the little dog so hard he squealed.

Shadow snarled at the nightmare vision out the back window. A dark twisty cloud fell from the sky and snapped at the car.

Rain and ice pounded the roof, sounding like many guns biting all at once. Shadow cringed. He watched wide eyed when September weaved through the doghouse barrels, aiming for the open barn door.

One of the doghouses lifted off the ground and tumbled away, and a second quickly followed as though kicked by a giant invisible foot. Young ones cowered and cried, flinching as hail thumped all around and hit them repeatedly.

Just as the car's nose poked through the barn door, a sonorous racket grew and the car lifted and smashed back down. Shadow wailed. He slammed against the side window, the new floor of the upside-down car. Nikki and Steven piled on top of him.

"Out, everyone out. Away from the door, hurry." September's shaky voice shouted over the wind noise. She opened the passenger door, now above their heads, and help Melinda out first. September passed the little dog to the girl, and then helped Steven through the crushed front seats. September clambered out and levered open the back passenger door.

"The dogs." Nikki's anguished voice rose over the wind.

"No, Nikki. We can't help them. Give me your hand." September reached in and Shadow licked her fingers. Nikki turned away and wiggled into the rear of the car. The crash had unlatched the hatchback. "Nikki wait."

"They'll die." The girl squeezed out of the back of the car, hunkered down, and sprinted toward the chained dogs.

# Chapter 26

The wind out-shouted September's screamed warning. She yelled again, but Nikki ducked her head and scurried to the first chained dog. She crouched beside the trembling youngster. The girl ignored the driving rain but flinched when the hail thumped the middle of her backpack. At least she had that minimal protection.

"What's she *doing?*" Melinda hugged Kinsler while Steven simply stared, silent with wide eyes. "The tornado will get her, what's the *matter* with her?"

"Go take cover. Go on." September gestured toward the dirt pit dug several feet deep in the center of the cement building. "Crouch down and cover your heads. Take Steven. I'm counting on you, Melinda. Go."

Melinda grabbed Steven's hand, and still clutching Kinsler, she headed for the pit.

September had to get Nikki to safety, but also protect Melinda and Steven. "Shadow, *go-to* Steven. Keep him safe." She gave him a quick hug, then squirmed into the crushed SUV. The car blocked the barn door completely. The only way out was through the open hatchback.

Her knee whined when it cracked against the car but she didn't listen. September narrowed her eyes against flying debris. She prayed the hail wouldn't knock either of them unconscious, and dashed to the girl. She yanked Nikki's backpack to get her attention. The storm's noise drowned out easy conversation.

Nikki's face reddened with frustrated effort. "I can't get it off." She screamed over the wind noise. "His collar's too stiff." The young tail-wagging Pit Bull pushed into Nikki's lap hampering her efforts.

"You'll get us killed." She tugged Nikki's arm, but the girl wrapped her arms around the pup, refusing to leave. With frantic fingers, September struggled with the pup's collar, too, but it was hopeless. "We'd need to cut it." She dug in her pocket for the knife Shadow had knocked out of Cassie's hand during the *show-me* game. Even with the sharp blade, it would take too long to saw through the stiff leather.

Nikki's smile lit up her face. She reached into her knapsack, and pulled out Doc Eugene's bolt cutters.

"What else you got in there?" September sheathed the knife back into her pocket with such force the blade sliced through fabric and caught in the padded batting lining. She took the bolt cutters from Nikki and cut the chain tethering the pup to the stake. "Now let's go."

Nikki shook her head, and mouthed something September couldn't hear, pointing to the next dog, and the next.

"Dammit! I'll do it. You go!" September waved the girl toward the barn when her screamed words tore away in the wind. She stood and grabbed Nikki by the arm, ready to drag her back, but the girl released her Pit Bull pup, pulled away and ran to the next dog.

Had she been alone, she'd not hesitate to rescue the dogs, so September fought grudging admiration for Nikki. As the adult, she had to put kids first, no matter what.

September sacrificed five seconds to consider options as the sky boiled black, and the swarming cicada-buzz grew deafening. Her ears popped with pressure change, but she couldn't tell the funnel's location. Hell, it could be a mile away or directly overhead, flatten the barn and leave her untouched. No way to predict, no way to get Nikki away from the dogs, and no way she could abandon the foolish child. *All you can do is the best you can do.* A sudden calm filled her with purpose, and she raced with the bolt cutters to the next dog.

Nikki soothed each dog and held collars steady for September's snick through the chain. At their release, the dogs slunk low to the ground, wagging and sticking close to their heels, either unaware of freedom or relishing the attention more.

The last dog, a massive adult male with a scarred head as wide as his chest, leaned into her arms as September cut him free. "Back to the barn." The storm out-shouted her words, but Nikki understood when September waved the bolt cutter.

The hail increased in size and velocity, pounding all around. The adult dogs, although frequently struck, made no sound but stayed close to Nikki and September as they hurried toward the shelter. An army of icy bullets machine-gunned the barn and Nikki squealed and covered her head. Then her arms dropped to her side, and the girl fell face forward onto the ground.

September stumbled and fell, surprised when her knees splashed into soggy ground salted with the chunks of ice. The roar of the storm out-shouted anything she might say. Bright crimson sheeted from the girl's scalp where hail had clubbed her brow.

The open rear hatch of the SUV beckoned. Before September could stagger upright to lift Nikki, Shadow leaped from the car and raced toward her. "No. *Wait.*" Heart in her throat, September also gave Shadow the *wait* hand signal, and breathed again, when he skidded to a stop.

The young Pit Bulls milled around her legs. At least the storm distracted them from aggressing toward each other, or Shadow. September had to get Nikki, herself and Shadow back through the SUV gateway. As she watched, one of the nearby dumpsters tipped over and blew hard against the barn, metal lid flapping like cardboard. The train-like chang-chang-chang-chang noise relentlessly approached. All but the scar-faced dog scattered.

September grunted as she hefted Nikki over one shoulder. Shadow hesitated, and then disobeyed and raced to meet her.

The Pit Bull eyed him, face and forelegs crisscrossed with a jigsaw puzzle of scars. Mangled ears pinned back, he offered a broken-toothed snarl, and stood foursquare braced and ready for a fight. Shadow put on the brakes but didn't take his eyes off the dog.

"No. Shadow, stay with me." She couldn't hear her own voice, and prayed he'd listen. No time left. Must choose. Prevent the fight...protect the girl. . .

The twister tore into view, uprooted trees like weeds and tossed the second dumpster across the yard. "Shadow, COME. Stay with me." Anguished, September left Shadow to race the last few yards to the

SUV, pushed Nikki's limp figure inside, and turned back to watch. "Shadow. Shadow, come boy, baby-dog, come on. Pleeeeese . . ." Her throat shredded raw with screams, shielding her eyes from debris, she watched Shadow's standoff from inside the SUV, willing her dog to run, run, return to her.

The Pit Bull would take him down if he turned tail. Shadow knew it, too.

The two dogs circled each other, Shadow backing away and turning his head as the older, more experienced fighter stalked him.

She couldn't abandon him. *Screw the storm.* September grabbed the bolt cutters to race to Shadow's defense. Then Nikki stirred and started to wail, and clutched September's arm.

"Don't leave me. It's coming, it's coming, don't leave me!" Frantic eyes wide, blood streamed from the child's sliced brow.

September dropped the tool, and gathered the girl into her arms. "I'm here, hold on, we're going to be okay, hold on." More debris flew past the SUV's open hatch. Shadow and the Pit Bull continued to circle each other.

Lightening staggered across the sky accompanied by a simultaneous "boom." A tree branch barely missed the open hatch of the SUV. It impaled the cement wall of the barn. Another one might not miss. September strained to see, but the two dogs had disappeared.

*Baby-dog, stay safe, God I'm so sorry, please forgive me . . .*

September wept as she pulled the hatch closed and thumbed the key-fob lock, praying she'd not cut off Shadow's only chance for survival.

# Chapter 27

The white dog scared Shadow more than the weird wind or thumping ice from the sky. The dog's body language threatened, and his tormented eyes and teeth promised pain.

He ached to follow September and Nikki back to the cement building, but couldn't allow this danger-dog to chase them. Shadow weighed less but the shorter dog's muscles, scars and smells told stories of bloody conquests. Shadow didn't dare turn away. He had to be brave and strong and create a furry barrier between the warrior dog and September. Nobody told him to do that. He simply knew.

Wind made it hard for a good-dog to hear. He strained to see September's progress. He wished he could smell or hear her but scent mixed together into swarms quickly scattered by rain. Ice hit him like Steven's fists during a rage, and Shadow winced and yelped with each blow. The white dog remained stoic and focused, though, ignoring cold thumps shooting from the sky, staring, staring hard at Shadow with pale eyes.

Shadow knew this territory belonged to the other dog. Shadow wouldn't want strangers in his place, either. He turned his head, and lowered his tail. He backed away, edging closer to the barn and September. With her out of sight, he didn't feel quite as brave.

The other dog stalked closer, snarling. His short white coat bristled, even the raw swollen wounds with little fur. He had only ragged stumps for ears, making it hard for Shadow to read his mood. The heavy chain swung from the dog's collar, and dragged furrows in the mud. He raised a forepaw, the leg crisscrossed with scars.

Shadow's brow wrinkled, he licked his lips and again turned away, a silent declaration: *no threat*. The white's close cropped ears and frantic tail said one thing while his offered paw contradicted the message. Shadow yawned, and backed away, his placating signals obvious.

The other dog charged, stopped short, and placed the paw heavily across Shadow's shoulders. Close up, the dog's sour stink of infection mixed with bitter rage.

The dog lunged at Shadow's throat.

Shadow ducked and whirled. A shattered tooth creased his skull and carved a ragged line down his cheek. Shadow snarled, his teeth snapped air, a warning despite the near miss.

The sky boomed. Big metal boxes tumbled and lurched toward him. Shadow yelped and danced sideways, but the cacophony elicited not even an eyelash twitched from the white dog. He stalked relentlessly forward, ignoring or unaware of the tower of black smoke twisting at the far end of the road. It chewed up and spit out trees, stones, and dirt as it staggered forward. Shadow's ears felt stuffed, so full they might burst.

Scarface sprang.

Shadow whirled, and left behind a mouthful of thick black fur in the other's jaws. When a branch scuttled across the ground, Shadow spun away from the massive wind-torn limb. It lifted into the air, clubbed the white dog and spun up into the sky.

Scarface screamed a choked eerie sound that rivaled the storm's shriek. He threw himself onto his back in a silent plea, eyes screwed tight. He didn't fight, just accepted the beating sure to come. The sharp aroma of dog pee rode the wind.

Before the white dog's confusion cleared and he scrambled away from the approaching funnel, Shadow fled in the opposite direction, back to the barn, to September. He needed to be with her, and keep September safe if Scarface returned. She'd know what to do about the black wind, and the ice balls that turned the ground white.

Shadow put paws up on the car's back window to peer inside. He barked, calling, pleading, *don't forget the dog.*

But he'd disobeyed. He'd only wanted to keep her safe from the white dog. That was his job. He barked again, but September didn't come. He pawed the glass, then hopped down and frantically searched for a way under or around the car.

The two remaining metal boxes banged against each other, their lids lifting and slamming closed like hungry mouths. Shadow cried out as two ice missiles hit his flank and the car glass simultaneously. September didn't come.

Shadow raced for the meager shelter of the dumpster tipped on its side. He timed his movement until wind lifted the cover a dog's width, and dove inside the metal box. Ice balls pounded and echoed as they tried to batter their way inside. The box stank of fear, feces and misery.

The box lifted slightly, and fell. Again, and then again it tumbled and rolled one way, and back the other direction. Shadow yelped, wailed, and finally fell silent. He crouched against a corner and curled into a tight ball of misery. No light penetrated the metal box, and the icy scabrous floor, filthy with animal stink and blood, made him shiver. Sounds of the outside storm echoed and hurt his ears as the wind raged.

After a long time, longer than a good-dog could say, the wind slowed and finally stopped. The plink-thump-CRACK! of ice missiles disappeared. Shadow stood and shook himself, and flinched and yelped at the bruises and the hot sting from the bite slicing his face. He nosed the heavy lid, but it stuck on something outside the box and wouldn't open. Shadow barked, and pawed the lid with frustration. Trapped.

A growl answered, followed by a whine and a hollow thumping sound. Shadow sniffed. His hackles rose. Another dog shared the big metal box.

# Chapter 28

A sudden eerie silence proved more frightening than the storm's violence, but September refused to move. She kept her eyes squeezed shut. She held Melinda circled tight in her arms, and the girl's trembling form in turn crouched protectively over Nikki and Steven. All remained silent, except for Kinsler, who keened and shivered.

September wanted to cry, too, but not in front of the kids. She couldn't think about Shadow, or would dissolve into a useless puddle. She had to be the adult. September cautiously opened her eyes and released her grip on Melinda. "Everyone okay?"

Melinda lifted her head. She turned loose of the kids and hugged herself. "Is it over? Will it come back?"

"Nikki, how's your head? Steven, you all right?" September waited impatiently for a response.

Steven remained silent, but Nikki nodded, then winced, and gingerly touched her blood-soaked hair. September pasted on a cheerful expression to hide her concern. Head wounds bled a lot, even when not serious. She hoped it wasn't serious.

Kinsler squirmed from beneath their feet, shook himself hard, and sniffed the bloodstained ground. The 18-foot square dogfight pit offered an ideal storm shelter. Three-foot-high plywood walls framed the space on two sides, reinforced by stair-step stacks of straw bales piled halfway to the loft.

Ironically, the same space had meant death or worse for the dogs forced to compete within its walls. The Pit Bulls she and Nikki had freed stood a better chance fighting the tornado than surviving this arena. September prayed they'd evaded the storm.

*And God, please let Shadow be all right.*

Any hope of finding Shadow hinged on escaping the barn. September scrambled to her feet to assess the damage.

Her SUV blocked the main entrance but the wall had collapsed around the vehicle. The car had taken out the loft ladder, too. Overhead, steady rain fell through where the metal roof peeled back like a pop-top lid.

The small loft above and three remaining cement block walls retained most of their integrity. A pushed-in section marred the back wall, where a small door and three shuttered windows suggested another way out.

"Melinda, watch the kids." The older girl had already begun to clean up Nikki's cut brow. Steven's attention remained glued to his tablet, probably playing a video game. Maybe her phone reception had returned. She checked, but had no bars.

September noted the scratch line in a corner of the square pen as she vaulted over the plywood wall. She tripped on a washtub positioned nearby, empty now but used to bathe fighting dogs before they entered the ring to be sure nobody "cheated" by putting poison on the fur. The opposite corner would have the same diagonal scratch mark, she knew, where the so-called "dog men" held their canine contenders at the ready before the "referee" gave the signal to release them and begin the fight. She shuddered.

Once past the divider, she saw more dogfight paraphernalia. A modified spring pole hung from an overhead beam, consisting of a length of rope and rubber tubing dogs were encouraged to grab and hang from to condition neck and jaw muscles. September knew BeeBo also provided a spring pole for his dogs to have fun, but she found nothing innocent about the contraption in this context. Out of place in the rustic surroundings, a modern electric-powered treadmill stood against one wall. The attached logging chain, similar to the ones she'd cut from the dogs' collars, made it clear the treadmill served as one more tool for conditioning the canine athletes for the blood sport.

The machine's presence meant power, if she could find a switch. Daylight faded early in February. With the SUV totaled, and storm still lurking, September had no intention of hiking out with a bunch of kids. Best to hunker down and wait for help. Lights would shine a welcome beacon to speed rescuers to find them, especially once the sun set. Only gray light filtered through the gash in the roof, but even as she watched, it grew dim.

On the wall behind the treadmill, September found a power bar with a bright orange weatherproof cord that trailed up the wall and disappeared through the ceiling into the loft. She toggled the switch, and floodlights blazed from the rafters, spotlighting the dog-fighting pit bright enough for an ESPN special.

Melinda stood up and cheered, and September turned back with a smile and a thumb's up. Nikki wobbled, though she kept a firm grip on Kinsler's collar. If she had a concussion, Nikki needed a doctor sooner rather than later.

"Let me see if I can get the back door open." September hurried to the far end of the barn.

The lights revealed the cat mill and she cringed. Designed like a miniature horse walker, trainers harnessed the dog to the long spoke projecting from a turn-style and lured him to chase the living bait held in a cage beyond his reach. This built up the dog's conditioning as well as increasing prey drive.

September hurried past, averting her eyes from the sad mound of fur trapped inside the cage. She gasped and stopped short when the fur moved. "Hey, there's a cat." And still alive, despite being cramped inside a space too small for it to stand.

"A kitty? Where?" Nikki finally roused, and stood up woozily.

September motioned to Nikki to stay put. "Keep hold of Kinsler or he'll scare it." She didn't want to explain to the kids about the cat, or God help her, the rape-stand over there used to keep breeding pairs of fighting dogs from killing each other.

The cat mewed and cheek-rubbed the side of its cage as she struggled to get the door open. He hadn't been inside long. She saw no waste in the cage or dropped beneath in the dirt of the barn floor. September knew that bait animals, often rabbits or cats, didn't last long, so this cat won the lottery. Otherwise, after the "training" session, the bait became the dog's reward. She'd like to "reward" the sickos with some of their own medicine.

The striking green-eyed cat sported a brown tabby "cap" on his head, tabby coat covering his back and tail, and underneath, snowy legs, chest, muzzle and tummy. His friendly demeanor had enabled the catnapping. The thieves hadn't even bothered removing his collar or nametag that clearly spelled out, "Boris Kitty."

She feared he'd run away—hell, she wouldn't blame him—but September couldn't bear to leave him inside the wire contraption. "Stay close, big guy." She crooned soothingly as she messed with the opening, hoping he wouldn't spook and zoom away. "When we get out of here, I'll do my best to get you back home."

As soon as the confinement opened, the cat leaped out of the wire basket, and scaled September's shoulder to nuzzle her cheek. He draped himself around her neck like a sack of potatoes, and the vibration of his purr made her smile for the first time in hours. "Guess that's as good a place as any. Hang on, Boris Kitty."

September fought the déjà vu sensation. Only eight weeks ago, she'd nearly died while trapped inside another barn when it caught fire. With the wooden loft drowned by the storm, not even a direct lightning strike would ignite this barn. Still, she didn't want to stay inside any longer than necessary. That the storm had abated didn't mean it couldn't return with renewed violence. As if in agreement, thunder boomed.

Keeping one hand on the cat as much to calm herself as to balance the perching animal, September hurried to the far wall. She tried the door, but it jammed from something wedged outside, and wouldn't budge. Long metal bars secured shutters covering each of the windows, effectively keeping any inside light contained. Scheduled fights likely took place at night. Whoever ran the show didn't want light leaking out and giving them away.

After removing the rebar brace, she swung open the first set of shutters. Glass had shattered from the outside in, and fell with a music box crinkling sound. A blue metal surface butted up solid against the opening, with no way through.

September moved to the next window, pulled away the brace, and found a repeat of the broken glass and blue wall. She banged on the metal with frustration, before moving to the third, final window.

Startled, the cat dug nervous claws into her coat collar. "Sorry, Boris Kitty. My bad. You're right, nothing gained by getting angry."

She pulled and tugged the final rebar until it released. September lost her balance and fell backward on the ground. She heard an answering thump from the blue metal.

The cat scrambled to keep his perch on her shoulders, and then abandoned her and ran. Wet soaked through her pants, and September put down a hand to brace herself. Where moments before the floor had been dry, now she sat in a wet spot that slowly grew as she watched, pooling from cracks in the cement blocks at the foundation level.

The banging came again, followed by faint shouts. September scrambled to her feet, and wrenched open the final set of shutters. The opening revealed the passenger side glass of a blue van pressed against the barn's shattered window. Willie Combs thumped and yelled from the front passenger seat, a dark haired younger girl peeking from behind him while a teenaged boy slumped behind the steering wheel, motionless.

# Chapter 29

Shadow cautiously sniffed the direction of the strange, spotted dog. Elevated levels of testosterone in the youngster's pee labeled him an adolescent. The pup crouched in the farthest corner of the dumpster, banging tail echoing in the metal box. A short length of metal loops hung from the pup's collar, and clanged against the filthy floor when he shifted. Shadow arched his neck and stretched his nose closer, and the pup whined and rolled onto his back, his tail whipping back and forth in an abject show of deference.

Shadow yawned and turned away, giving the youngster a chance to compose himself. When the pup slunk forward, crawling to reach Shadow, whimpering as he came, Shadow stood stiff and slowly waved his own tail. He allowed the youngster to lick his face and eyes. The spotted pup dropped to his back without prompting, and wriggled as he offered Shadow an up-close personal sniff. Recognizing the pup posed no threat, Shadow gave him space to stand. The dog rolled happily to his feet, dripping from the pooled water in the bottom of the metal box, and shook, spraying wet in the close space.

Happy to have a new dog friend, Shadow rested his chin on the smaller dog's shoulders for a moment before turning to the exit. He needed to find September. His paws splashed in the puddles that got deeper inside the box, and Shadow nose-nudged the edge of the plastic door-lid beside him. It should be above him, except that the metal box had tipped on its side. It wouldn't move. Something pressed against the plastic from the other side, so that he couldn't budge the covering. Now water leaked into the bottom of the metal box from the saturated ground outside. As he watched, a steady stream ran inside.

Shadow followed the bottom edge of the door lid, and push-tested every few inches until he reached the far corner where it gave a bit more. He pushed harder and managed to stick his nose through the opening. He pulled back when it tightened on his neck, and tried to jerk free. Shadow pawed the plastic, thumping and clawing to no avail. His feet stung with cold, and he splashed with each step.

The pup shouldered beside him, and pressed a blunt muzzle to the base of the plastic. He dug paws for traction and leaned one shoulder against the plastic surface. When it gave a bit more, Shadow wasted no time, and pushed his nose, then face, and finally shoulders through before it tightened and held him in its jaws.

Whining with sudden concern, Shadow struggled but couldn't move. He backpedaled, but couldn't pull himself free that way, either. A big tree outside held the dumpster lid shut.

He had to get out-out-OUT, and find September. Shadow yelped and struggled, but the plastic held tight.

Behind him inside the metal box where he couldn't see, the younger dog leaned against his flank, and Shadow stiffened with concern. He couldn't defend himself, or get out of the way. Shadow panicked when the pup scramble under him. He pedaled and flailed when the smaller body wiggled beneath his tummy. But the youngster didn't make a sound, only squirmed and clawed in the mud until he'd escaped through the door-space held open by Shadow's body.

Shadow closed his eyes when the pup again licked his face. He pulled and tugged and squirmed, but still couldn't get free.

His jerking efforts to escape startled the pup so much, the youngster dodged away, but stopped short. Shadow stared, and cocked his head. The dangling chain from the collar caught on something, and held the spotted pup in place. Shadow sniffed the metal links, and twisted to see them disappear beside him under the plastic lid cover. The pup yelped, and tugged, and the lid cover jostled.

Struggling but now silent, the young Pit Bull braced his paws, ignoring the water that had risen knee deep. He pulled, pulled, and pulled again. With each tug, the pup's neck and shoulder muscles bunched and relaxed, and Shadow felt the lid shift, slightly releasing pressure that clamped him in place. Shadow dug his own claws for purchase, and when the pup gave one more wrenching yank on his collar chain, Shadow pushed out of the metal box the same moment as the pup's chain popped free.

Shadow shook himself hard, and briefly nose-touched the pup. He saw the metal box still rested against the hard wall of the barn. September's car poked out the doorway. He needed to find her.

As Shadow splashed his way to the car, the spotted puppy whined, and lifted each paw in turn in reaction to the deepening water. The youngster scrambled onto the fallen tree that leaned next to the dumpster they'd escaped, heavy chain still dangling from his collar.

After a quick sniff around September's car, Shadow knew she hadn't come out yet. But he could find no way into the building. The water level flowed around the base of the barn, more from one side than the other, and instinctively Shadow headed toward the higher elevation past the dumpster, uphill to the water source.

He had to duck and weave to find a pathway through scrubby trees that sheltered the side of the stone building. A loud metal noise sounded overhead, and Shadow flinched when the roof waffled in the wind. Would it take flight like a bird and soar away? He'd seen big birds grab little animals. Would the roof-bird chase a good-dog and carry him off, too? Shadow hugged tight to the building, and hurried to reach the back of the barn.

The ground became steeper when he rounded the corner. The barn backed up against a big hill covered with grass and scrubby trees. A dark scar cut down one side of the hill. It looked like a dog had dug for varmints. Now water ran down the trench, overflowed, and bled mud across the grass.

A big boxy car, bigger than September's, sat at the end of the channel and Shadow wondered how it got there without a car path to ride. It leaned against the backside of the barn. Someone moved inside the car. Shadow cocked his head when someone shouted from the barn.

"Get back. Cover your face."

He recognized September's voice when she called from inside the barn. Shadow charged ahead despite the scary thump-thump-crash-crunch sound as he raced toward the big car. He barked, and barked again, frantic for a way to get past the car and into the barn to reach September.

Despite his barks, September never answered. Instead, she waited until the boy inside the van shook off pieces of glass. She helped him climbed out the car window into the barn, and never looked at Shadow at all. That made his tummy hurt with worry.

Maybe September couldn't hear or see him. The water's noise covered up a good-dog's barks, and he knew people couldn't hear as well as dogs. Shadow dodged to one side as the van shifted when a small girl also climbed out. He froze in momentary shock when September crawled out the barn window into the van. Shadow whined and licked his lips, relief mixed with concern for her safety. She'd come for him, after all! He expected her to call to him, make eye contact and tell him what to do. But she only crouched over the motionless driver.

The van shuddered and slid forward, riding a sudden shift in the ground. Shadow's surprised barks mixed with frightened yelps as a rush of deeper cold sluiced over his paws. Above him, the hill moved, turf sliding downward like a green blanket unmaking a bed. Water spilled over the top and sides of the dark flayed wounds. The hill split. One side fell away.

Shadow leaped high, as high as a good-dog could, and landed on the slick front surface of the car. He scrambled to keep his footing as the van surged and bucked in churning water. His throat ached and tummy soured with distress that only contact with September could soothe. He barked, his warnings louder when September still ignored him. She had to hear, it was a good-dog's job to keep his person safe.

She hadn't come before when he called. But he'd disobeyed her *go-to* Steven command. Maybe she didn't want him anymore?

Shadow dug at the splintered windshield and bit at the crystal fragments that glittered and broke away. His bark escalated to a scream that sprayed the glass with bloody saliva as the van shifted and lurched, battered by the rising tide of the flash flood.

# Chapter 30

*He's okay, thank you God, Shadow's all right.* The relief made her want to shout, but September had to trust he'd stay safe until she could get Lenny into the barn. The van shifted again, taking the windows out of plumb. She had to hurry or the passage into the barn would slam shut.

She hunted for and found a pulse. Lenny's blue lips and labored breathing scared her more than his bruised face. He'd not worn a seatbelt, and the old van had no airbags. The impact not only cracked his head on the windshield, the steering wheel probably caused internal damage. Moving could kill him.

The van lurched, and Shadow's barks turned hysterical. "I hear you, baby-dog." God, she had to get the kid out, and help Shadow. "I won't leave you again."

No choice, she had to move Lenny now, or they'd all die. September yanked and tugged to drag him from behind the wheel. She looped his arm over her shoulders and supported Lenny's waist with her other arm.

Water carved twin channels down the sides of the reservoir's breached dirt dam. The gushing stream eroded the van's precarious perch and it lifted with a stomach-dropping action.

Shadow shrieked. His paws clawed for purchase as he surfed the hood of the van. "Hang on, baby-dog." September prayed he'd keep his grip. Once they got inside, the old cement structure should buffer the strong current. She pulled the boy with all her strength and thrust his head and shoulders through the opening.

"Grab his shoulders, pull-pull-pull." September knelt on the seat, and eyed the water spilling into the bottom of the van. She shoved Lenny's legs through the aligned windows as Melinda and Willie pulled the lanky teenager into the barn.

The van bumped with a sudden herky-jerk movement with the loss of Lenny's weight. September grabbed to steady herself, angrier than scared when the barn window slipped out of sight.

Shadow yelped, still clinging to the hood of the van. "Good-dog, what a brave boy." At her voice, he slicked back his ears, and nosed the ragged opening in the windshield. If she could knock out the rest of the glass and climb onto the roof, maybe they could ride out the flood together. Staying inside risked entombment in a watery coffin if the van toppled in the current. Shadow would never survive.

September pushed at the windshield, and immediately realized the futility. Hail or impact with the barn created starburst splinters, but laminate held the safety glass together. It would take time and tools to remove the entire window, which likely would knock Shadow off in the process.

The van jerked again, and September screamed. It caught on something, and slowly spun before slamming back into the wall. Shadow somehow maintained his wobbly balance, and she gasped with relief.

The water kept rising. The next surge would take them.

With the windshield holding her captive and the passenger window flush against the barn's cement wall, the driver's window offered the only escape. Every movement she made risked unsettling the van's temporary anchor and launching Shadow into the flood. September carefully shifted her weight, knelt on the driver's seat and tried to roll down the window. It wouldn't budge.

She'd used the rebar to break the van window, but had dropped it inside the barn. September searched for something else that would work. Other than a few candy wrappers on the wet floor, the van was clean. She popped the glove box, and again came up empty.

The van canted backwards. Water settled in the back half of the vehicle. Shadow barked and pawed the windshield, then climbed halfway up the spidered glass as it shifted to near horizontal. She had to get out. Now.

She hammered the window with the heels of her palms and then fists. Shadow barked with each blow. The window didn't budge. September searched the dashboard for something, anything to use. She pulled out the van's keys from the ignition, and jabbed them at the window, then tried her own SUV keys using the casing from Macy's laser pointer. She felt for the knife in her pocket, but after slicing through the fabric, it nested between inch-thick padding. After failing to extricate the blade, she gripped the knife through the coat fabric and stabbed the glass. The tip of the blade punched through the fabric, but the bare metal tip broke off and barely left a scratch. Nothing worked. She scooped up a handful of change, tried to score the glass with a quarter, and then threw it at the window with a scream of frustration.

The van lurched and settled. Water lapped above the seat. The current increased. September spied something white on the seat between her knees, picked it up and reacted with horror at the bloodstained porcelain tooth torn from Lenny's mouth. With revulsion, she hurled it away. It pinged the glass.

The driver's side window shattered.

Without hesitation, never questioning what had happened, September crawled out of the window. The van began to roll. She scrambled to get free of the vehicle and used the sill as a step to vault onto the roof of the van.

Shadow already waited for her there, wagging and crying. "Good-dog, what a brave boy." She grasped his collar with one hand and the roof rack with the other to get her bearings. The van roof, only a temporary island of safety, would either sink, flip them off or spin away on the growing rush water.

Beside and above them, the loft offered the only hope. The tornado had sheared away part of the roof and wall. Good luck for them, since it offered access they otherwise wouldn't have. September carefully stood. That put the raw edge of the loft at shoulder height.

"Shadow." She kept her voice upbeat more for herself than for him. He'd easily read her terror, but she had to be resolute so he'd trust to do what she asked. She wouldn't leave him behind again, but there'd only be one chance to save them both.

Once Shadow made eye contact, she patted the high-placed floor of the loft. She prayed she'd keep her balance, her bad knee wouldn't betray her, and that the van's modest anchor held for another thirty seconds. He'd made vaults higher than this. She patted the loft floor again. "Shadow, JUMP."

He didn't hesitate. Shadow vaulted, stretched front paws and clawed for purchase when they caught the loft floor. September boosted his haunches the last little bit.

Relief flooded September, but she couldn't waste time. She heard the remainder of the dam crumble behind her and a wall of water gush forward.

She leaped for her life, and grabbed hold, forearms braced on the loft floor. Below her dangling boots, the van tipped over, and spun away in the deluge. September inched forward, swinging her good leg up and catching her heel on the edge until hot breath and teeth tugged her collar. Shadow's boost provided the extra needed to roll into the loft.

Panting, she lay on her back. Shadow stood over top of her, licking her face and making crying dog sounds.

September sat up and pushed the dog away. The sounds were not Shadow, but from below, inside the barn. Mixed with Kinsler's howls, kids screamed.

# Chapter 31

The hail switched off as the heavens called a temporary truce, but Combs didn't move. He hunkered on the floor of Doc Eugene's storage closet, knees drawn up and face pillowed in his arms. The pain and denial grew, not wanting to believe September's message. Willie, his bright, exuberant son, so young, strong, and happy...no. He wouldn't let his imagination go there.

Damn the dog. Damn the storm. And double-damn September for failing Willie.

Lights flickered back to life, but Combs kept his head down. He heard the others labor to their feet, and surreptitiously scrubbed tears from his cheeks before taking three or four gulping breaths and lifting his head.

"Let's see the damage." Doc Eugene opened the door and exited the tiny room, closely followed by Robin. "We're still standing." He disappeared into the front of the vet clinic, his footsteps sneaker soft as he canvased the building. Robin trailed him.

Gonzales held out a hand to help Combs up. "You look like hell. Storm's over. For now, anyway."

Combs jerked away, and stalked out of the room. His throat ached. "Over for us. Willie's still out there." He couldn't tell Gonzales about September's call. To say it out loud made it real. Magical thinking, sure, but he didn't care.

"What did September say? She didn't find him?" Gonzales took out his phone, checked it and grimaced. "Still no bars."

He turned away, and grudgingly spoke. "The message broke up. Wasn't clear." Combs clung to that thin thread and the hope that September wouldn't relegate such news to a voice mail.

Doc Eugene came back into the room. "Lots of limbs blew down, some power lines, too. Robin's car looks like someone worked it over with a baseball bat. Don't know if yours will start or not. But my SUV has barely a scratch, except a honey locust branch scratched one side." He sniffed. "Bizarre weather keeps getting more and more strange." He saw Combs checking his phone. "The office landline is dead, too."

"I'll check the car." Gonzales turned to Combs. "Better touch base with Doty on the radio, find out the state of the county. I don't care if the car's a lumpy-bumpy mess, if it runs." He squeezed Combs's arm. "I got kids, too. We'll find him." He hurried out the door.

Doc Eugene raised his eyebrows.

Combs answered. "Willie's out in the storm."

"For heaven's sake, why would he do that?" Doc Eugene held out a palm in a placating gesture. "Forget I said that. He's a kid. Doesn't need a reason."

"He went after his dog. September's tracking with Shadow, but I can't reach her." Combs shrugged. "Her last message mentioned Willie, but was garbled."

Gonzales returned. "Car's got two flats. I reached Doty, though. Cell towers are down all over North Texas, and flooding disrupted cable between those still standing." He held up his mobile phone. "Meet my high-dollar paperweight." He pocketed the device. "Told Doty about your boy and she promised to get a team out ASAP. But she said lots of people need help." He cleared his throat. "Headquarters got a tip about the dogfight ring. They're set to go. Tonight, in a couple hours. She tapped us to follow up."

"My son's out there. She expects us to check some half ass tip when Willie's missing?" Combs barked a humorless laugh. "She can go screw herself."

"Is the Internet still up?" Doc Eugene hurried to the reception area and booted the computer. "I shut it down during the storm, it'll be a minute."

"The 'net probably is hit or miss, depending on your provider." Gonzales took a step toward Combs's angry pacing. "About that tip. Doty said every account in the department got an email from some hacker calling himself Kid Kewl that detailed the time and location. Some old barn off of FM 691."

Combs wanted to punch something. Punch someone. Doty's face would do.

Gonzales gnawed his mustache, and hesitated. "Isn't that the area September headed?"

He nodded. "But nothing's happening tonight. No dogfight, no drug deals. Doty's bust won't happen, none of the players will be out in this weather." Combs spoke with forced politeness. "Do what you need to do, Gonzales, but right now I could care less about Doty or my job. I'm going after Willie."

Doc Eugene interrupted. "If the Internet works, you can track Shadow by his GPS collar. I know he wears one. You said September mentioned Willie by name, and Shadow never leaves her side. Find Shadow, you'll find Willie."

Combs remembered the GPS system they'd used before. "She's got her house defined as the home territory. When September's pets wander beyond that designated area, her email gets an alert."

It worked similar to Amber Alert tracking systems used to keep kids safe, something Combs wished he'd got for Willie. Parents could get updates sent to a computer or smart phone about the child's location every minute or so and track movements 24/7, even define new areas for after school events or vacation destinations. For pets, the bare bones design used a combination of cell phone towers and GPS to track movement. It worked with a handheld reader.

Gonzales sounded hopeful. "We can give the barn a once over and work the GPS angle at the same time. Doty won't have to know."

Combs moved closer to the computer. "The hand held device has a two-mile range. A desktop won't cut it. We'd need a laptop or tablet with mobile hot spot. Last time our friend Theodore Williams, the geriatric hacker, set that up but since his wife died, he's not been around much."

The computer started up and Doc Eugene launched the browser. The icon spun forever, but nothing came up. "You're right, that's not going to work." He stuck his hand in his pocket, and plucked out his car keys. "But I remember the way to Teddy's house. Let's go."

# Chapter 32

Lightening clawed the sky, but September didn't flinch, numbed by what had come before. She only gritted her teeth and shivered when the clouds once again turned on the spigot. Shadow pressed close beside her.

From her vantage, she saw the tank's partially breached dam continue spewing water. Two-thirds of the dike held the rest of the water at bay, but as she watched, the artificial current down each side chewed at the barrier. She swiveled, gauging the rate of rising water inside the barn, its rush buffered by cement block walls already weakened in the storm. Once the dike surrendered—not *if*, but *when*—anything inside would drown.

The roof and loft already sliced and diced by the tornado exposed the barn interior to punishing rain. The low windows she'd opened to reach the kids now allowed water to sluice inside like a dam's open floodgates. Her elevated view mimicked first balcony seats at a macabre theater production, and she carefully edged forward and craned her neck when the kids screamed again.

Melinda, Willie, and Steven clung together. Lenny sprawled unmoving at their feet. The little group hunkered on the first level of an island of stacked straw bales that abutted one side of an eight-foot-long horse panel, a wire grid barrier defining that side of the dogfight pit. The rising water lifted the bale and the kids rocked a bit before climbing to the next tier to join Boris Kitty. They left Lenny, and September worried the boy might roll off into the water.

Willie wailed again. "He wiggled and slipped out. Get him. Please, get him, Nikki." He jerked his arm but couldn't escape his sister's grip. "I can't swim, please get Kinsler."

September followed Willie's gaze, and her stomach lurched. A bucket floated by, banged against her SUV that still blocked the exit, and performed a drunken pirouette before the current sucked it beneath the car. Nikki slowly plodded through the rising water toward a bobbing white bundle.

Shadow woofed under his breath. He watched with interest, but kept a wary distance from the edge of the drop off.

It only took a few inches of rushing water to knock adults off their feet, and a little girl like Nikki wouldn't have a chance. If the dam broke, the surge of additional water would batter her against, or trap her beneath the car. Once sucked through the narrow breach and tumbled out the other side, not even an Olympic swimmer would survive.

Nikki didn't understand the risks. Her empathy for stray cats nearly got Nikki killed in the burning barn, too. September quelled the urge to shout, "Hurry up," because slow and steady offered better footing. "One step at a time, don't trip, Nikki."

"I'm okay. But his head's under water." Nikki stopped, scooped up the dripping dog and turned back to the bales. Limp and unresponsive, Kinsler flopped in the girl's arms, and September's heart sank.

"Is he okay? Is Kinsler going to be okay?" Willie scrubbed anguished tears from his eyes. He pulled away from his sister's restraint, but fear of the water kept him rooted in place.

September didn't blame the boy. Water made her queasy, too. She couldn't bear to put her face in it. "Everyone, stay right where you are." Her voice whip-cracked with authority. "Nikki, hook your hands in the wire grid on the horse panel. That's right, that's the way." She held her breath until the girl slogged close enough to roll the small dog up onto the level where the kids crouched.

"He's not breathing." Willie stroked long white fur away from Kinsler's face. "He's not breathing." Willie hovered over his dog, and his sister helped Nikki climb out of the chilly water.

The boy's pleading expression unnerved September. In his world, adults had all the answers, and were supposed to make everything better. Poor kid. First the divorce, then his mother's illness, and now he'd watch his dog die. She hated adding another failure onto his young shoulders, but she had no time to waste on a hopeless cause. The kids' safety and getting them into the loft before the dam broke took priority.

"Listen to me. The water's going to get worse really fast. Everyone must get up high, quick as you can." Straw stacks gave them height, but the bales floated, and would become unstable once the dam broke. The loft was the safest location, but her SUV smashed the loft's stairway.

The spring pole's rope moved back and forth in the breeze. Able to sustain the ferocious grip and gyrations of a Pit Bull hanging by his jaws, it certainly could support the weight of each child. But the lowest end hung a good five feet above ground now covered with over a foot of water. Rope-climb drills in Phys. Ed. class when she was a girl spawned universal kid nightmares. September doubted she'd be able to do it, let alone tiny Tracy. They needed something foolproof. Like a ladder.

Even then, the kids couldn't lift Lenny. Shock alone could kill the boy, if his injuries hadn't already. "Melinda, there's a couple of horse blankets on one of those top bales. Yep, where Boris Kitty is resting. We've got to keep Lenny warm."

Willie remained focused on his dog. "Nikki, you work for a vet." His voice trembled, the implications clear. "There's stuff you can do to save him. I saw it on TV about pet CPR."

"I never learned how. September knows." Nikki leaned over Kinsler and felt his chest, then held her palm in front of his nose. "He's not breathing. And I can't feel his heart." She jutted her chin. "September, tell me what to do."

September fumed. They couldn't waste the time. At least Melinda had covered up Lenny as best she could. The orange cat Willie called Waffles decided to snuggle beneath the injured boy's neck. Maybe they could secure the bale in place—

"My dog, what about Kinsler?" Willie yelled, frantic.

Shadow whined. He hated raised voices. More to placate Willie and keep him busy than with any hope for success, September barked out instructions. "Melinda, you're the tallest. Pick up Kinsler by his rear legs. That's right, upside down. Now swing him. Back and forth. With more energy." That often jump-started breathing. Chest compressions required a flat firm surface, not spongy straw bales, and even a veterinarian had trouble performing the ideal 100-120 compressions per minute under the best of conditions.

With Willie's urging, Melinda took the dog by his hocks and swung him back and forth several times. The white dog flopped and dripped water like a sodden stuffed toy.

Nikki interrupted. "It's not working. What about mouth to mouth? Doc Eugene promised to show me but—"

September didn't wait for her to finish. *No time, no time, she had to get the kids to safety.* "Nikki, you still have your bolt cutters? Good. Willie, you work on Kinsler. The rest of you do exactly what I say, no questions and no hesitation. Got it?" She couldn't get down there to do the work, so they'd have to pull together.

They all agreed, eyes wide and frightened.

"Willie, sit down and put your dog in your lap on his back." As he situated himself, September pointed to the metal grid next to the stacked straw bales. "Nikki, those panels come in sections. Cut one loose. It'll be about four bale lengths apart, probably wired together."

"I'm ready, now what?" Willie cradled Kinsler and waited, ignoring Nikki as the girl carefully climbed back into the water and searched for the far edge of the horse panel.

September turned to the two youngest. "Steven and Tracy, you need to help, too. Melinda, work with them. Cut free the baling twine that holds together the bales. Choose the ones that won't matter if they fall apart, we need the twine."

"What do I do about Kinsler?" Willie sounded panicked.

"Willie, do nose-to-mouth rescue breathing. Kinsler's mouth won't seal right so wrap your hands around his muzzle. Yes, that's right. Now open your mouth, and put it over top of his nostrils and mouth." The boy didn't hesitate. "Keep his neck straight so it's a direct shot into his lungs. Gently blow two quick breaths, like you're blowing up a paper bag."

He did it and then pulled away. "His chest moved."

"That's good, Willie. After every two breath-puffs, pull away to let the air come back out. Keep doing that. Don't stop." Sometimes it took quite a while before pets breathed on their own. Sometimes they didn't. But she couldn't tell him that. Better that he remained focused. And calm.

"I got one end cut." Nikki splashed to the other end of the wire grid panel while the first part sagged in deepening current. September wondered why the girl didn't shiver in the cold water. Adrenalin kept them all warm, she guessed.

"Stay close to the bales, and keep a hand on a safe anchor." September told herself that would give Nikki time to escape if the breach came. The truth was, she didn't know. But they didn't have any choice.

Melinda tugged ineffectually at the sisal on one of the bales. She screamed her frustration. "I need a knife!"

The broken knife still poked through one side of September's coat. She grabbed the handle through the fabric and tried to work the blade free. She'd toss it to the kids, and pray her aim wouldn't hit them or fall short and drop it into the water.

Nikki continued to struggle to cut loose the other end of the panel. Without the horse panel, they wouldn't need the twine, and without the twine, they couldn't use the panel. September checked the state of the dike, and her breath quickened. No wonder the water level increased. The rest of the barrier could go at any moment. And the damn knife wouldn't come free.

Steven brought a two-foot scrap of twine he'd found and pushed it into Melinda's hands. Her brow furrowed. She wouldn't take it at first, until he began to singsong instructions.

*"See-saw, Margery-Daw,*
*Cut the thing with the string.*
*See it saw, Like a claw,*
*Make a sling, Cut the string…"*

September frowned. Maybe he had learned this trick at the theater. Worth a shot. "Melinda, do what Steven says. Take that bit of twine, slip one end under the bale strap. Now grab both ends of your piece and pull up. That's what he means, *make a sling*. The weight of the bale holds it taut, you see? Now use your short piece and saw back and forth."

Melinda's face lit up when the maneuver cut through the strap like butter, and then she stiffened. Boris Kitty had climbed up her pant leg and draped himself around her neck. She dumped him off.

"Good job, what a team. Melinda, you cut them, and Tracy and Steven collect them." September balled her fists, frustrated she couldn't lend a hand. "Next, tie all the pieces together, end to end, to make two strands long enough to stretch from here," she patted the loft floor, "clear down to the ground. Hurry." Best to have enough and double or even triple that amount of twine to add strength. She'd not yet worked out how to get the twine up to her level.

Boris Kitty once again vaulted high, this time clawing up Melinda's back. With a cry, the girl twisted, stood, and tried to shake him loose but he kept his grip and shimmied to reach her shoulders. She peeled him off and set him none too gently on the bale beside her.

"Done." Nikki stood with one hand still clutching the bolt cutters, and the other entwined in one end of the horse panel to keep it from sinking into the tugging current. "Now what?"

Willie yelled with frustration, his face red from worry and exertion. "It's not working. He's still not breathing." September winced at the accusation in his voice.

She saw a bit of sharp wire sticking out from the panel. Desperate times call for Hail Mary measures . . . "Nikki, cut off that wire, and straighten it out like a needle. You're going to do acupuncture on Kinsler."

Willie's eyes grew large. To Nikki's credit, she acted excited. She followed September's directions explicitly. "Take the sharp end, and jab it to the bone in the midway point of Kinsler's philtrum. That's the slit below the nose and above the lips. Jab it HARD and wiggle back and forth." Needling this alarm point stimulated the release of adrenalin—veterinarians call the drug epinephrine. That might be enough to jump-start the dog's heart. "Don't stop, keep wiggling it and pressing hard."

Ten seconds become a lifetime watching for signs of life in someone you love. When Kinsler gasped, Nikki jumped backwards with a squeal. The dog took another breath, and then yelped. He struggled weakly in Willie's happy embrace.

Melinda shouted, too, and Shadow barked with excitement in what September thought to be celebration. But no. It was Boris Kitty again, this time perched atop Melinda's head, a climbing maniac determined to scale the heights.

September smiled. She knew exactly how to get the twine into the loft.

# Chapter 33

The spring pole system, anchored with a triple-wrap of steel cable, sprouted from a crossbeam even with the loft floor. The attached industrial-size spring looked like it came from a garage door. A well-worn rope hooked to the spring, and ended with a frayed, chewed up double knot that swung slowly back and forth.

September checked below. Steven and Tracy sat beside Willie who kept a firm grip on Kinsler's collar. The little dog appeared recovered, and September didn't want to tell the boy Kinsler could still collapse. All near drownings needed follow up medical care, but at this point, that was the least of their worries. She still hadn't a clue how to get Lenny up into the loft. *Concentrate on those you can help.*

The two girls pushed one of the floating bales directly beneath the suspended rope while dragging the metal horse panel grid behind them. September knew the panel only weighed about fifteen pounds, but the eight-foot-by-fifty-inch dimensions made it a pain to manipulate. It'd make a keen ladder, though, something all the kids could climb. They'd hoist it up with twine and secure it to the crossbeam, once they got the twine up to September.

"Nikki, stay low on the bale. Help steady it for Melinda." The older girl wore Boris Kitty like a stole, and his tail thumped with agitation. September didn't blame the cat. If she had a tail, it'd be bottlebrush with fear.

Melinda carefully stood on the floating bale, directly below the spring pole rope. The kids had already threaded one end of the twine through Boris Kitty's collar. Melinda grabbed the end of the swinging rope, using it to steady her own balance, and then held it next to her neck. Nothing happened.

"What'll I do now? He won't go." Melinda peeled the cat off her shoulders with one hand, and tried to hang him onto the rope. He twisted and clawed at her shirt.

"No, don't try to force him. It has to be the cat's idea." September watched in horror when the girl lost her grip and Boris Kitty fell into the water. The current immediately whisked the feline toward the swirling exit. "The twine, catch the twine." September prayed the collar wouldn't give way. Many cat collars break away, for safety reasons, so a cat wouldn't catch on something and strangle.

Nikki caught up the end of the long spool of twine they'd gathered, and towed the hissing cat back. Before she could collect his furious form, he clawed his own way onto the floating straw bale, shook himself and each foot in turn, and leaped for Melinda's pant leg.

She squealed as he climbed her body, scratch graffiti testament to his displeasure. This time Boris Kitty didn't stop at Melinda's shoulders. He spat in her face, paw-clutched the rope she still held steady in one hand, and scaled it quicker than a furry Tarzan, the lightweight baling twine trailing from his collar.

"It worked. Now what?" Nikki stood in the water beside the bobbing bale, and grabbed the other side of the metal grid.

The soaked cat, met by Shadow's inquisitive nose, smacked the dog soundly and streaked across the loft floor. Shadow started to follow. "No, Shadow. *Wait.*" Cowed, he did as she asked. September wanted to shout with joy, but still needed to retrieve the hissed off cat and collect the twine. He'd vaulted to the top of a stack of wardrobe boxes stored in one corner.

The cat ignored her. Shadow whined with concern as September walked the balance beam to reach the other side of the barn. "Hey there, Boris Kitty. Can I call you BK? What a brave cat, and such an athlete." She crooned to him and avoided eye contact, crossing to him in a curving pattern. One wrong move and the spooked feline might self-launch into the rafters, destroying their plans.

But for once, luck was a lady. BK ignored her to studiously groom away water from his soaked fur. She picked up the trailing end of the twine, and collected it hand-over-hand as she approached the cat until able to untie the string from his collar. He purred his forgiveness. "Aren't you a handsome, brave fellow?" He mewed, head-bumped her hand, and returned to his tongue bath.

Shadow woofed and pranced where he waited on the far side of the loft. September planned to set up the makeshift ladder on the far side, but time had run out. She'd need to tie it off on this side, and quickly.

"Girls, weave twine back and forth through the end of the grid. Do it now." She watched impatiently. "That's right. Now tie it off. A couple of knots are fine, I'll do more once it's up here. Y'all lift and support the bottom, feed it up as I pull from this end."

They lifted and all eight feet of the flexible fence snaked out of the water. September gathered the twine into a pile beside her. "Good, good, now hold it steady while I secure the top."

The makeshift ladder wasn't ideal but the best she could do. September wrapped twine around the crossbeam, through the wire grids and back again, doubling and tripling the strands. The kids watched from below, finally understanding what she had in mind. This side of the barn actually worked better, because a double tier of straw rested directly beneath the panel making the first step up an easier reach.

They heard the roar when the dam broke. The surge of water rocked Nikki and Melinda's bale, and the girls shrieked. They clung together when the straw surfed backwards. It smashed into the other bales where the other children perched.

"Hang on. Everyone, stay together." September watched helplessly as the bales lifted in the sudden swell. Shadow rushed to her side.

The flood uncorked the SUV from the bottleneck at the barn's doorway, bulldozing it away. Lenny's straw bale, closest to the exit, bobbled and twirled. Steven lurched; his tablet flew from his hands and landed between Lenny's legs, startling the small orange cat that still nestled on Lenny's chest.

Steven grabbed for Lenny's sleeve, but missed, slipped, and pitched into the water. Steven never made a sound, but his mouth opened in a shocked "o" of horror. He dog paddled to keep his head above water, but the current battered him like a cat playing with a mouse.

"God, no!"

When September screamed, Shadow pressed hard against her side. She hugged him tight and trembled, but her muscles refused to obey the mental command to go after the boy. Save him, save Steven. It's what any normal mother would do.

Shadow stared into her face, gently licked September's tears, and pulled out of her embrace. He whirled, and without hesitation, Shadow dove off the loft floor into the water below.

September screeched as her dog—her heart—disappeared beneath dirty swirls of water. The water depth had risen past his shoulders, running so swiftly it easily knocked him off his feet. She leaned forward, staring, ivory knuckles clutching the edge of the loft.

She couldn't catch her breath. Her hands, feet, even her legs tingled. September willed Shadow to reach Steven. Her pulse drummed so loudly in her ears, it out-shouted the flood.

He lunged, snapped and snagged Steven's jacket. Shadow's grip swerved the boy's trajectory enough to lob Steven against Lenny's floating bale. Steven managed to claw a grip into Lenny's bale strap with frantic fingers.

The bale bobbed, dipped, and disappeared out the barn door with the two boys, Shadow helplessly swept in its wake. As if to underline the blackness of despair, the overhead floodlights sputtered out.

# Chapter 34

Nikki shrugged off Melinda's weeping embrace. She had to shout over the rush of water. "What do we do?" They couldn't go after Lenny and Steven. But they couldn't stay here, either. Their perch on the straw stack bobbled.

The other kids stared anywhere but at Nikki, the way kids avoided eye contact if a teacher asked a difficult question. Willie clutched his dog with one hand and held tight to Melinda with the other. Tracy hugged her dinosaur and rocked. They were no help.

"What do we do? The flood's getting worse." September didn't answer. Nikki craned to see into the loft, but September had moved back from the edge out of sight. Maybe working on some kind of plan? "Hey, September, where are you?" She hoped the woman wouldn't do something stupid, the way grownups sometimes did out of desperation. Nikki wanted to cry.

The bales heaved upward and tipped, and everybody squealed, even Nikki. "September, we got to do something now." The whole stack shifted toward the open doorway, a hayride gone terribly wrong. One more big wave and the water would squirt them out like jelly from a doughnut. They couldn't wait for September. They had to finish her plan themselves.

The crazy ladder beckoned, but the bales had shifted so much, they'd have to wade yards of water to reach it. Nikki caught up the extra baling twine—they'd cut far more than they needed—and patted Melinda's arm.

"What?" The older girl shivered uncontrollably and whimpered. Her tangled hair and runny mascara turned her face into a freaky Halloween mask. The collective bales, now a floating island, bobbed sideways. The whole stack slowly traveled toward the open barn door, and hung because the top tier of the straw wedding cake proved too high to pass through. It might scrape off any minute, though. The mountain of straw ground against the dirt floor. Flood pressure pushed from one side and sucked from the other, creating a temporary dam that slowed the outflow. When the top scraped off, they'd stream away with the rest of the bales.

Nikki thrust the twine at Melinda. "You're biggest, you have to go first. Tie one end to your belt loop. Then you." She poked Willie. "Put Kinsler inside your jacket and zip it. You'll need both hands."

"What are you talking about?" Melinda's attention sharpened. "Go first?" But she threaded the end of the twin through belt loops, without being prompted a second time.

"I'm next to tallest so I go last." Nikki had grown a bunch in the past two months, and stood a head taller than Willie despite being the same age. "Tracy goes ahead of me, because she's littlest."

Nikki's hands shook and her tongue wanted to stick to the roof of her mouth. At least she knew how to swim. Willie said he didn't know how, and there was no way Tracy could cross the water without help. Nikki scanned the loft again. She hoped September would be there when they climbed into the loft.

Now that the bales had moved, the swaying horse panel's eight-foot length still left a four-foot gap to the floor of the barn. Nikki measured the best route with her eyes. A direct path, though shorter, risked the tug and push of the current. Better to sidle off the bales and use them like anchors as they moved to the far wall first. "There." She pointed, and explained as the other kids finished stringing themselves together. "September has the ladder all ready. We just have to reach it without getting drowned."

Willie snorted. "Yeah, getting drowned would suck. Ask Kinsler." The dog's head poked outside his jacket like Wack-A-Mole and Willie pushed Kinsler's head back down. Willie's complexion matched Kinsler's pale fur.

Nikki figured she wasn't at her best, either. Her favorite shoes looked ruined, and her jacket would never recover, but at least she wasn't swept away like Steven and Lenny. And Shadow. Before she could dissolve into a blubbering baby mess, Nikki pinched herself, hard. That hurt. But it worked.

Their bales shifted again. Nikki reached out and grabbed Tracy to keep her steady. The little girl didn't notice, simply clutched her soaked dinosaur and rocked faster and faster. "We've got to go. Now."

Nikki gave Melinda a shove. "Wait, you mean into the water?" Melinda wrinkled her nose.

"It's either that or fly. Go ahead, step off real careful. Willie, give her your hand." Nikki paused, and when Melinda hesitated, her tone sharpened. "You want to die? You want all of us to die?"

"Okay, I'll do it. Willie, don't let go." Melinda sat on the edge of the bale, and let her feet drop into the cold brown water. "Nasty, stinks like a sewer. I'm going, already." She clung to Willie's hand and slid off to stand in the water, adjusting to the tug of the current. If the stack of straw let loose in the doorway, the current would turn into a water shoot and blast them out.

"Steady yourself against the bales." Nikki had already been in the water and knew what to do. Melinda gained confidence after a couple of steps. "Get to the wall, and wait for Willie. Once he's there, follow the wall until you reach the metal wire fence."

Melinda nodded, but said nothing, biting her lip in concentration. She reached the wall, and waited for her brother to draw near.

Willie joined his sister. "Go ahead, Melinda." Nikki talked as loud as she could without screaming, so they could hear her. "Hug the wall, and be real careful you don't slip because there's nothing to catch you. That's the reason for the tether, see? It's our contingency." Dad always said a contingency was the most important part of any plan. Dad was the smartest person she knew. Well, Doc Eugene was super smart, too, being a veterinarian and all.

Melinda moved more quickly. She reached the near edge of the suspended fencing and grasped the wire, but tripped and went chest-deep in the water.

Willie yelled and started toward his sister.

"Stay where you are, Willie. Keep the twine tight so you can reel her in!" Nikki held her breath.

"I'm okay." The older girl dragged herself upright, spitting and making a face after getting a mouthful of the runoff. "Willie, don't go toward the middle. There's a rut or something in the ground." Melinda turned back to Nikki. "What about the little one?"

Nikki had it all figured out. She spoke softly to Tracy, explaining exactly what would happen. She wasn't sure if the girl understood but talking worked with the spooky feral cats at the clinic, and they didn't understand people talk, either. Doc Eugene and September said tone of voice meant more than words, so she spoke with confident encouragement and hoped Tracy understood.

Tracy stopped rocking long enough to let Nikki lift her. With the girl's legs and arms firmly wrapped around her waist and neck, Grooby trailing down her back, Nikki took a first careful step into the water. She moved sideways, clawing deep with both hands into the bales to anchor herself along the way, until she reached Willie.

"Now you. Along the wall, Willie, to Melinda at the grid." He made hurried progress and soon joined his sister. "Melinda, how about you moved to the far edge of the fence to hold it steady, while Willie holds his side. Hang on tight, though." She waited until they sloshed into position. Was it her imagination or had the water got deeper, but the current slowed? Whatever. They couldn't stop now.

"I need some help here. Willie, make sure you have a good grip on the panel. Yeah, that's good, hook an arm through. Now find your end of the twine, and keep it tight as I come to you."

If she slipped while holding Tracy, they'd both head out to sea unless the twine held. September said it would hold. But they only had a single strand, while September used multiple thicknesses to secure the fence-ladder. "We don't weigh much, though, do we Tracy?" The little girl squeezed her neck, and Nikki smiled. "I'll take that as a yes." She took a breath. *Here we go.*

The tether tension Willie provided, along with leaning one shoulder hard against the barn wall, gave Nikki enough extra balance. She only slipped once, and thank goodness, quickly recovered. Finally, they all stood beneath the suspended horse panel. Water now reached Melinda's butt and stood well over Willie's waist.

"Now what?" Melinda waited for direction.

Nikki examined the cross beam above. It wouldn't be easy to climb the metal fence, and tricky to get from the beam to the solid floor of the loft. They'd come this far, though, and she wouldn't give the other kids any reason to doubt their ability. Dad said that, too. You had to believe, before you could do. *I believe, Daddy.*

"Tracy first." Nikki unwrapped the girl's arms from her neck. "You can do this. I'm going to hold you up to grab hold, and Melinda and Willie will hold the bottom steady. Climb, and don't look down. Climb like you do the monkey bars at the playground, okay?"

Nikki worried the girl would freeze, or cling to her and yell or something equally dumb. She was clean out of ideas if that happened. But happily, Tracy gripped Grooby between her teeth, and scrambled quick as a squirrel up the ladder contraption. "Wow, good job. Tracy, you're a champ." She turned to Willie. "You next. Watch out for the dog."

"Got it covered." Willie had tucked his jacket into the waist of his pants to secure Kinsler. "If Tracy can do it, so can I."

Nikki didn't appreciate the girl-slam, but at least it gave Willie incentive. Real heroes got scared, too. They didn't let the brain freeze shut them down. "So make like a monkey already."

He made a face, and hooted his chimp impression, but let Melinda give him a boost up before he quickly climbed the fence.

Nikki's shoulders relaxed. September's idea worked great.

"Now you." Melinda wiped hair out of her eyes. "I'm the tallest, like you said. I can get up that first step on my own, but you'll need me to give the first boost. And I'm the oldest. You've done enough; I got to step up, too." She dropped her voice. "Girl power, right?"

"Girl power." Nikki smiled. "Okay, we got this." She searched with her foot under the water to find Melinda's braced knee, balanced briefly on one foot while grabbing the wire, and pulled herself up.

With only one person steadying the make-do ladder, it wanted to shimmy as Nikki climbed. It took her twice as long to reach the loft as the first two kids, but her arms already ached from holding Tracy. Finally, she grabbed the beam, and crab-walked to the solid loft floor.

Nikki sank to her knees, so relieved she wanted to cry. She looked around, and saw the other kids around September, who sat in one corner of the loft with her knees drawn up, shaking and crying and acting totally weirded out.

She wanted to find out what was wrong, but had to wait for Melinda. Just as the older girl grabbed the wire handholds, the topmost wedding-cake bales broke off. The straw stopper unplugged and the rest of the bales washed out the barn door like bumper cars. The sudden outflow swept Melinda off her feet.

# Chapter 35

The water tasted of dirt, animal dung and dead bugs, fermented grass and bitter bark. Shadow sputtered, struggled to keep his head above the tumbling torrent, and lunged once more. He grabbed and latched onto cloth. A familiar scent, one never forgotten, filled him with confusion.

Protectiveness. Affection. Distrust. Fear. Memory of the "otherness" of his-boy pointing the gun that bit a good-dog's ear.

He gulped air in panting breaths. Small scared whimpers escaped but he didn't dare let go his grip on the coat. Nose thrust hard against Steven's back, Shadow's jaws ached with tension and his stomach churned. When his flank smashed into something hidden beneath the rush of dark water, he nearly lost his grip, but didn't yelp. Shadow drew his paws up tight, helpless, riding the whims of the water.

His-boy's odor crinkled Shadow's nose, the bite-sharp terror spilled through Steven's clothing more potent than the cat pee dribbling from the little orange cat. Smells choked his throat. Water filled his ears, muffling the flood's roar and cat's screams. Shadow wanted to shake his head. But he clenched his jaws and hung on.

Bam!

The sodden bale hit, stopped, tipped downward. One of Lenny's arms flopped into the water. Shadow's hold broke loose when the bale reared high, a legless horse vaulting a hidden obstacle.

He flailed; paws churned to find solid purchase, and turned water to filthy froth. The wet, muddy bank beckoned, only a dog-length distant. Current tugged him away.

Steven's arm whipped out. His-boy grabbed Shadow's collar, and kept his other fist latched onto Lenny's bale. Steven had grown in the time away, and his legs were much longer than Shadow's. When he found his feet, Steven stood chest deep and braced himself against the surge.

Shadow reluctantly met Steven's eyes. Neither of them liked eye contact with strangers, and after all the time that had passed, they were strangers. But something had changed. The "other-ness" in Steven's eyes remained but it no longer spoke of danger.

The floating bale bucked again. Shadow's collar tightened. Steven swung him through the water closer to the bank where shallow water pooled.

Shadow didn't think. As his paws touched, he clawed and scrambled out of the water. He shook himself so hard, he nearly fell over. He panted and shivered at the same time, then in one convulsive heave, threw up.

The current continued to push wreckage along the water's surface. An underwater tree had hooked the bottom of the bale. The tree bobbed up and down in the current. When down, the bale tried to squeak over the branch, which then boosted it up again.

Steven waited until the bale dipped low, then grabbed something shiny and flat from between Lenny's legs. With a smooth gesture, he Frisbee'd it toward Shadow.

Shadow lunged and caught it. He recognized it from the earlier *show-me* game. Steven didn't smile, but sensed his-boy's approval. He wagged.

Shadow cocked his head when the orange cat yowled with each bounce of the floating bale. He wondered why the cat didn't jump off and race to higher ground. Macy-cat picked a safe tree to climb and wait for Shadow to *seek* and bring him home. But this cat didn't move, merely kept his claws secured in Lenny's shirt, and burrowed closer to the boy.

Steven clung to the bale, wading with careful small steps to reach the bank. He had to let go of the bale to climb up like Shadow, but kept slipping back into the water. The bank's soggy mud turned loose of trees and grass so there was nothing his-boy could grab. Boys don't have claws like dogs.

Shadow put down the tablet he'd caught, and slowly put one paw and then another on the fallen tree. His weight held it steady. When Steven reached out, Shadow stretched his neck and grabbed the end of Steven's coat sleeve, and tugged.

That gave his-boy enough help to scramble up on the tree limb. With both Steven and Shadow standing on the slender trunk, though, the limb sank further beneath the current, bouncing the straw bale and giving it enough leeway to pass over the temporary snag.

Steven sprang at Shadow, and Shadow nearly dodged away. But something told him to stay still.

"Good-dog."

Shadow pricked his ears with surprise. His-boy had never told him that before.

He held still, marveling at Steven's gentle touch. His-boy quickly pulled off Shadow's collar and tossed it toward Lenny, just as the current again captured the bale and swirled Lenny and the cat out of sight.

# Chapter 36

*September screwed her eyes tight against the flames. Her flesh blistered, charred and fell away. She struggled to breathe in the super-heated furnace of the burning barn. Her legs, cocooned in an ever-tightening noose, strangled every effort to escape. She clawed, flailed and bucked to get out, crawl away, to survive. A heavy weight crushed the air from her chest and pinned September to the hard pack dirt.*

*From far away Shadow yelped, followed by an anguished howl. Oh God, don't let him burn, too! Wet flame licked her face, and September screamed, screamed, screamed for a lifetime and only fell silent when her raw throat and heaving lungs failed. The relentless heat bathed her face again and again. Barks and whines cut through the fog of horror, hot air fanned her neck, and she recoiled — then recognized the sensation with a sob of relief. Not a furnace blast, but anxious dog panting. Canine whimpers sounded a counterpoint rhythm to each attention-seeking slurp-kiss aimed at her eyes and mouth. His icy nose shocked her out of the flashback.*

Her heart still hammered its marathon sprint, and her entire body shook with chills despite the heat flushing her face. September kept her eyes closed. She told herself to breathe slowly, and managed to curtail gasps and unclench still tingling hands. Thank God, she had

Shadow, her sweet baby-dog, to keep her safe, to anchor her in the real world.

"Good-dog, I'm okay." Shadow knew better, but saying the words gave her a goal. She put up a hand to block his enthusiastic face kisses. His wet fur was wrong.

Kinsler, the white terrier mix, got in one more slurp before she pushed him away. Shadow? She sat up with a gasp, disoriented.

Still in the barn. A different barn. Cold and wet, no choking smoke or flame. Tornado. The flood. The kids. Lenny. Steven.

A choked sob caught deep in her lungs. Her fault, her terrible fault. Steven, her dirty reminder, fruit of the trauma she'd never ever escape. But she'd never wished him ill, even put her life on the line to save him.

Then Steven was gone. And she was glad.

She was a monster. Only just for God to punish her, she deserved it, the taint on her soul she'd never scrub clean. But not Shadow, why punish him? His loyalty, his love, his innocence. They shared one heart. She'd bleed to death from his loss. The mind-numbing grief threatened to suck her back into the void.

Kinsler nose-poked her again, and more of her surroundings came into focus. Willie rode her legs like a pony. "Willie, get off."

The little dog scampered around, as the boy dismounted. "You were moaning and flailing around, and I didn't want you to roll off the loft."

Her scowl silenced him. She pushed away the dizzy hopelessness before she fell back down the rabbit hole. September steeled herself. Get over it. Life wasn't fair. She wasn't meant to love, or be loved. *Accept it. Move on.*

"How'd you get up here?" She was afraid to ask about the other kids. She had no more grief to spend.

"It worked. That ladder thing we built, it worked." Willie couldn't stand still, excited and happy, a kid on an adventure. "Nikki made us work together. Tracy's over there," he pointed to a corner of the loft, "and Nikki's helping Melinda climb up. Everyone's okay. Well, except for Lenny and Steven." His smile faded but his words remained hopeful. "Maybe they'll be okay, too."

She didn't answer. Easier to accept their deaths, ignore the hollow emptiness, and work to save the living. There'd be time later for a lifetime of regrets.

She wanted to scream to the heavens the depth of her loss. But she wouldn't dare, not when children's lives were lost. Her silence would be the worst betrayal of Shadow's trust.

The wooden floor and upper walls reverberated as if a semi rammed the structure. Dust and straw sifted from the ridgepole. Water gush increased to a roar.

September scrambled to her feet. "What was that?"

"No no no!" Nikki crouched above the makeshift ladder. She nearly lost her balance when the floor shuddered. "Hang on, Melinda." Her frantic expression implored help.

September rushed to Nikki's side. Below, Melinda had a double-fisted grip on the bottom "rungs" of the horse panel, but her legs trailed in the water that poured out the open barn door so fast, the girl couldn't stand up.

"I'm slipping. I'm going to fall." Melinda's shriek made the rafters ring.

"No. You will *not* fall." September's temple throbbed and fists clenched, damned if she'd lose another kid. "Nikki, move back." September searched the loft for something, anything, to help.

Across the loft, Tracy poked around a stack of dusty wardrobe boxes. "Dammit, what are you doing? Leave that alone, Tracy." For the first time September noticed the baling twine that trailed from Tracy's waist across the floor. She looked sharply at the other kids. "Are y'all tied together?"

Nikki nodded, pointing to twine that dangled from her waist over the edge of the loft. If Melinda lost her grip and water yanked her away, Nikki and the rest of the kids would jerk along like the tail of a kite. It worked both ways, though. They could give Melinda a toehold if they could keep from tumbling off the edge.

In the dark corner above the boxes hung a metal contraption with a large pulley that ran on an overhead track attached to a high beam. September had seen fancy multi-pulley contraptions re-purposed into lamps in antique stores, but this hay trolley worked. Melinda needed the extra boost to get her footing. This would work. Because it had to work.

"Nikki, cut loose that twine, but hang on to the end for all your worth." September rushed to the trolley as she spoke, caught and tugged the end until it followed, jerking along the overhead track. "Now give me your twine."

"I'm slipping. My hands feel numb." Melinda twisted and turned in the current.

"Don't try to stand, not yet. Going to get you some help, sweetie, hang on." Working fast, September threaded Nikki's end of the twine through and over the large metal pulley. "Melinda, when I say NOW, I want you to pull as hard as you can and grab the next rung up. Okay?"

Gathering the slack, September wrapped the twine around both hands, shouted, "NOW!" and pulled down with all her strength. The twine cut both palms, but the reel gathered the twine and levered Melinda upwards. September released one hand to get a grip further up, and sensed Willie take up the excess cord behind her and add his weight. She couldn't see Melinda's progress, but the weight and steady movement told her the girl must be moving. When Melinda's red head poked over the edge, September dropped the twine to grasp the girl's arm and pull her the rest of the way up. Willie grabbed her other arm, and the two fell into each other's arms.

September sat down on the wet floor, hardly noticing the burning cuts. She put her face in her hands, but had no more tears. Numb was good. Numb didn't hurt. If she started feeling again, her heart would shatter.

At least the kids were safe. She had to let Combs know and tell Claire she found Tracy. She wondered if Nikki's folks knew where she was. Happy endings for some, numb for the rest.

Her phone still had no signal. Even if it didn't go through, she sent a text to both Combs and Claire.

One of the wardrobe boxes, nearly as tall as Tracy, toppled as the little girl pulled threadbare clothes off the hanger bar inside. Rattling pill bottles spilled out all over the floor. Tracy crowed and danced around the loft with Grooby. "Told you so, Willie, told you told you. Magic pills."

# Chapter 37

Claire sat statue still in the passenger side of Sunny's green truck. The woman hadn't said a word since leaving the convenience store. Finally, Claire could stand the silence no longer. "Where are we going?"

"Shut up. I'm thinking." Sunny stared at the sky, clearly worried. She finally glared at Claire. "I know you heard. You were in the bathroom."

Instead of terror, the weight of uncertainty lifted and a calm clarity descended. She lied, and prayed the near truth would suffice. "I only heard the last part, something about a barn and the kids. And dropping me off somewhere." Claire puffed herself up, knew she had to play this right. "I won't get in the way. I don't care about anything except getting my daughter back."

Sunny's face darkened. Claire wondered how she'd ever thought the woman beautiful. Sunny's high cheekbones could slice skin and her snarl bared feral teeth, but she only pressed harder on the gas.

Claire recognized the sign for Rabbit Run Road. Within minutes, the big truck pulled up behind Claire's ramshackle car parked outside of September's gated drive.

"Get out." Sunny sat stony faced.

"I want to go with you, and find my daughter. And Lenny. They're out of medicine by now. You can't handle both at the same time." She unbuckled her seatbelt, gambling the woman wouldn't hurt her. She had no choice.

"Go. Now. Before I change my mind." A small vein throbbed in Sunny's neck. "That wall cloud's ready to birth serious weather. Take my advice, and get under cover."

Claire spoke earnestly, but her nostrils flared. "If you had kids, you'd understand. A mom does anything for her kids to keep them safe. Anything."

Sunny reacted as if slapped. A flush climbed her throat.

Claire didn't stop. "You wouldn't know about that. TV star and model perfect, probably everything comes easy for you. Okay, fine. I'm going, I'm going." She climbed out, slammed the truck door and ducked her head against the returning rain. After thumbing the key fob, she climbed into her car, and shouted over the rising wind. "You can't stop me from following in my car."

Sunny rolled down her window and pointed a gun with a barrel the size of Texas. "You don't know me, bitch."

Claire wailed. She slammed the door, and covered her head with both hands. *Stupid, stupid.* She fumbled for her phone. Two shots popped, not nearly as loud as she expected. Her car shifted. Sunny had shot the tires.

Another shot and the driver's window shattered, spraying glass over Claire's crouched form. The fourth came with an explosion of white-hot pain that bloomed below her right shoulder and came out her front. Claire screamed, screamed again, and waited for the final shot that would end her life.

"Shit." The truck's engine roared, and it raced away.

She didn't move. It hurt to breathe, so she knew she wasn't dead. Her phone. Call the cops. Stop Sunny, or she'd hurt the kids.

Claire grabbed the steering wheel with her left hand to lever herself upright. Slicing heat traversed her chest. The bullet had entered her back and exited below her right breast. Blood soaked her coat. It smelled raw and rich, a meaty aroma that made her gag. Retching, nothing coming out. Gasped until she caught her breath. Claire wadded and rolled the bottom of her jacket, picked up her right hand and placed it over the wad, commanding herself to hold it tight.

Her phone pinged, blinking on the seat between her knees. She picked it up, read the text message from September, and began to cry. Claire didn't question or care how it happened; only that Tracy was safe.

She coughed, and tasted blood. She might die. She might never see Tracy again. Claire had to speak to her, hear Tracy's voice, one time, that's all she wanted. Carefully, Claire balanced the phone on her knee, scrolled to find September's number and dialed.

September answered at once. "Claire? Claire, thank God the phone's working, don't know for how long. You got my text? Tracy's fine."

"My daughter, want to talk to her." Hard to breathe or to speak. The whole side of her body weighed a million pounds. It didn't hurt so badly now, though.

"I need you to call the police. Ask for Detective Jeff Combs. Tell him—" The connection filled with static before again clearing. "...barn loft. Don't know how long it'll stand, the tornado hit us hard. Hello? Hello, are you there?"

Hail the size of gumdrops pattered the windshield, quickly growing in size and velocity. The sky blackened and temperature dropped twenty degrees in the space of ninety seconds. No wonder Sunny raced away. "Tornado. Coming at me."

"Claire! Where are you? Take cover."

"My car. At your house."

"Get out, get out, cars are deathtraps, go to the house. Damn, you'll never get inside, I made that house a frigging fortress."

The shattered window glass fell from her lap in a glittery heap as Claire stepped from the car. She thumbed the phone onto speaker, and dropped it into her coat's breast pocket. September's frantic voice continued to yell instructions. "The garage, go to the garage. Hurry."

"Need to tell you." Claire held both hands over the bloody hole beneath her breast, amazed she could still move or speak or breathe. "Sunny works for the Doctor. She's coming to the barn to get the pills. Tell Tracy I love her." She reached the side of the house, and leaned there to catch her breath. And couldn't. "Can you hear me?" She staggered against the wind, no longer ducking or even acknowledging the hail. "Sunny shot me." Another push, the garage over there, only a little farther to reach safety.

The tornado hit, taking the entire garage and half of September's house with it. Roses lifted into the air with clods of black, and swirled in a delicate dance. Claire's car sat untouched.

# Chapter 38

September redialed when the connection failed, but Claire's number went to voice mail. She prayed the woman reached cover on time. Her garage, actually an old-fashioned carriage house, had withstood nearly a century of weather, after all.

Sunny Babcock's involvement made no sense. September didn't know the woman, had only briefly met her after the debacle involving the hog hunting reality show. Combs met Sunny there, too. And when she reached out to Combs this morning for P.I. help—had it only been this morning?—he sent Sunny.

A horrible idea reared its ugly head. When Combs arrived at BeeBo's, he'd been angrier than she'd ever seen, more than her presence justified. Last year, the Doctor and his mother had an insider on the police force, Combs's own partner. . .

The kids surrounded the stacked boxes of Damenia pills, chattering with excitement, especially Tracy. The bounty would relieve Claire's financial worries, too.

Steven no longer took Damenia. She hadn't wanted to know about his treatment, wanted nothing to do with the child. He reminded her of an ugliness she'd never erase, but it wasn't Steven's fault. Too late to make it up to the boy—or herself.

According to Claire, Sunny could show up at any moment. She'd have no compunction about eliminating witnesses, even kids. September squared her shoulders. Too late for Steven, but saving these kids might save her soul, if God even listened anymore. After losing Shadow, she doubted the Big Guy had any time for her. It was all on her.

For now, they were safe from the flood. But with no way out of the loft, they might as well have taped bullseyes to their backs.

It worked both ways, though. Sunny had no way to get into the loft, and didn't know they were here. They could hide. Claire's call to the police would bring Combs to the rescue.

"Tracy, leave that alone. It's evidence." The little girl stuffed a double handful of pill bottles into her jacket pockets, while Boris Kitty sat inside the open box, batting vials around.

"It's *her* medicine." Nikki sounded defensive. "That's why she and Lenny drove all the way from Chicago. Finders keepers." She put her hands on narrow hips.

Tracy ignored September and stuck several more vials in her pockets. "Eighty-four pills per bottle times 30 bottles, two pills a day, 1260 days 180 weeks 45 months 3.75 years. Not enough." She abruptly sat on the dusty floor of the loft, and pulled out her tablet from an inner pocket. "Internet is up." She fiddled with the screen.

No need to argue. Let her keep the medicine, for now. Hiding the kids took priority. "The man who made the medicine—"

"The Doctor." Nikki had appointed herself spokesperson for the little group. "That's what Tracy said." Her gaze shifted up and to the left, telling September the girl fudged the truth. As if to cover sudden nerves, Nikki fished Boris Kitty from the box and draped him over her shoulders.

September didn't care how or where Nikki got her information. "Tracy's mom called. Someone's coming to collect the pills. We need to hide, or it could get dangerous." She scanned the loft. A pair of ramshackle bookcases, one against a wall and the other shattered across the floor, spilled back issues of Sporting Dog Journal and Certified Contender Report across the loft. Illegal as hell, the publications recorded which dogs won and tracked winning bloodlines. A few cardboard cartons filled with who knows what sat nearby. None were large enough to hide one kid, let alone the whole group.

"The storm blew everything to smithereens." Nikki scratched under the cat's chin. "Only place to hide is behind the stack of boxes. Or inside them." She rolled her eyes.

Smiling, September hugged Nikki. "You're brilliant."

"Careful of the cat." Nikki turned away, incredulous. "You don't mean actually get *inside* the boxes. We won't fit, they're full of stinky old clothes and Tracy's medicine. We can't throw it out, or she'd see." She pet the cat, defiant.

"She? You know who's coming?" September grabbed Nikki's arm when she tried to walk away.

"Uh, no. How could I know that?" Nikki looked away again. "She, he, whoever. There's nowhere to dump the clothes so *the person* wouldn't see and suspect something."

"Sunny "The Babe" Babcock. It's a she. Will be here in six-and-a-half minutes. That's 390 seconds." Tracy kept fiddling with her tablet.

September stared, then grabbed the tablet from Tracy, expecting a CSI-like satellite view of a car speeding toward them. Instead, she saw a rudimentary BBS where posters could message each other. It reminded her of early days on the Internet.

Nikki snatched it back before she could read anything. "That's private." She returned it to Tracy. "It's a kid thing, our secret club. We're not allowed to go on Facebook. We're not hurting anything." She spoke too fast, and blushed.

She dismissed the childhood angst. She had no clue how Tracy knew about Sunny, but the fact she did lent credence to the predicted arrival. September stared toward the road. It sat thirty feet away, and nearly level with the loft elevation. Six more minutes and Sunny would be here.

"Everyone, quickly dump clothes from the boxes out the back of the loft into the water. Hide the pills in these magazine cartons. That'll make room for you to get inside." The Doctor transported the medication in mislabeled wardrobe boxes so nobody would search past the musty clothes.

"There are five boxes but six of us if you count Kinsler." Willie stuck out his jaw and she could see his dad in his belligerent pose. He clutched the dog and looked ready to argue his cause if anyone suggested leaving Kinsler behind.

"Kinsler goes with you. I'm too big for the box. It's getting dark, she won't see me. I've got a plan." She didn't like it, but had no choice.

September upended the two shabby cartons. Medical supplies spilled from one, including syringes, hemostats and suture material probably used to patch up dogs. The other carton contained a dozen or more plastic dagger-like objects, some with bite marks and blood on them. Break sticks, inserted behind the gripping dog's premolars to persuade him to release, usually were made from wood. September dumped them onto the floor with distaste.

The pill bottles overflowed the empty cartons, testament to the many customers the Doctor still controlled. September set the cartons atop the toppled bookcase, scooped the remainder into the prone shelves, and scattered armfuls of the fight publications to cover them up.

"Quickly now. Inside, everyone inside." September lifted Tracy into of the first box. "Turn off your tablet. If it makes noise and Sunny hears, we're sunk." She shut the lid, and reused the old tape to secure it closed.

"You next, Willie. I'll hand Kinsler to you once you're inside. Promise to keep him quiet." Willie folded himself into a Buddha pose and she handed the subdued dog to him.

Nikki and Melinda hopped into their respective boxes after September cupped hands for a boost up. "You sure this will work?" Nikki stared up at her from the bottom of the box, thin arms hugging her knees. "Where will you hide?" Worry etched her brow.

"I'll hang out. Literally. I want to try out that homemade ladder. Y'all got to climb it, and now it's my turn." September tried to smile, but quickly gave up. "I don't know what sort of equipment Sunny has. I'm banking on her taking the boxes one by one."

Clouds finally had started to break apart. The nearly full moon offered the only illumination, streaking the loft with sinister gloom. Good.

"Sit real quiet, like mice. Cover up your mouths if you need to when she moves your box." September shivered. "Melinda, she'll probably leave keys in her truck. Once everyone's out and Sunny comes back for the last box, y'all take off."

Nikki shook her head, and started to pop back out of her box. "Leave you? That's not happening." Her lip trembled.

"That is SO happening, Nikki. Go to the police, drive like your lives depend on it." September shut their boxes and loosely taped them shut like the others, so they could easily get out.

From inside the closed wardrobe, Nikki yelled. "What about the cat?" Boris Kitty meowed, and hopped onto the top of the highest box.

Headlights pierced the gloom. "Too late, she's here." September stage whispered, not sure how far her voice would carry, now the storm had passed. A green truck with a high rack-hunting rig tooled down the road, and jerked to a stop.

# Chapter 39

When the big truck rumbled down the road toward the barn, Shadow followed Steven and hid with his-boy behind a stand of scrubby trees until it passed. He poked his long, black nose out to scent-test the wind. The engine sounded familiar and made Shadow's hackles rise, but he didn't know why.

Shadow wanted to race back to the barn. September waited for him there. She'd be worried, and he grew more anxious the longer they stayed apart.

The water had carried them a long way. They'd only walked back a short distance because Steven couldn't run as fast as dogs. Boys don't have as many paws. But September wouldn't want him to leave Steven, and above all, Shadow wanted to please her.

Steven found a big rock and sat on it, shivering in his wet clothes while he stared and poked at the shiny Frisbee-tablet. Shadow whined, wanting to follow the truck. Maybe the driver would find September and the other kids. That would be a good thing. Still, the wet fur on the back of his neck itched and quivered, increasing his unease.

He put a paw on Steven's knee, but the boy nudged it aside. Shadow whined again, and then woofed sharply.

"Shhh." Steven made the hush-sound again.

Yawning with nervous frustration, Shadow peered from Steven to the distant barn. September waited for them. Why was his-boy sitting there, shivering? Going back to the barn meant finding September. She always knew what to do. His tummy grew warm when he thought of her, even though his wet fur chilled him in the wind. With exasperation, Shadow nose-poked Steven, using his muzzle to lever his-boy's hands away from the device. September always laughed when he did that. It was his job to tell her when she needed a break.

"No-no-no! Like I say, go away." Steven clutched the tablet before it fell. "Ready to yell for show and tell. Go away, right now, today." He slapped Shadow's nose.

Shadow squeezed shut his eyes. The slap didn't hurt. But it reminded him of Steven in the long ago time, when his-boy got so angry Shadow had to lie down and hold him and never flinch away from his fists. September taught him what to do. Now when September cried out and flailed at invisible threats, Shadow did the same to keep her safe.

He debated what to do. His-boy was safe, out of the water. And Steven said go away. It was a good-dog's job to do what people said. He still didn't feel right about leaving.

In the distance, the truck door slammed and a woman cursed. That decided Shadow, and raced to reach the big truck.

It sat at the edge of the broken car path, a short distance from where water cut the road in half. The driver stood in the brightness of the truck's eyelights, talking into her phone. Her voice sounded familiar, but only when the wind shifted and he caught her scent did Shadow recognize the woman. She'd visited that morning, smelling of gunpowder and death.

# **Chapter 40**

Kelvin recognized the caller and answered immediately. He quelled his first impulse to rip her a new one. Sunny should have checked in long ago. The plan had been flawless, until she screwed it up. He'd grown more and more flustered the longer he sat with the Doctor virtually breathing down his neck. The crazy-eyed bastard had begun polishing his gun twenty minutes ago.

"Who calls?" The Doctor moved from his post in front of the closed office door, to hover like a vulture spying a meal. He leaned on the desk, the gun dangling from the other fist.

"Sunny." Kelvin struggled not to shrink away.

The Doctor held out an imperative hand, but Kelvin shook his head and turned away to talk. He could still salvage the situation. Maybe she had good news. He forced himself to speak calmly. "I want you to—"

"Kelvin, I don't care what you want." Wind buffeted Sunny's phone. "Is the Doctor there? Tell him there's no way to retrieve the product."

Done, screwed, over and out. Kelvin shouted into the phone. "Tell him yourself." He switched the phone to speaker, clunked it down on the desk and backed away, distancing himself from Sunny's failure.

She spit the words, a cornered cat with claws extended. "I'm at the barn. Correction, I'm parked on the last bit of road, at least 20 feet away. The road washed out, it's all under water. No way to get to the barn." She laughed bitterly. "There'll be no big show tonight, sweetheart, not with all the dogs drowned. Everything's under water. Hell, half the loft is gone. Tornado probably took the drugs, too."

The Doctor's free hand rose to his scalp, grasped a lock of silver hair, and twisted. "Promises made," he whispered.

Kelvin parried with persuasion and sympathy. "Sorry about the dogs, Sunny. But we made a deal. You don't have a choice."

"Forget the dogs." She snorted. "Hell, most were has-beens, only a few good prospects. Kelvin, there's always more dogs. And the Doctor can make more pills."

"Find. A. Way." Had they been fists, Kelvin's words would have bloodied her face. "If it's there, get it out. That's why you're being paid." She had no idea what tightrope they walked. The venal bitch cared most about money, so he'd use the only leverage he had.

"I already got paid. Most of it, anyway." She paused, amusement in her voice. "The Doctor's making you all flustered. Take a chill pill, Kelvin. Maybe he'll loan you some meds."

"Sunny "The Babe" Babcock, you have been paid for services not yet rendered." The Doctor yanked a twist of hair from his head, and idly painted the gun with the hank.

"Yeah, well, the tornado had other plans." Her sarcastic retort made Kelvin's stomach drop. She thought distance kept her safe. He took another step backwards.

Twist, yank. Another silver lock fell. "You will arrange for another event to fulfill our agreement. And you will secure the product for this future event, at your own time and expense."

"Why should I?" She taunted the man, clearly enjoying herself. "It's your party, Doc. Give me one reason I shouldn't pack up and leave you to clean up your own mess."

Kelvin took another step backwards. If he could reach the door . . . He stopped when the Doctor raised his gun.

"I'll give you two reasons, Sunny Babcock. Reason number one. Do this and I will pay you Kelvin's share as well."

Licking his lips, Kelvin slowly shook his head as the Doctor pointed his gun. No chance to change his mind. He could see the Doctor's decision in his pale eyes.

For the first time, Sunny sounded cautious. "Kelvin might object. What's the second reason?"

In concert with the gun's "pop-pop-pop" Kelvin's knees unhinged. The triple-punch blazed fire into his middle. He pressed both hands to his gut, wobbled, and then keeled over. His face smooshed against the floor. The carpet smelled of mouse turds.

"Reason number two. The police will discover you killed Kelvin for his share, unless you finish the assigned task."

Another "pop-pop" sounded, followed by the opening squeak and rattle of the top desk drawer dumped to the floor. Kelvin's money-stuffed yellow sock rolled under the desk. From his vantage, he watched the Doctor scoop up the blood money he'd never get to spend. The money never mattered, not really.

The Doctor picked up the phone, talking as he walked, until his fancy snakeskin boots stood inches from Kelvin's face. He closed his eyes and held still when the man's toe nudged his neck. Possum time.

"Since I no longer have confidence in your trustworthiness, Sunny Babcock, I will meet you at the event destination. You will transfer the rescued product into my safekeeping. Don't disappoint me." The Doctor's pointed boots moved away, then the office door opened. "Broken promises reap punishment." He tossed the phone at the desk, and slammed the office door.

Kelvin's eyes flew open. His phone. He'd be dead soon. But there was still time. To do what mattered most. To be a hero.

***

Shadow watched the woman's back stiffen. Her fist clenched and she shoved the phone back into her pocket. Then her shoulders slumped, and she paced back and forth in the eyelight beams, looking first at the barn and then at her big truck.

Shadow watched curiously when she backed the truck dangerously close to the road's chewed up edge. She got out and climbed into the back of the truck bed and began adjusting things. Metal pings and thunks made loud clattering and he slicked down his ears. She squatted and with a grunt, lifted a metal rack contraption upward until a clacking sound locked it in place.

Shadow cocked his head and he huffed beneath his breath when she climbed the platform sprouting from the truck's bed. A long metal ladder was heaved upward, too. Shadow knew about ladders.

But she didn't prop the ladder against anything. Instead, she balanced the ladder on the top platform and then tugged and pulled a rope contraption until the ladder grew. Shadow nearly barked with surprise when it kept expanding, sticking out like a tree limb. It clanked down with a muted thud on the top of the open dumpster but kept growing longer and longer.

Shadow had never seen a ladder move sideways through the air instead of up against a wall. It stopped growing when the end touched the cement wall just below the open side of the loft.

The woman at the truck took a careful step onto the ladder, balanced herself, and then hurried along the metal pathway she'd created, graceful as a cat on a fence. She reached the end of the ladder, grabbed the edge of the loft, and hiked herself inside.

# Chapter 41

Combs sat in the passenger side of Doc Eugene's SUV, bracing himself as Gonzales pushed the car's limits. The veterinarian sat in the back, probably wishing he hadn't insisted on coming.

The GPS idea to find Shadow should have worked. *Should* being the operative word. They'd arrived at Teddy William's house in good time only to discover several days' worth of newspapers stuffed in the front door. Combs had his cell number, but with the towers down, no way to reach him. Without someone like Teddy massaging the technical side, they'd wasted their time.

Gonzales slammed the brakes, and both Combs and Doc Eugene stifled curses. Half a bois d'arc tree blocked the road. He shoved the SUV into a lower gear, cranked the steering wheel, and plowed off the road around the barrier, scraping up the car's side on his way around.

"Sorry, Doc. Now you've got matching scratches." Gonzales took off again.

"Insurance covers storm damage." Doc hung onto the back of Combs's seat. "Lucky we didn't slide into the water, though."

The county road barely cleared runoff that surged alongside the drainage ditches on either side, spilling over the road in each low spot. Combs stiffened every time they slowed to clamber through one of these runoffs. It didn't take much to hydroplane off the highway.

Somebody's phone buzzed. "Hey, that's my phone." Doc Eugene answered, and quickly shut it off with a grimace. "Robin checking in. She's heading out to check on a friend."

Combs dug out his phone to call September. He looked at messages first. One from Kelvin, the P.I. he'd referred to September, but nothing from her. He scrolled through text messages next.

Gonzales's phone beeped. "Yeah this is Gonzales." He pulled the phone away, and whispered, "It's Doty."

"Tell her to—" Combs cut off the rude comment when he saw September's text. He read it again, and then a third time, suddenly realizing he'd stopped breathing. Without a word, he reached out a hand to grip Gonzales's shoulder. His face split with the biggest, sappiest grin of his entire life.

Gonzales mouthed, *what?* "Uh, hold a minute." He held his phone against his thigh. "Willie?" He took his foot off the gas, letting the car coast.

At first, Combs couldn't speak. "Text from September. Don't know when it came in, but she says Melinda and Willie are with her. They're fine. The dog, too." Combs thought he might cry, and didn't care. "What is Melinda doing with her?" He didn't care about that, either. His kids were okay. Safe. And so was September. That mattered, too. A lot.

Doc Eugene leaned forward to pat Combs on the arm. "Where are they?"

"Didn't say. Her house, I guess." Combs leaned back, and felt his tightly wound spine crack and relax for the first time in hours.

The car drifted to a stop, and Gonzales shoved it into park in the middle of the county road. No danger with the highway deserted. Residents knew to stay inside during tornadoes, and the clouds hinted the weather might return.

"Let me get back to Doty before she chews me a new one." Gonzales slapped the steering wheel. "Now we won't have to kill ourselves to find this barn. Hell, we're already in the neighborhood." He picked up the phone.

While Gonzales dealt with Doty, Combs tried to call September but only got voice mail. He left a brief message. Later, he'd show her the extent of his gratitude. Curious, he thumbed the voice message left by Kelvin, and frowned when he only heard a long silence followed by heavy breathing. "That's weird. I got a heavy breather call from Kelvin." Gonzales's pissed expression stopped the banter before it began. "What?"

"Doty was at Kelvin's office. He's dead. Shot."

"What the hell?" The euphoria over his kids' safety evaporated.

Doc Eugene leaned forward again. "Do I know this Kelvin fellow?"

Gonzales ignored the veterinarian. "Kelvin always aspired to get ahead. This time, he must have sucked up to the wrong players." He put the car back into gear. "Doty said they found a dog tag in BeeBo's hand. Belonged to Kelvin's mutt." He smoothed his mustache. "He was up to his BVDs in this dogfight stuff. Kelvin had a wadded up map in his fist, with directions to that same barn our tipster shared."

Combs grunted. Didn't sound like the dog-loving Kelvin he knew. "Money makes people do crazy-ass evil. Let's drop Doc Eugene somewhere." Now his kids were safe, he could focus on the job.

"No, I'm fine. I'll ride along. Won't get in your way. Robin locked up the clinic, but nobody's coming by with this storm." The veterinarian leaned back and crossed his arms. "Besides, it's my car."

Much as Combs liked Doc Eugene and appreciated his help, they couldn't worry about a civilian and work, too. "We'll leave you with September and I can check my kids. It's on the way."

Gonzales chewed his lip. "Where'd you say she they holed up? Hope it wasn't her house. That whole area got hit by the storm."

Combs's gut clenched.

Gonzales wouldn't meet Combs's eyes. "We'll swing by. Like you said, it's on the way."

# Chapter 42

September watched Sunny through a crack in the loft wall. The streaming headlights sparkled the water, and revealed an insurmountable path from the barn to the truck. She'd nearly decided to let the kids out of the boxes—no way Sunny could collect them without a fire truck—when the hunting rig rose and a hunter's spotlight turned twilight to day.

The ingenious jerry-rigged affair looked precarious. Sunny somehow had secured the foot-end of the extension ladder to the top of the hunting rig. From there, it stretched horizontally toward the loft, supported at the midway point by the dumpster's rim. The ladder extended further from there to reach the barn wall, ending about three feet lower than the loft opening.

That meant the boxes containing the kids must drop off the loft floor, land on the horizontal ladder, and be scooted the entire length back to the truck. Missed aim at any point would send the boxed kid into the floodwaters, below.

What a stupid idea, to hide the kids in the boxes! Even if Sunny had a gun, it would have been better to surprise ambush her.

Sunny's balance beam performance rated a perfect ten as she danced along the ladder toward the loft.

Crap. Too late to change plans even if she wanted to.

Just before Sunny reached the barn, September climbed down the makeshift wire ladder. As long as Sunny focused on the boxes, she'd be safe.

But almost immediately, footsteps approached September's hidden roost. She clambered around to the other side of the grillwork, putting the floor between her and a clear sight line. Her arms trembled, making the grate shimmy back and forth.

Sunny focused overhead, though, and grabbed twine that still hung from the hay trolley. She rolled it along the overhead tracks probably back to its original position over the wooden pallet of stacked boxes.

The woman muttered and cursed. Moving straps creaked and the metal rollers squealed. "I ought to shove the whole mess into the water. That'd show him. Blackmail me, will you?"

Alarmed, September climbed higher and cautiously peeked over the edge. Sunny shed her jacket, flung it angrily across the floor, and her truck keys spilled out and scattered the collection of break sticks.

So much for Melinda driving the truck to safety.

Boris Kitty lounged on the highest box, a feline king surveying his domain. "Shoo, cat. Get the hell away." Sunny poked at the cat until he hissed and jumped off. "Hate cats. Even BeeBo had a stinking cat."

Sunny's back strained with each tug on the rope she'd strung from the leather harness cradling the pallet. As she pulled, the pallet shifted, tipped, but finally rose enough to clear the wooden floor. Sunny booted the pallet to swing it over and out of the loft.

It took four tries before the pendulum swung far enough, and Sunny let the rope drop. The pallet thudded against the outside of the cement wall on the backward swing. September heard a muffled yelp. She winced, prayed Sunny hadn't heard, and that Willie could keep his dog quiet a bit longer.

Sunny kept working. Her bare arms flexed as she slowly lowered the pallet onto the ladder. Once in place, she released the rope, and bent, hands on her knees to catch her breath. September saw three parallel red stripes on her neck. Cat scratches.

The truck keys glinted. Teased. She had to get them to the kids.

Sunny gingerly stepped off onto the ladder. September heard her grunt again, and the soft scree of the wood pallet shoved across metal.

"Screw this. One by one, then."

September peeked out, and started when Boris Kitty stared at her, front paws tucked under and sitting only a few feet away. She continued to sneak peeks as Sunny nudged the first box off the pallet, and shoved it steadily on metal ladder "tracks" to reach her truck's platform. September pulled herself up onto the loft floor to be out of sight when Sunny returned, and worried there wouldn't be room for all of the boxes on the high rack platform. Sunny confirmed her worst fears when she bent her knees, lifted and then dropped the box into the truck bed several feet below.

One gasp or scream from inside the box, and Sunny would know. September held her breath, but whichever kid hid inside the first Trojan box must have stayed silent.

Sunny hurried back up the ladder to retrieve the next box, and September timed her descent to stay out of sight. Back and forth the woman toiled, tugging and pushing boxes and dumping them into the bed of her truck. The cat crept closer to the opening in the loft floor until he peered down at September, tail flicking. She hoped Sunny's obvious dislike of cats would keep her from investigating Boris Kitty's interest.

September's up-and-down exertion made her biceps throb and hands sting from clutching the thin wire. The truck keys rested well out of reach. Maybe she could climb up and grab them the next time Sunny went to the truck. But if caught, she couldn't match the athletic woman, and the gun would come out. No, better to wait until the final kid-in-the-box reached the truck. She couldn't fail these kids, the way she'd failed Lenny and Steven. And Shadow.

Boris Kitty stared at her. His tail thumped, jostling one of the break sticks so it rolled a few inches along the floor. Maybe the cat could help.

September grappled in her pocket for her SUV keys. She switched on the laser light Macy loved. Aiming the red dot at the floor right in front of the cat, she held her breath and then smiled when Boris Kitty followed the lure, pouncing and chasing it across the dusty floor. Once he reached the far side of Sunny's keys, September jiggled the laser on them. He obliged by pouncing and swatting the rattling bundle across the loft closer to her. Another paw-swipe like that, and she'd be able to snag them.

Not winded in the least, Sunny ran lightly up the ladder toward the final box. Instead of the repeat of past efforts, she vaulted back into the loft and crossed to collect her jacket. And keys. Sunny saw the cat, and aimed a foot to boot Boris Kitty off the loft into the floodwaters below.

The cat spit and dodged, the kick missed. The laser light fell into the water. September lunged and grabbed Sunny's ankle, toppling her to the floor.

Sunny shrieked, caught herself on her palms, and immediately rolled onto her shoulder and back to her feet.

September grabbed for the truck keys.

Sunny kicked them. They slid and jangled across the loft, and stopped near the final wardrobe box. The cat chased them down, and crouched over the keys, growling. Sunny straightened, ignored the cat, and drew a knife from her boot.

September scrambled to stand. Her hand closed on one of the breaking sticks, and she crouched low, jabbing it toward the other woman.

Sunny laughed. "When I bite, I don't let go." She feinted with the knife, smiling when September twisted and fell as her knee failed. Sunny moved in quickly, grabbed a handful of September's hair, and shook her like a dog worrying prey.

September screamed. Her scalp caught fire, and blinding tears filled her eyes.

"Let her go!"

Oh God, Melinda had climbed out of the box. "Get out of here. Call your dad."

"What the hell?" Sunny pivoted, yanking September's hair while keeping the knife at her throat.

"I did, I already called Daddy. Let her go, the police are on the way." Melinda's gaze slid up and to the left. A lie. Maybe Sunny didn't see.

The keys. The keys, there on the floor, right next to Melinda, guarded by the cat.

"One word, one move, I slit her throat." Sunny growled the words.

Melinda's eyes grew big.

The cold blade pressed harder, hot pain laced September's skin.

"Jeff Combs's kid." It wasn't a question.

The knife cut deeper. Scalding warmth trickled from her neck. September struggled to stay still.

"Damn Doty. If that bitch detective hadn't sicced BeeBo on us, we'd be free and clear."

Detective Kimberlane Doty had sent BeeBo undercover, not Combs after all. September stifled a sob. He'd been killed by Sunny, someone he considered a friend.

September widened her eyes, and purposefully stared from Melinda to the cat on the floor, and back again. Boris Kitty fell on his side to bunny-kick the jingling set of keys. Back and forth, she stared, girl to cat, until Melinda followed her gaze. The girl tightened her lips and nodded understanding.

"Now!" September yelled.

Melinda dove for the keys, snagging them away from the cat. Reflexively, Boris Kitty grabbed Melinda's collar, and hugged the girl's neck as she awkwardly clambered back out of the loft onto the ladder.

In the same instant, September used both hands to drive the point of the break stick backwards, deep into Sunny's thigh.

Sunny shrieked. Her knife plunged into the churning water. The woman tumbled backwards, following her knife. One hand entwined in September's dark mane jerked September to the floor.

She acted like a human anchor, holding Sunny aloft as she dangled by September's hair. Scalp screeching, September's fingernails tore against chinks in the wooden floor. She slid ever closer to the edge.

Something hard pressed through September's coat.

"You're coming with me, bitch." Sunny's face twisted with determination and hate.

September punched the knife's broken blade through the coat's hem, and slashed as she pitched over the side.

## Chapter 43

Shadow watched and worried as the woman brought boxes from the barn. Each time, the truck lurched when she dropped them into the back. He waited, though, hoping to see September emerge from the loft.

When the shrieks came, Shadow exploded from his hiding spot beneath the truck. He raced to the edge of the road. How to reach September? Water surrounded the barn, making it an island impossible to reach. The ladder offered a path, but hung far over his head. Not even Shadow could leap that high into the stranger's truck.

Shadow's heart banged hard in his chest. He danced forward, close as he could get to the edge of the water. He didn't like the cold wet. But he had to reach September.

A disturbance made him look up. Kids appeared in the back of the truck, silent as they watched Melinda scurry along the ladder. She moved with jerks, fits and starts, not like the smooth dance of the strange woman. And she wore a fur collar around her neck. It moved and smelled like cat.

Melinda jumped down from the high platform into the back of the truck to join the other kids. They yelled and cried out so loud it hurt a good-dog's ears and made it hard to understand.

Melinda yelled louder than all the others. "We're going."

Willie wailed. "You don't know how to drive."

"I'll learn." She ran to the truck cab, and the other kids noisily followed.

Shadow swiveled his attention between the loud kids and the quiet loft.

The truck growled to life, made a grinding sound, and jerked into motion. Its tires spit mud and sticks at Shadow when it sped away. One end of the ladder fell out the back and thud-splattered in the mud. The truck disappeared down the road, taking the light with it.

Another scream pealed from the barn. Shadow barked, and barked again, crying out to September. A woman dangled over the water, holding fast with both hands to something overhead.

September? He couldn't tell. Shadow ran to the fallen ladder, now within reach, and sniffed the metal. Different than the wooden one in his garden. But he had to try.

Something shiny-bright flashed above the dangling woman's hands. Her yell choked off when she plunged into the water. Another woman, this one with short hair, spilled after her through the loft hole, but caught on the metal grid. Clouds blew apart and moon glow shined down.

"Shadow? Baby-dog, is that you?" September's raw voice overflowed with disbelief, hope, and then elation. "Thank you God, you're alive."

He howled again. His forepaws tested the ladder. She was there, so close. He *needed* to be with her.

"*Wait,* Shadow. Good-dog, *wait* for me."

He hated that word. But he trusted September. She knew things dogs didn't know. He could relax now she took charge. The relief in her voice made his heart sing, and he sat down to wait for her. He panted anxiously, yearning for her touch, wanted to taste her face. He wanted a nap. And maybe some bacon. Shadow licked his lips, and yawned.

Mud splattered his fur at the same instant he heard the POP!

Shadow jerked away. He'd focused so hard on September that the rumble of a car running without lights snuck up on him. The gun reached out again to bite him, and he dove into the brush on the other side of the road.

He snarled as the boy-thief climbed out of the car, the gun gripped in one hand and Steven in the other.

# Chapter 44

Her head throbbed and September fought dizziness from the near scalping. Her jagged knife-cut hair fell in her eyes, blinding her as she clung to the horse panel. She'd lost her knife, but survived. Sunny had disappeared, swept away by the waters.

Seeing Shadow made her want to laugh and cry at the same time. Weak with relief and arms trembling, September dragged herself up the horse panel back into the loft. She had to reach Shadow, hold his solid warmth in her arms, and never ever let him go. September carefully stepped from the loft onto the ladder, just in time to see Shadow dart out of sight.

A heartbeat later, the strange car pulled up and disgorged her worst nightmare. The Doctor who haunted her nightmares yanked Steven from the car. September choked back a cry. Steven lived! She sank to her knees with relief. Maybe she wasn't such a monster after all.

The real monster stood below. The Doctor raised the gun, and as he fired, Steven squirmed enough to skew his aim. A bullet splintered the cement block beside her.

She reflexively covered her head. He shot again, this time on her other side. Playing with her. September forced herself to stand. The moonlight shined the metal ladder, and water reflected its glow, illuminating her as clearly as a spotlight. If she tried to duck back into the loft, he'd kill her before she reached safety. She wouldn't give him the satisfaction of cowering.

He aimed again, and then cocked his head and lowered the gun. "I'm going to kill you, September Day. No more interfering. Medicine must be delivered to save the children." He ignored Steven's struggles, the tiny boy less than a gnat of annoyance. He raised the gun again.

"I'll dump this ladder. Then try to get your precious poison." She could do it. September shifted her weight, and the ladder shuddered and clanged. The once horizontal ladder now canted at about a thirty-degree angle, barely clinging to the corner of the open dumpster at its midway point. Knocking it off meant there'd be no way to get to the loft until water receded.

"Sunny Babcock retrieved the product at my behest. She likes money. People do anything for money."

"Sunny failed, you miserable mental defective. I've got your product right here." Nothing to lose. "And you'll lose, too." If she could prod him enough, maybe he'd come after her and let Steven go.

"So the product remains in storage." It was a statement, not a question. September imagined his brain clicking away, mental gears calculating what that meant.

She shifted backwards a bit, so when she kicked away the ladder, she'd have a chance to pull herself inside. "Let Steven go, right now, or I'll take down your only chance to recover your *product*." She sneered the final word.

His bloodless smile chilled her. "I can make more. Delay means more children suffer. More blood on your interfering hands." He flexed the gun back and forth, back and forth. Stimming. The self-comforting repetitive behavior increased with stress. Maybe the Doctor needed another dose of his miracle drug.

She taunted. "It's not about the kids, it's never been about the kids. Or the money. It's playing god, turning people into puppets to make you important." *C'mon, get mad.* "You give nice, decent autistic people a bad name." He might be brilliant but his stunted emotions offered a weakness she'd used before. Get him riled enough, and like dogs and cats, analytical thought couldn't function alongside fear or fury.

She rocked the ladder, and it shifted closer to the edge of the dumpster. The green box rocked as water continued to surge around it. "You scared, Gerald-baby? Should be. I beat you before, put your sicko bag of scabs Mommy away. You're only brave shooting unarmed women. And abusing dogs. How's it feel, knowing you'll never see your Mommy again?"

The stimming grew worse. Steven squealed, his arm in a vise.

This time, she wouldn't let him get away, even if she had to use herself as bait. He vanished too easily, and had resources nobody could match. And by God, she owed it to all the lives he'd ruined, to Lenny and to Claire. To her sister, and Steven and Tracy, and so many more.

If she could get him into the loft, she could dump the ladder and trap him until the police arrived. When Combs arrived. She'd been wrong about him, wrong about so many things.

"What you going to do, you sick bastard? Son of a bitch, go on, make your move."

"Bad language, lazy language. Shut up shut up shut up!" He shook Steven into submission, steadied his hand and aimed the gun.

# Chapter 45

The boy-thief's posture changed. Before, he'd been relaxed and unhurried. Now his shoulders hunched, breath panted and his scent screamed DANGER! and made Shadow bristle and bare his teeth.

September stood over there, up high on the ladder against the loft. But Shadow knew guns could reach out and bite from far away. His notched ear twitched at the thought, and his tummy tightened when the pale man steadied his wobbly hand, and pointed the gun.

At September.

He didn't wait for direction, his heart told him what to do. He sprang, paws digging deep in the muddy soil, and leaped high to muzzle-punch the gun away.

At the last second, the man spun, flinging Steven to the ground. He adjusted his stance, ignoring September to aim at Shadow.

Shadow grabbed for the gun. So did Steven. The gun spat.

Steven squealed, swinging from the boy-thief's arm. He'd jogged the gun enough for aim to go wide.

"Steven, run!" September screamed and rushed down the clanging ladder, but Shadow didn't move his eyes from the pale man. "Shadow, good-dog, *go-to* Steven."

His ears rang from the shot, making September sound far away. He snarled at the gun's acrid oily stink.

"Demon dog bit me." The tall man's voice shook. "Sick of dogs. Sick of ungrateful kids." He brushed off Steven, set his legs apart, and aimed with both hands. The empty eye of the gun stared back and followed when Shadow danced forward and back.

September cried out with desperation. "Run, Steven, get away. Please Shadow, please go."

But Shadow didn't budge. Sometimes dogs knew better than people. Even smart people like September. As long as the gun sniffed after him, it couldn't bite September or his-boy Steven.

The man reeked, the whites of his eyes shined bright as the moon. Shadow heard the man's heart thud so hard and loud it might come out of his chest and his pungent breath wheezed like Bear-toy's broken squeak.

Steven ducked around the man's spider legs, and dashed for September on the metal ladder.

"No, no, no, run away." September's anguished voice shook, her hands waved Steven away.

The boy-thief tracked Steven's scrambling escape and Shadow's challenge at the same time, head moving side to side.

Shadow's lips curled when the man's concentration wavered. He adjusted his posture so his head, neck and back flowed in one smooth line. His tail, only the tip, jerked as he watched the pale man's eyes return to him. Once the bad man's attention moved from Shadow's family, calm descended, surrounding him like September's embrace.

Good-dogs don't bite. But Shadow wanted to be a bad-dog if it meant protecting September and Steven. This man needed biting. He remembered the dry taste of fabric, the flex and give of muscle, the salt-bright blood smell. He wanted that taste on his tongue again, to rend this man's flesh. To punish. To protect his family.

Shadow dodged left, ducked right, and charged. The gun popped, and white-hot pain creased his neck. But his teeth crunched, bones broke, and he tasted blood. Shadow shook the hand and pulled hard, snarling without releasing his grip, relishing grim satisfaction at the man's ratcheting screams. The gun fell in the dirt.

"Shadow, good-dog. Hold him." September moved to meet Steven at the halfway point on the ladder.

He put down his ears and wagged at her happy encouragement. And hung on. September would make everything right.

The boy-thief kicked Shadow hard in the stomach. With a gasp, he let go, and struggled to catch his breath. His stomach cramped.

"I'll kill you dead dead dead!" He shrieked so loud, Shadow winced. When he scrabbled with his good hand for the gun, Shadow snapped the air in warning. He didn't want to bite again. The man tasted bad.

The pale man's expression changed. The pain in Shadow's gut and neck slowed his reaction. He couldn't stop the man's spider climb up the ladder toward Steven and September.

# Chapter 46

Almost before the SUV stopped, Combs bounded from the car to climb over, around and under trees tumbled across the front of September's property. The gate hung by one hinge, and a battered old car he didn't recognize sat nearby.

The tornado's pick-up-sticks game left the proud brick fortress in rubble. Barely half the house stood, the rest blown away to God knows where. The old carriage house on one side had vanished.

A rescue worker tried to stop him, until he flashed his badge. "Who's in charge?" The man pointed, and Combs raced to a cluster of firefighters and two police officers, their expressions grim. "Anyone? Did you find any survivors?" Combs stuffed his hands in his pockets to keep them from shaking. September said his kids were fine. Now this?

"No sir, Detective Combs." The firefighter scanned the area. "Found one body. Female, dark hair, early to mid-thirties."

Combs slumped against the wall as Gonzales caught up to him. "They found September." He croaked the words, tongue thick. "No sign of the kids." Doc Eugene trotted up, too, but Combs didn't care enough to make him leave.

"Uh, Detective? Sorry, I understand you knew her. We're waiting on the team to process the crime scene. We've not moved the body."

His eyebrows rose. "Show me." Combs followed the man, Gonzales in his wake. Doc Eugene trailed them until Combs glared and the veterinarian stepped back.

The body—*too small for September*—sprawled face down. Sudden relief switched to worry, wondering where she'd gone. This woman had been shot, the bloody wound clearly visible. The tornado probably finished the job. "Who is she?"

"Claire O'Dell. That's the I.D. in the car by the gate, anyway, but she doesn't resemble her license anymore. There's blood in the car, too. The wound is through and through, so the bullet could still be in the car."

"O'Dell. Where do I know that name?" Gonzales scribbled notes in his ever-present pad.

One of the firefighters yelled, bent over, and picked up something dark that struggled and then settled in his arms. "Found a cat."

Combs motioned Doc Eugene forward. "Must be Macy. That cat has nine lives." September would be relieved, once he found her. And his kids. "Take care of Macy for us, Doc?"

The veterinarian cradled the big Maine Coon in his arms. "We'll wait for you in the car. Lucky I came along after all, eh?"

Gonzales stayed to talk with the first responders, while Combs followed the veterinarian to the road to examine O'Dell's car. It wasn't locked. He opened the passenger door, pulling on gloves first. Keys remained in the ignition. Despite the bunged up appearance from the hail, the inside of the car was tidy, except for broken window glass and the dark stain against the driver's seat back. He poked the hole in the upholstery, noting it went clear through. Perhaps they'd find the bullet in the back.

Combs opened the glove box, and leafed through the papers. He found registration and insurance naming Mike and Claire O'Dell. A purse on the floor produced a wallet with a few crumpled bills, and the driver's license of a pretty snub-nosed woman. He also found an intricate picture, probably drawn by one of the woman's kids. He frowned, reading the inscription.

No worry Tracy and me fix.

Two kids in a van. One with a pill bottle. He squinted, and held the page under the overhead light. Everything clicked when he focused on one tiny detail. The pill bottle label named the patient, Tracy O'Dell, and the medication. Damenia.

"Gonzales," Combs yelled, "We gotta go." He slammed the car door, taking the colored picture with him. When he hit redial again, the number still went to September's voice mail.

The smaller man ran from the destroyed house and they met at the SUV. Combs thrust the drawing at Gonzales. "You can't see it without a light, but trust me. The pill bottle with that little kid says Damenia."

"No shit." Gonzales handed back the picture. "Her kids?"

"I think so, yes." He slapped his forehead. "That's why O'Dell sounded familiar. Claire O'Dell was one of the parents we questioned at the Rebirth Gathering last November."

"Right. There were nearly 200 kids, all with at least one parent, and not one said a word. And that was a single Gathering, we don't know how many others came before." Gonzales opened the car door and climbed behind the wheel.

About one out of every 88 children fell into the Spectrum, a 78 percent increase in the last ten years. Parents of these kids were ripe for the Doctor's pitch. "Her kids must have run away, like Doty said. O'Dell figured out they headed here, and contacted September to help. That's why she wanted the P.I." He paused, and snapped his fingers.

"Kelvin." They said the name at the same time.

"Kelvin already had a shady deal going with the Doctor. Bet you my pension the Doctor killed Kelvin." Combs's phone rang. Maybe it was September. He answered without looking. "Combs here."

"My guy says you're at your girlfriend's house searching for AWOL kids." Doty, in a perpetual state of pissed, sounded ready to explode. "A whole shit-load of delinquents just got pulled over driving some god-awful pick-'em-up truck without a license." She breathed heavily. "Now you're all caught up on your freaking family ties, are you ready to do your job, Detective?"

"Wait. What?" Combs ran a hand through his hair. "You found my kids?"

"Found your son, your daughter, couple of pets and their joy-riding friends." She laughed without humor. "Patrol saw them weaving all over the road, with some sort of high metal rig hanging off the back. Redheaded girl behind the wheel said she belonged to you." She grudgingly added, "They appeared to be fine, but I instructed Patrol to transport to the hospital and check everyone out."

Combs closed his eyes, and breathed with relief.

"They tell a wild story we gotta sort out, and mentioned Pit Bulls. And September." She continued, acerbic as ever. "Why is she always involved when something goes sideways? Don't know what you see in her, Combs. But according to your kids, they weathered the storm with September in a barn. So you and Gonzales get out there, now."

The news made his heart sing despite Doty's prickly tone. He didn't know how or why she'd ended up there, but he had no doubt they'd find September at the barn. Combs quickly brought Doty up to speed on the O'Dell woman's identity, and what it meant, and disconnected. Doty promised to send backup.

Doc Eugene leaned forward. "Did I hear right? The kids are fine?"

Combs nodded. "Let's go get us a bad guy."

Gonzales started the car. "Hang on tight, Doc. What do you know about dogfights?"

## Chapter 47

September crouched to keep her balance on the ladder but finally fell to her knees as the crab-climbing Doctor wobbled it side to side. It clinked and clanged a broken bell chorus, and barely clung to the corner of the dumpster.

Steven scurried higher, with the Doctor in plodding pursuit. If she could get the boy into the loft, she'd dump the ladder, sending the Doctor to join Sunny in the hellish flood.

"Take my hand." September reached for Steven, careful not to move too far and tip them all off. Better to let Steven come to her.

Shadow ran back and forth at the far end of the ladder. He'd been silent before. Now his barks became yodels of frustration. Her joy at his survival turned to fear he'd be killed, and then fierce pride how the uncertain puppy had become a confident protector. She hadn't taught him that, but he'd improvised when needed. God, how she loved him.

September had to trust Shadow to protect himself while she focused on Steven's safety. The kids must have called Combs by now. She could hang on until the cavalry arrived. Didn't have a choice.

The Doctor couldn't grip with his savaged right hand. He still made creepy progress bracing his elbow and gripping with the good hand. He stopped, grabbed one edge of the ladder, and shook it until Steven's small hands lost their grip, and slid backwards within the Doctor's reach. Steven yelled and kicked at the pale man's face.

"Hang on, Steven. I'm coming." September scooted on her butt in an urgent race to reach Steven before he fell. The Doctor showed his teeth in what passed for a smile, grabbed Steven's ankle and yanked.

The ladder rocked, still barely gripping the dumpster's edge. The metal box bobbled and dipped, halfway floating in the tide. Only their weight held the ladder in place.

September caught a cloying stench of animal feces, infection and wet dog. Something white moved inside the dumpster, but she couldn't take the time to look.

She grabbed one of Steven's hands. "Let go of him, you bastard." Her hands ached but she couldn't let go.

Steven became a tug-toy between her and the killer. The child's soprano screams sang discordant counterpoint to Shadow's baritone yodels.

Then the dog fell silent. The ladder shook. Behind the Doctor's oblivious form, Shadow crawled up the ladder one careful paw-tread at a time. A raw scrape bisected his head; a bloody crease carved an opening in the side of his neck, and his face dripped blood into the water below.

September screamed again, this time to keep the Doctor's attention. One unknowing kick would knock Shadow into the water.

Shadow had returned to her twice. He couldn't survive another immersion, not with such severe injuries.

Steven kicked the Doctor in the teeth, knocking the Reaper's grin off his face and September wanted to cheer. He recoiled backwards, and Shadow's jaws snapped closed on his ankle. The man gasped and released Steven. The Doctor tried to regain his balance, but fell sideways from the ladder, dragging Shadow with him.

The Doctor belly flopped, folded across the edge of the foul dumpster, head inside and legs dangling outside. Shadow still clung to the shrieking man's ankle, rear paws trailing in the floodwaters. Suddenly the man's screams cut off. He shuddered, and fell limp.

September poised to dive after Shadow. It was her turn to save him. But when the dumpster began to move, she reflexively grabbed Steven. The ladder tipped sideways, and they hung for an endless moment before splashing into the icy flood. To save Shadow, she'd have to let go of Steven.

The dumpster drifted with the water. Shadow's jaws remained clamped on the Doctor's leg.

Shadow's big brown eyes met September's with an expression of acceptance that seemed to last forever. She had no words, but he knew. He always knew. His eyes closed, he unclamped his teeth, and sank beneath the water. The metal dumpster floated the Doctor away.

September clung one-handed to the partially submerged ladder. She struggled to keep Steven's head above water. Moon glow cast diamonds over the frigid flood. She'd had no choice, and no more tears to give. Only prayers.

*Please God, take care of my dog.*

# Chapter 48

Combs stood aghast when he saw the barn. Or what was left of it.

The cement frame carried less than half a roof, leaving most of the wooden loft open to the weather. The flood swelled four feet high around the base, turning it into an island that might wash away any minute. The sibilant sound of the water reminded him of snakes. He hated snakes. Floods flushed out all kinds of creepy crawlies. Now that Willie and Melinda were safe, worry for September knotted his gut.

Uprooted trees and other debris created beaver dams that clogged the new waterway, hitching along in fits and starts before pieces broke loose and surfed away. Nobody could survive unless able to anchor to something solid.

Combs, Gonzales and Doc Eugene slowly climbed out of the SUV. The veterinarian collected an odd-looking gun from the back of his car that Combs knew held tranquilizer darts, in case Pit Bulls posed a problem. He and Gonzales both carried flashlights. So far, though, he detected no sign of life.

Gonzales walked closer to the edge of the road, and peered up and down. "If they held dogfights here, the water has done a number on any evidence." He headed to the abandoned sedan, with the driver's door still open, and poked his head inside. "Keys in the ignition. An iPad on the passenger seat. Is this September's car?"

Combs shook his head. And Shadow, he never left September's side. He gazed up at the distant loft. If she was there, they'd need a hook and ladder to get her out. "Hellooooo! September, you there?"

A dog yelped. "Shadow? Hey boy." Combs searched for the author of the sound, his flashlight spearing the gloom. On the far corner of the barn, nearly out of sight, slanted green metal thrust up out of the water, a fallen tree partially obstructing and holding it in place. "There, is that a dumpster?" It had overturned, and a white dog with spots clung to the top.

Doc Eugene adjusted his glasses. "It's a pup. What do you know; we've got a dogfight survivor after all. Somebody cut its chain." Heavy links hooked to the dog's oversize collar clanked and chattered against the metal box. "No way to reach him, though. Smart not to swim. The chain would drag him down."

"Have to wait for the level to drop." Gonzales examined the sky. "The rain stopped for now. If it doesn't start up anytime soon, flood water recedes pretty quickly."

Combs eyeballed the debris field both on the ground and in the water surrounding the barn, searching for any motion. Hope tightened his throat when he saw the bundle of clothes, then recognized hangars stuck in the mass caught on an extension ladder half submerged in the flood. Damn. Just showed how tornadoes created havoc, dumping the contents of someone's closet from miles away.

Gonzales, still at the strange car, examined scuffmarks in the ground, and then reached for his gun. "Combs, I got shell casings. It's a .45, consistent with a semi-automatic, same as at Kelvin's office."

"Doc Eugene, go back to the car." Combs pulled his own gun, and speared his light over the ground. "The Doctor had a Remington Rand." There were lots of those World War Two surplus guns still in circulation. "Here's another shell. And another." He scanned left and right, and then hurried toward the brink of the drop off. "I got the gun." It sat in a puddle next to the road.

Gonzales cocked his head. "Hear that, Combs?" He surveyed the area, brow wrinkled in concentration. "I could swear somebody's singing."

"...*down came the rain,*
*and washed the spider out...*"

***

She imagined voices, including the bark of a dog. Not Shadow, she knew his voice.

September stirred, tried to raise her head, and gave up. She'd managed to pull Steven onto her lap, one arm locked around him while she hooked the other through the overhead ladder rungs. She didn't have the strength to pull them both out, and wanted to hang on and catch her breath.

When dumped clothing from the wardrobe boxes swam out of the barn, she'd been grateful it covered them both. She didn't fight the sodden mess. By comparison, the worn material kept cold wind from further chilling their forms.

Steven still shuddered with cold, but September felt warm. She'd stopped shivering. And wanted in the worst way to close her eyes for a nice nap. But not yet. Not until he was safe. "Steven. Steven." She tried to shake him a little, and panicked when she nearly lost her grip on the boy. "You have to climb out. Can you do that? Grip the ladder rungs, and climb out."

She wondered why her words slurred. Steven acted like he didn't hear her or understand. But even a little kid should be able to manage. "Up up up, climb out. Ona ladder, get in the car." He'd be warmer, safer inside the Doctor's car. The Doctor wouldn't need it anymore. That thought made her want to giggle, but it took too much effort.

The police would come soon. Somebody called them. Couldn't remember who. "A little nap..." They'd wake her when they came. Her eyes drifted closed.

Steven started to sing. Little boy soprano, like an angel. Rude audience, shouldn't talk . . .

If the voices would stop, she could sleep. Asleep, she could dream. About Shadow. Her baby-dog. He'd gone away, hadn't he? She'd done something to make him go away, couldn't remember what. The deep ache of loss hurt, hurt, hurt, God please, she wanted to hold him one more time, tell him sorry, so very sorry. She'd laugh and he'd lick her face, and beg to chase Frisbee and shake his Bear-toy and play sniff-the-cat to drive Macy nuts and wag-wag-wag so hard his tail hurt when it hit her legs and she didn't care but God, the love and acceptance in his big brown eyes, no blame, no judgment, only love and more love and silly sweet baby-dog cocking his head and sticking toys in her face to make her laugh.

September held out her arms. She could feel him, his furry black warmth in her arms, and clung tight to him, happy again, never wanted to let him go, but still he slipped away, away, away . . .

***

"She's there. End of the damn ladder. Doc, hold it steady." Combs couldn't believe he'd nearly missed her.

September trailed in the water, barely floating and anchored only by one elbow hooked over a rung. Her waist-length hair had been hacked off, ragged, close to her scalp. The child, could that be Steven? clung to her, repeating the singsong nursery rhyme.

"September, hang on, I'm coming." Her blue lips never moved, and her eyes remained closed.

Doc Eugene and Gonzales held the end of the extension ladder while Combs climbed to reach the pair. He had to pry Steven from September's arm, and then handed him back to Gonzales. Steven continued to sing as Doc Eugene wrapped him in a blanket and carried him to the warm SUV.

Combs slipped into the water to reach September. He gasped at the temperature and his teeth chattered. He could stand in the four-foot flood, but the current greedily sucked and dragged, eager to swallow him up. He hand-walked the overhead rungs, and kept one hand gripped on the ladder, and gently unhooked September's arm. Her icy skin shocked him.

"Doc, call the paramedics." They had to warm her up. "You got anything for hypothermia?"

She stirred in his arms. Her green eyes didn't focus. September began to cry. "He's gone he's gone he's gone, oh God, he's gone, my fault." She looked around wildly. "Steven. Lenny? Did you find Lenny, he's a kid. And Shadow, oh my poor baby-dog." She wept.

"Steven's safe. Put your arms around my neck. Come on, put your arms around me, honey." Combs looped his left arm about her waist, and used his right on the ladder to pull them along.

September tried to hook one arm on his waist, but it kept slipping off. The temperature quickly sapped his strength, and he wondered how long she'd been in the water. Combs reached the bank, and handed her up to Gonzales.

He pulled himself out and as soon as their weight came off, the ladder slid from the dirt bank and sank beneath the filthy water.

"Let me." Combs took the blanket Gonzales offered and cocooned it around September. "Come on, honey, talk to me." He shook her. "Talk to me, September."

September blinked, and recognized him. "Are you real?"

With a cry, he hugged her. "Yes, I'm real. You're safe, the ambulance is on the way. Steven's okay, too. All are okay." He smiled, holding and rocking her. "Now that I found you, September, I won't ever let you go. I love you."

But her eyes overflowed. "I love you too, Jeff. But I've lost Shadow." She turned her face into his chest, sobbing.

# Chapter 49

September hugged Macy. He cheek-rubbed her face and nuzzled her short wavy hair as though they'd been apart for years instead of a single day. Six days ago, the hospital insisted she stay, but she'd signed herself out after one night against the doctor's orders. She'd been frantic to reunite with her cat, the only thing left of her family, and had visited Macy every day since.

"He missed you." Doc Eugene smiled.

"Thanks for keeping him." She forced a return smile. "Mom isn't a cat person." *Or a dog person. Not that it mattered any more.*

"No problem. He's welcome to stay as long as you want. Macy has become a favorite around here."

"What's Robin think of that?" September hadn't noticed the sour woman the past few days.

"Had to let her go. She wanted more than I could give."

"A raise?"

He hesitated. "She'd been helping herself to more than the cash drawer. Pills missing, and a whole stack of my prescription pad. The local pharmacists called when my signature looked off. I'd already caught her mishandling a couple of the dogs." He shook his head sadly. "Did you know she was BeeBo's cousin? Makes you wonder what turns some people on the wrong path. Anyway, I turned her in but I don't think they've caught up to her, yet."

"I'm sorry." She knew about misplaced trust and betrayal, had experienced enough to last nine lives. She looked around the clinic, still stroking Macy. "Guess you'll need a new office manager, huh?"

He chuckled. "Nikki's already campaigning for the job. That kid can't get enough of the animals, especially the cats. She loves showing Macy off. Surprises the heck out of clients when he takes his medicine without a fuss." He took off his glasses and polished them on his smock as he spoke, avoiding her eyes. "I'm sorry about Shadow. But he's the reason we found Lenny. Well, with help from Steven's mad computer skills."

She stiffened, and then made herself relax. Doc Eugene meant to make her feel better.

She'd been out of her mind with grief, and insisted they search for Shadow's GPS signal. They'd found the dog's collar looped over Lenny's ankle, when Steven used his iPad to track the signal as neatly as any computer geek quadruple his age.

Lenny had floated over a mile on his straw bale before it hung up on a tree. He suffered internal injuries but would survive, in part due to the protective warmth of the young orange cat that refused to leave him. A miracle. The boy's parents agreed that Lenny could keep the little cat Willie insisted they name Waffles.

Mom wouldn't stop talking about her genius grandson. Despite Steven's irksome rhymes, September made an effort to connect. She needed to, for herself as much as him.

Of course, Mom got on her nerves even more. Nothing new there. It sucked not having a car. Or a house. She hadn't decided whether to repair, rebuild or relocate. A clean break would put distance between her and painful memories. Besides, Heartland wasn't truly home, and hadn't been for years. She couldn't pretend any more. Even her family acted uncomfortable around her, and she couldn't blame them. Coming back to Heartland had been running from the past, and she no longer needed to run. Now she could choose. Live in the present, and plan a future.

But until the insurance claims processed, she'd put up with being an uncomfortable guest in her parent's home. Mom treated her like a fifteen-year-old again, before all the bad stuff happened. But she'd put up with it, for now. Mom couldn't compare to the conflict she'd already survived.

These days, September walked eggshells without Shadow to keep her grounded. Surprisingly, she'd suffered no flashbacks. Stress and memories triggered the attacks, and both were a package deal with her family, another good reason for a fresh start. Even the rescued animals conjured memories. That's why she'd turned down the offer to take BeeBo's dogs.

After the news broke, pet lovers rallied to adopt the furry victims, including Kelvin's sweet dog Hercules. September wanted to scream when they found Sunny two days ago trying to sneak across the Mexican border. It wasn't fair a murderer survived when Shadow had perished saving innocent lives.

Sunny even tried to blame Kelvin for BeeBo's death, and might have gotten away with it, if not for the torn claw festering in her neck. September had no doubt forensics would confirm the claw came from the kitten BeeBo rescued. Fuzzit now lived the life of Riley as Doc Eugene's clinic cat.

Boris Kitty and his person celebrated a joyous reunion filmed by local TV news crews, and started a blog featuring the hero cat. Delays continued over the spotted Pit Bull puppy's adoption, though a waiting list clamored for the honor. The police considered him evidence. Samples of his blood, sent to the Pit Bull DNA database, would trace his bloodlines back to breeders and others for prosecution in the sordid dogfight business. A forensic veterinary team continued to collect evidence at the barn.

Her phone rang, and she checked before answering. Parker Belk again, the orchestra conductor from the theater. She sighed and let it go to voice mail. She'd already told him she wasn't interested. Thankfully, the other cellist recovered enough to play the rest of the Secret Garden run. She'd pick up Harmony later. Macy and her cello were the only two things of value she had from her old life. Time to start a new one. Maybe even tonight.

The front door binged bringing a warm glow of anticipation. She handed Macy to Doc Eugene as Combs appeared.

"Ready?" He crossed to shake the veterinarian's hand before turning back to her. "I like your hair. Different, but I like it."

Mom insisted on a makeover: hair, makeup, the works, even a new outfit with a tailored emerald blouse to match her eyes, and a slinky white skirt. But September drew the line at dying the white streak. It looked even more pronounced with the short hairstyle.

September blushed when Combs put an arm around her waist, and brushed her cheek with a kiss. But she liked it. "Yes, I'm ready." They had a long overdue Valentine's make-up date.

She'd promised herself she'd smile and act happy, despite her aching sorrow. For Combs. He deserved that, and she did care for him. Loved him, in fact. She had a hard time saying so, or showing it. Tonight, though, she'd show him. Or try to. Wasn't sure she knew how. She blushed again.

"I've got news first. Not to spoil the mood or anything." Combs scratched Macy's ears, and the cat purred. "We found Larry Pitts."

"Who?" Doc Eugene leaned forward.

"September found him first, I think." Combs turned to her. "Remember when Shadow tracked Kinsler?"

"Oh my God. The hand." The dog had perched on top of a body. How had she forgotten?

"That was Larry Pitts. Young high school kid, only seventeen. Found his car swamped not too far from his body. He had scratches on his back and neck consistent with dog claws." He rubbed his face. "Haven't told Melinda yet, not sure what to say. It's different, when you have kids."

September touched his arm. "I know. And I'm sorry."

Doc Eugene frowned. "But you don't think Kinsler—"

"No, he's too little. Larry had been missing before Kinsler went AWOL." Combs snorted. "Damn dog still goes nuts for the squirrels, but now we've Kinsler-proofed the fence." He cleared his throat. "We also found the Doctor." He nodded at September. "Just like you said. Dead."

"Good." *Another chapter closed.* "Where?" She wouldn't apologize for being glad.

"About six miles from the barn." Combs kept petting Macy as he spoke. "Inside a floating dumpster, an appropriate coffin for a very bad piece of garbage. He'd been mauled." He avoided meeting September's eyes. "No sign of the dog. Or dogs. Forensics will figure it out."

"Shadow saved me. He died for me. But he didn't kill the Doctor." She stuck out her chin. "I'm glad that evil man got what he deserved. Poetic justice, if one of his canine victims sent him to hell." She sounded like a monster, and for once, she didn't care. "Did you find the drugs?"

He scowled. "Not a trace. Must have all floated away when the loft collapsed. I'm thankful you and the kids were well away by then."

She forced a smile. "I'm ready if you are. Let's go."

September liked the weight of his arm around her shoulders. She leaned against Combs as they walked together to his car. "Where are we going?"

"To a secret garden." He smiled, and took her hand, lacing their fingers together before opening the car door for her. He waited as she pulled her long skirt inside. "I hope you like it, that it's okay." He shut the door, and cracked his knuckles.

*He's as nervous as me.* Somehow, that made September relax.

They drove in companionable silence until she recognized the route. When he turned on Rabbit Run Road, she finally spoke. "My house? But there's nothing left. You said so."

He shrugged. "There's some of it left. Enough of the important parts, anyway." He cleared his throat. "I know with everything that's happened, you've got no choice except to move forward. To do that, you have to start somewhere. Right? Put the past in perspective so you can build on it and make a new future?" He rubbed his face. "Hell, I don't know what I'm saying. Maybe this was a bad idea."

Although puzzled, she reassured him. "It's fine. I want to go, need to see. Only I wasn't planning on it tonight." She reviewed her outfit, carefully chosen for a romantic evening, and sighed. September steeled herself, but still wasn't ready.

The old Victorian had stood for over a hundred years. Previous owners let it go to seed. It had been the designated witchy house when she was a kid, but had always intrigued her and made her sad, like an old dog once loved and now neglected. So, when September returned to Heartland last year, she'd bought the place, determined to restore it to its former glory.

In the process of creating her own personal safe haven, she'd created a gorgeous, glorious prison. The tornado had torn away the locks, ripped bars off stained glass windows, and destroyed the fancy security system. Only the shell of the haunted house remained. She wondered if ghosts ever stopped haunting the living.

They drove through the broken front gate, pulled into the circle drive and stopped. Combs waited, silent.

She took a big breath, smiled at him and pushed open the car door. "Since we're here, why not look, right?"

He got out, and hurried to meet her. "It's not all wrecked." He took her hand, and tugged her across the brick sidewalk past the missing carriage house to the back of the house. "Wait." He dropped her hand, hurried over to the damaged wall, and flipped a switch. Outside lights lit the back garden.

September's mouth fell open. A gentle breeze moved dozens of wind chimes, creating fairy music. A stained glass table from her kitchen now sat on the grass, and held two place settings. A picnic basket waited for them, and a small stained glass lamp shined a cheery kaleidoscope on the brick walkway. "I can't believe anything survived."

"Like I said, not everything was trashed. Your brother's lamp and the table were untouched. The living room, too. The piano didn't make it, though. Sorry."

"Oh my heavens, the roses. That perfume. I wanted to rip them out. But now, oh my." She walked quickly to a busy plant covered with tiny pink blossoms, and another nearby boasting white starbursts. "The rain, all that cursed rain. It brought the roses back to life."

"Ripped some away, too." Combs pointed out several bare spots sandblasted by the storm. "And there." He pointed up, and she saw a bright rambler transplanted to the eaves, spilling a profusion of butter-colored petals in the wind.

Awed, she sighed. "That's Fortune's Double Yellow. Way too early for it to bloom."

Combs smiled. "Texas roses are tenacious; they bloom and grow wherever they land."

"Guess the bare spots make room for the new. For the future, maybe?"

He smiled, and held out his hand. "There's food. Don't worry, it's catered, I wouldn't dare try to cook. But it smells pretty yummy."

Before she'd taken two steps toward the table, a sound stopped her cold. "Did you hear that?"

"Hear what?" He held the chair for her, but cocked his head. "September?"

It came again, a soughing carried on the wind she felt more than heard. She took another step toward him. "You must hear that. Please, tell me I'm not crazy." Her breath quickened. *Please, not now.* But it didn't feel like any flashback she'd had.

"Are you okay? I'm here." Combs wrapped her in his arms. And then he stiffened when it came again.

"You heard it too. You did." And she tore out of his arms, running, running, stumbling, getting up and racing toward the sound, the whimpering cry, the voice she'd heard every night in her dreams for a week, certain it would never come again. "I'm coming, I'm coming!"

Combs raced with her, matching her step for step, their breath as one. There. Now louder. He stopped when they saw him. Combs let her go on by herself.

Shadow stood on the other side of the garden fence. Covered in caked mud from paw to shoulder, muzzle and neck stained with blood, she could count his ribs. He couldn't get through to reach her, but tried with all his might to force his way in. His voice nearly gone, he still warbled his happiness with garbled, heart-breaking gasps.

September dropped to her knees as close as she could get. "Oh baby-dog, my sweet boy." She pushed her arms through the fence, trying to hold him, to touch him, but the bars kept them apart. Her hand came back red with blood. "He's hurt."

Combs grabbed her waist and lifted her, and she struggled. "No, no, no I can't leave him; we have to get him help." And he set her gently down on the other side of the fence.

Then Shadow was in her arms, burrowing his head into her neck, licking her face, tail bruising her—oh, bliss. And Combs had leaped the fence.

"I'm not leaving either of you." His strong arms encircled them both. "You're my family. This is where we begin."

## Chapter 50

Nikki hurried to the mailbox. It would come today, it had to come today. Kid Kewl told her exactly what to do.

Her parents had been scared at first, then madder than she'd ever seen. She couldn't explain why, either, and that made it worse. At least she hadn't been driving when the cops pulled them over. Melinda being a cop's kid meant she embarrassed her dad. That couldn't be good.

At first, Mom said Nikki couldn't volunteer at the vet clinic anymore. She thought she'd die. Nikki called up Doc Eugene to tell him, and instead Robin got on the phone and gave her what for. Doc Eugene must have found out, because then he came over and talked to her folks, said how much he depended on her, especially now that Rotten Robin was gone. Wow. How lucky, to have a friend like him, otherwise, she'd still be grounded until she was old, like thirty or something.

But after today, it'd be worth all the upset. Between the money they'd found in Sunny's truck, and the cash Steven found in the Doctor's car, her parents would be rich.

It made her guilty the others insisted she take it all. Melinda called it blood money, and said she couldn't touch it because it could get her dad in hellacious trouble if somebody found out. Tracy and Lenny only wanted pills. Nikki guessed that's what happened when you got addicted.

She could care less if the money had blood on it, or not. It spent the same. But Nikki knew her parents would question where it came from. Kid Kewl had promised to help. So, she asked him what to do.

*"Send a little in a letter,*
*And that riddle makes it better.*
*A bit won't alarm or do any harm.*
*A little at a time will be just fine."*

So she decided to mail cash, a few hundred dollars at a time, to her parents. She used Doc Eugene's printer to address a bunch of envelopes. And every couple of weeks, she'd stick one in the mail from the clinic, addressed to her folks.

Kid Kewl said he read the idea in a fiction book. He must be really smart. She saw the mail truck coming down the street. Now, she and her parents wouldn't be a charity case anymore. Heck, they could even *give* to charity if they wanted to.

***

Tracy ran and jumped into Daddy's arms and hugged him tight-tight-tight. Too bad he still acted sad all the time, and she wondered when Mommy would come home.

He hadn't asked how she got so many bottles of magic pills. A bunch spilled out somewhere during the adventure, and the police people tried to take them from her. So, she made lots of noise and screamed and Grooby might even have bit someone. But they let her keep two bottles.

Kid Kewl said it was enough. He said twice-exceptional kids like them made exceptional things happen. She liked being a 2e kid.

Tracy excelled at numbers the same way Lenny aced maps and other kids shined at different stuff like peeping inside long-distance computers, tracking phone calls and postal codes, making art and singing, and bunches of other things Tracy didn't understand. Twice-exceptional, her teacher said. But that was okay. A single kid alone got ignored. But all together they fixed things for their parents and for themselves.

Grownups said she and Lenny and the others were different than everybody else like it was a bad thing, but Tracy knew better. *We're exactly the same, only different.* With their magic pills, they'd still be twice-exceptional kewl-kids, too. Tracy couldn't wait.

Daddy set her down without a word, and walked to the clock on the counter. It had stopped. He wound it up tight, so it made the tick-tick-tick sound she liked. "Time to take your medicine, Tracy."

She smiled, and ran to him and opened her mouth. Instead of one pill every twelve hours, she'd take 1/2 pill every eight hours. She'd number-juggled the days-minutes-seconds for new medicine times. Before long, she'd need less and less. And soon, very soon, no more pills at all. Kid Kewl had everything planned.

She still hadn't told Daddy about the secret. The adventure had barely begun.

## EPILOGUE

Shadow whimpered, and leaned hard against September's leg. He liked Doc Eugene, but the hospital smelled of strangers, and resounded with cries of scared cats and dogs. Not even petting and treats made up for all he endured, shivering but stoic while the doctor took care of his many hurts. Now, the thru-thrump of September's heartbeat jittered like a puppy gallop, making Shadow's tummy flutter in sympathy.

"He'll be fine, September. Healing nicely, and lucky he only lost one toe to frostbite. We saved his tail, and the fur should grow back soon. There's just this one stubborn place he won't leave alone. It's got to come off before he does more damage." The man scowled, and Shadow flattened his ears, and thumped his tail.

September stroked Shadow's brow. "Can I be with him?" Her heart still raced. "I mean, just as you put him under for the surgery?"

She held him steady on the cloth-covered table, her scent a balm calming him even before the medicine made him yawn. Shadow leaned against September, safe in her arms, his-person, his everything. Eyes fell closed, muscles relaxed, and the clinic faded away...

Shadow dreamed. Dreamed of another place. Of a different girl. Dreamed of Lia saving a good-dog from the hungry flood. And of the beautiful, sweet-smelling puppy-girl Karma, who warmed his heart....

Have you read all of September and Shadow series? Ask your favorite booksellers for your copies today!

Wonder what happened to Shadow during his lost week? The adventure continues in book #4, FIGHT OR FLIGHT, introducing Lia and Karma!

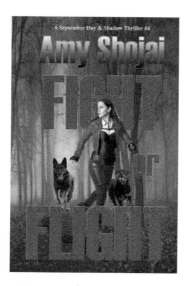

# FACT, FICTION & ACKNOWLEDGEMENTS

Thank you for reading SHOW AND TELL, and I hope you enjoyed this third book in the September Day series that began with LOST AND FOUND and continued with HIDE AND SEEK. I feel like I've won the lottery, to write about my passion and share these stories with the world. There never would have been a second book, and now a third one, without YOU adopting these books. (Can you see my virtual tail wag?)

My writing pedigree tips heavily toward the nonfiction side of things, so when I began writing novels, the journalist on my shoulder continually whispered in my ear. Fiction by definition is, as September would say, made up crappiocca. But in order for readers to suspend their disbelief, there needs to be a scaffold of truth holding it together. My first fiction publisher Bob Mayer writes "factual fiction" and I love that concept so much, I'm stealing it. Below, you'll find the Cliff's Notes version of what's real and what's fantasy.

As with the other books in the series, much of SHOW AND TELL is based on science, especially dog and cat behavior and learning theory, the benefits of service dogs, and the horror and reality of dogfights. Suspense and thriller novels by definition include mayhem, but as an animal advocate, I make a conscious choice to NOT show a pet's death in my books. All bets are off with the human characters, though.

I rely on a vast number of veterinarians, behaviorists, consultants, trainers, and pet-centric writers and rescue organizations that share their incredible resources and support to make my stories as believable as possible. Find out more information at IAABC.org, APDT.com, DWAA.org and CatWriters.com.

**FACT:** The *show-me* game is real, created by trainer Kayce Cover as a vocabulary game used with a variety of animals, which my own dog loves to play (http://kaycecover.synalia.com)

**FICTION:** Shadow's viewpoint chapters are pure speculation, although I would love to able to read doggy minds. However, every attempt has been made to base all animal characters' motivations and actions on what is known about canine and feline body language, scent discrimination, and the science behind the human-animal bond.

**FACT:** Real-life pets inspire some of the pet characters in SHOW AND TELL. I've held a "Name That Dog/Name That Cat" contest for each of the three novels thus far in the series. This most recent contest resulted in 46 dog and 81 cat name nominations and a total of 16,930 votes.

Patricia H. named **Hercules,** the Mastiff belonging to Kelvin, based on a dog she met during pet sitting. Debbie Glovatsky's yellow tabby boy **Waffles** won the honor of being rescued by Willie and later saving the life of Lenny—Waffles is a blogging star known to have an extra-long tail and an adventurous mancat nature. Another cat blogging star, Kelly Hoffman's feline alter ego **Boris Kitty** (a kitty from da hood) shines in the "Tarzan cat" scenes and, I'm told, is also a climber, leaper, shoulder-percher extraordinaire. Karyl Cunningham suggested the name **Fuzzit** for BeeBo's rescue kitten in honor of her 18-year-old cat Anubis, nicknamed Fuzzit, a real-life friend of **Simba,** also mentioned in the story. For BeeBo's dogs, Lynette George suggested **Teddy,** a beloved protective red Pit Bull from her childhood, and Kristi Brashier nominated **Dot,** a glamour girl rescued Pit Bull who is also a diabetes alert service dog. Finally, Theresa Littlefield's squirrel-fanatic dog **Kinsler** won the honor to be Willie's run away dog. Congratulations and THANK YOU to all the winners. I think they all deserve treats. Maybe even bacon!

**FACT**: Therapy dogs can work wonders when partnered with autistic individuals. Emotional Support Animals (ESA) also partner with a variety of people, from children to adults, including those suffering from post-traumatic stress disorder (PTSD). Only dogs and guide horses for the blind can be service animals trained to perform a specific function for their human partner, from becoming the ears for the deaf, eyes for the blind, support for other-abled and alert animals for health and physically challenged individuals. Learn about the differences and the benefits of pet-people partnerships at http://petpartners.org. You can also find out about "fake" credentialing services that hurt legitimate partnerships in this blog post: http://amyshojai.com/fake-service-dog-credentials/

**FACT**: Dogfights are a sad reality in much of the world. All of the paraphernalia described, from break sticks to the cat gin, spring poles to rape stands, are real. It's also true that law enforcement now has veterinary forensic specialists available—think of it as animal CSI—to nail these bad actors. The flood in SHOW AND TELL would be problematic but tests from the living dogs or any remains found could help find out a great deal. Animal fighting is already a federal crime and dog fighting is a felony in all 50 states. That's due in part to the relationship between the fighting events and illegal gambling, guns and drugs. Here in Texas, it's still quite a problem where sometimes whole families attend including little kids. Children brought up in the culture of dogfights consider them normal, and perpetuate the horror. To combat the crime of dogfights, the Missouri Humane Society, the ASPCA, the Louisiana SPCA, and the UC Davis Veterinary Genetics Laboratory collaborated to establish the first ever database. Find out more about Canine CODIS here:

http://www.vgl.ucdavis.edu/forensics/CANINECODIS.php

**FACT**: Pit Bulls are not inherently "evil" or "aggressive." Because of their heritage, these dogs have an increased propensity for dog-on-dog aggression, as do many other terrier breeds. Pit Bulls do not bite people more readily than other breeds. Sadly, that statistical distinction goes to German Shepherds. (Don't tell Shadow!) All dogs bite, and every breed has challenges, so be educated and prepared for whatever animal friend steals your heart.

**FACT**: Kinsler's resuscitation accurately depicts nose-to-mouth rescue breathing. The acupuncture "alarm point" does work, and has been known to resuscitate stillborn puppies and kittens up to twenty minutes after pronounced dead.

**FACT**: The porcelain cap from Lenny's tooth used to break the van window theoretically could work. Windows designed to withstand blunt force, like car windows, can break a household knife. Any sharp sudden strike with the right force and location could cause the glass to shatter. I just liked the idea of using the tooth, after seeing this YouTube video, enjoy! https://www.youtube.com/watch?v=llu-ckEe5cQ

**FACT**: According to the CDC and others, Autism Spectrum Disorder (ASD) affects about one percent of the world population, and about one in 68 children. The challenges facing these children and their families vary from mild to severe, and can prove devastating to those who love them. Some of these gifted individuals rise far above their challenges (think of Temple Grandin and Albert Einstein for example). These types of characters make great fodder for fiction authors, even if "twice exceptional" or 2e children may not be the average. After putting Steven, Tracy, Lenny and their parents through hell in the first book LOST AND FOUND, it seemed only fair to turn SHOW AND TELL over to them for their heroics to shine through. Refer to these resources for more information on ASD: http://www.cdc.gov/ncbddd/autism/data.html http://psychcentral.com/lib/autistic-and-gifted-supporting-the-twice-exceptional-child/

**FICTION**: I created the fictional drug Damenia supposedly borrowed from an Alzheimer's treatment. However, drugs for dementia and psychotropic drugs offer mixed results when treating autism. Off-label drug use in children is controversial but does happen, particularly with informed consent of parents. At times, the benefits are enormous and other times potentially devastating. Some psychotropic drugs cause psychosis, and oftentimes, abrupt withdrawal from a drug protocol causes unexpected consequences. However, there is no evidence to support the notion that withdrawal from an approved ASD treatment would cause any of the outcomes described in my thrillers. I made it all up.

**FACT**: Court cases have convicted people based on animal evidence, such as Fuzzit's torn claw embedded in Sunny's neck, or cat hair found on the defendant. Actually, I wanted to use cat hair DNA evidence, but after Sunny spent so much time in the water, that idea didn't wash. Literally.

**FACT:** Both dumpsters and straw bales float. I checked.

**FACT:** This book would not have happened without an incredible support team of friends, family and accomplished colleagues. Cool Gus Publishing, Jennifer Talty and Bob Mayer made these thrillers with "dog viewpoint" a reality when many in the publishing industry howled at the notion. Special thanks to my first readers Kristi Brashier, Carol Shenold and Frank Steele for your eagle eyes, spot-on comments and unflagging encouragement and support. Wags and purrs to my Triple-A Team (Amy's Audacious Allies) for all your help sharing the word about all my books. Youse guyz rock!

I continued to be indebted to the International Thriller Writers organization, which launched my fiction career by welcoming me into the Debut Authors Program. Wow, just look, now I have three books in a series! The authors, readers and industry mavens who make up this organization are some of the most generous and supportive people I have ever met. Long live the bunny slippers with teeth (and the rhinestone #1-Bitch Pin).

Finally, I am grateful to all the cats and dogs I've met over the years who have shared my heart and oftentimes my pillow. Nine year old Magical-Dawg (the inspiration for Shadow) and nineteen-year-old Seren-Kitty, along with newcomer Karma-Kat inspire me daily.

I never would have been a reader and now a writer if not for my fantastic parents who instilled in me a love of the written word, and never looked askance when my stuffed animals and invisible wolf friend told fantastical stories. And of course, my deepest thanks to my husband Mahmoud, who continues to support my writing passion, even when he doesn't always understand it.

I love hearing from you! Please drop me a line at my blog http://AmyShojai.com or my website http://www.shojai.com where you can subscribe to my PET PEEVES newsletter (and maybe win some pet books!). Follow me on twitter @amyshojai and like me on Facebook: http://www.facebook.com/amyshojai.cabc

# ABOUT THE AUTHOR

Amy Shojai is a certified animal behavior consultant, and the award-winning author of more than 30 bestselling pet books that cover furry babies to old fogies, first aid to natural healing, and behavior/training to Chicken Soupicity. She has been featured as an expert in hundreds of print venues including The New York times, Reader's Digest, and Family Circle, as well as television networks such as CNN, and Animal Planet's DOGS 101 and CATS 101. Amy brings her unique pet-centric viewpoint to public appearances. She is also a playwright and co-author of STRAYS, THE MUSICAL and the author of the critically acclaimed September Day pet-centric thriller series. Stay up to date with new books and appearances by subscribing to Amy's Pets Peeves newsletter at www.SHOJAI.com.

Made in the USA
Middletown, DE
11 July 2023